The Adventures of Freak the Mighty

RODMAN PHILBRICK

SCHOLASTIC INC.
New York Toronto London Auckland Sydney
Mexico City New Delhi Hong Kong Buenos Aires

Freak the Mighty, ISBN 0-590-47413-8, copyright © 1993 by Rodman Philbrick. Originally published in hardcover by the Blue Sky Press in 1993.

Max the Mighty, ISBN 0-590-57964-9, copyright © 1998 by Rodman Philbrick. Originally published in hardcover by the Blue Sky Press in 1998.

12 11 10 9 8 7 6 5 4 3 2 1 4 5 6 7 8 9/0

Printed in the U.S.A. 01

This edition created exclusively for Barnes & Noble, Inc.

2004 Barnes & Noble Books

ISBN 0-7607-6334-8

First compilation printing, November 2004

Contents

Freak the Mighty

To the real Kevin, and the real Gwen,
with love.

1.
The Unvanquished Truth

I never had a brain until Freak came along and let me borrow his for a while, and that's the truth, the whole truth. The unvanquished truth, is how Freak would say it, and for a long time it was him who did the talking. Except I had a way of saying things with my fists and my feet even before we became Freak the Mighty, slaying dragons and fools and walking high above the world.

Called me Kicker for a time — this was day care, the year Gram and Grim took me over — and I had a thing about booting anyone who dared to touch me. Because they were *always* trying to throw a hug on me, like it was a medicine I needed.

Gram and Grim, bless their pointed little heads, they're my mother's people, *her* parents, and they figured whoa! better put this little critter with other little critters his own age, maybe it will improve his temper.

Yeah, right! Instead, what happened, I invented games like kick-boxing and kick-knees and kick-faces and kick-teachers, and kick-the-other-little-day-care-critters, because I knew what a rotten lie that hug stuff was. Oh, I *knew*.

That's when I got my first look at Freak, that year of the phony hugs. He didn't look so different back then, we were all of us pretty small, right? But he wasn't in the playroom with us every day, just now and then he'd show up. Looking sort of fierce, is how I remember him. Except later it was Freak himself who taught me that remembering is a great invention of the mind, and if you try hard enough you can remember anything, whether it really happened or not.

So maybe he wasn't really all *that* fierce in day care, except I'm pretty sure he did hit a kid with his crutch once, whacked the little brat pretty good. And for some reason little Kicker never got around to kicking little Freak.

Maybe it was those crutches kept me from lashing out at him, man those crutches were cool. I wanted a pair for myself. And when little Freak showed up one day with these shiny braces strapped to his crooked legs, metal tubes right up to his hips, why those were even *more* cool than crutches.

"I'm Robot Man," little Freak would go, making these weird robot noises as he humped himself around the playground. *Rrrr . . . rrrr . . . rrrr . . .* like he had robot motors inside his legs, going *rrrrr . . . rrrr . . . rrrr*, and this look, like don't mess with me, man, maybe I got a laser cannon hidden inside these leg braces, smoke a hole right through you. No question, Freak was hooked on robots even back then, this little guy two feet tall, and already he knew what he wanted.

Then for a long time I never saw Freak anymore, one day he just never came back to day care, and the next thing I remember I'm like in the third grade or something and I catch a glimpse of this yellow-haired kid scowling at me from one of those cripple vans. Man, they were death-ray eyes, and I think, hey, that's him, the robot boy, and it was like whoa! because I'd forgotten all about him, day care was a blank place in my head, and nobody had called me Kicker for a long time.

Mad Max they were calling me, or Max Factor, or this one butthead in L.D. class called me Maxi Pad, until I persuaded him otherwise. Gram and Grim always called me Maxwell, though, which is supposed to be my real name, and sometimes I hated that worst of all. Maxwell, ugh.

Grim out in the kitchen one night, after supper whispering to Gram had she noticed how much Maxwell was getting to look like *Him*? Which is the way he always talked about my father, who had married his dear departed daughter and produced, eek eek, Maxwell. Grim never says my father's name, just *Him*, like his name is too scary to say.

It's more than just the way Maxwell resembles

him, Grim says that night in the kitchen, the boy is *like* him, we'd better watch out, you never know what he might do while we're sleeping. Like his father did. And Gram right away shushes him and says don't ever say that, because little pictures have big ears, which makes me run to the mirror to see if it is my big ears made me look like *Him*.

What a butthead, huh?

Well, I *was* a butthead, because like I said, I never had a brain until Freak moved down the street. The summer before eighth grade, right? That's the summer I grew so fast that Grim said we'd best let the boy go barefoot, he's exploding out of his shoes. That barefoot summer when I fell down a lot, and the weirdo robot boy with his white-yellow hair and his weird fierce eyes moved into the duplex down the block with his beautiful brown-haired mom, the Fair Gwen of Air.

Only a falling-down goon would think that was her real name, right?

Like I said.

Are you paying attention here? Because you don't even know yet how we got to be Freak the Mighty. Which was pretty cool, even if I do say so myself.

2.
Up from the Down Under

That summer, let's see, I'm still living in the basement, my own private down under, in the little room Grim built for me there. Glued up this cheap paneling, right? It sort of buckles away from the concrete cellar walls, a regular ripple effect, but do I complain about the crummy paneling, or the rug that smells like low tide? I do not. Because I *like* it in the down under, got the place all to myself and no fear of Gram sticking her head in the door and saying Maxwell dear, what *are* you doing?

Not that I ever *do* much of anything. Grim has it fixed in his head I'm at a dangerous age and they need to keep me under observation. Like I might make bombs or start a fire. Or whack out the local pets with my trusty slingshot or whatever — except I never *had* a slingshot, it was Grim who had one when he was my age. The proof is right there in the family photo album. You can see this blurry little miniature Grim with no front teeth, grinning at the camera and yanking back on this prehistoric slingshot. Good for whacking mastodons, probably. "Just proper targets," Grim says, closing up the photo album, end of discussion. Like, oops, better hide the evidence. Don't want to give the dangerous boy any ideas.

Not that I *have* any ideas. My brain is vacant, okay? I'm just this critter hiding out in the basement, drooling in my comic books or whatever. All right, I never actually *drool*, but you get the picture.

Anyhow, this is the first day of July, already counting down for the Fourth and wondering where can I get an M80, which is supposed to have the explosive power of a quarter stick of dynamite or something, and when it goes off your heart thuds to a stop for a microsecond, *wham*. Which is probably what Grim is afraid of, eek eek, Maxwell armed with dynamite.

So finally I get bored in the down under and I'm hanging out in the so-called back yard, your basic chunk of chain-link heaven. Grim keeps this crummy little mower in the shed, but what's the point of mowing dirt, right? Okay, I'm out there messing around and that's when I see the moving van. Not your mainstream, nationwide, brand-name mover, either, just some cheapo local outfit. These big bearded dudes in their sweaty undershirts lugging stuff into the duplex half that's been vacant since last Christmas, when the dope fiend who lived there finally got busted.

At first I'm thinking the dope fiend is back, he's out of jail or whatever, and he's moving his stuff back in. Then I see the Fair Gwen. Not that I knew her name, that was a little while later. At first she's a glimpse, caught her going between the van and the front door, talking to the beards. I'm thinking, *hey I know her*, and then I'm thinking, *no way, butthead, no way you'd know a female that beautiful.*

Because she looks like some kind of movie star. Wearing these old jeans and a baggy T-shirt, and her long hair is tied back and she's probably sweating, but she *still* looks like a movie star. Like she has this glow, a secret spotlight that follows her around and makes her eyes light up.

And I'm thinking, well *this* improves the old neighborhood. You're thinking, yeah right, the goon is barely out of seventh grade, who does he think he is? All I'm saying, the Fair Gwen had star quality, and even a total moron can see it. And the reason she looked familiar is, I must have seen her bringing Freak to day care, way back in the dark ages, because the next thing I notice is this crippled-up yellow-haired midget kid strutting around the sidewalk, giving orders to the beards.

He's going: "Hey you, Doofus! Yeah, you with the hairy face, take it easy with that box. That box contains a computer, you know what a computer is?"

I can't believe it. By then I'm sneaking along

the street to see what's going on, and there's this weird-looking little dude, he's got a normal-sized head, but the rest of him is shorter than a yardstick and kind of twisted in a way that means he can't stand up straight and makes his chest puff out, and he's waving his crutches around and yelling up at the movers.

"Hey, Gwen," one of the beards says, "can't you give this kid a pill or something? He's driving us nuts."

So Gwen comes out of the house and pushes the hair out of her big brown eyes and she goes, "Kevin, go play in the back yard, okay?"

"But my computer."

"Your computer is fine. Leave the men alone. They'll be done soon and then we can have lunch."

By this time I'm hunkering along in front of the place, trying to maintain a casual attitude, except like I said my feet are going wild that year and I keep tripping over everything. Cracks in the sidewalk, ants on the sidewalk, shadows, anything.

Then the strange little dude jerks himself around and he catches sight of me and he lifts a crutch and points it up at my heart and he goes, "Identify yourself, earthling."

I'm busy keeping my feet from tripping and don't get it that he means me.

"I said identify yourself, earthling, or suffer the consequences."

I'm like, what? And before I can decide

whether or not to tell him my name, or *which* name, because by now I recognize him as the weird little robot kid from day care and maybe he remembers me as Kicker, anyhow before I can say a word he pulls the trigger on that crutch and makes a weapon noise, and he goes, "Then die, earthling, die!"

I motor out of there without saying a word. Because I'm pretty sure he really means it. The way he points that crutch is only part of it. You have to see the look in his eye. Man, that little dude really hates me.

He *wants* me to die.

3.
American Flyer

Okay, back to the down under, right? My room in the basement. Scuttle into your dim hole in the ground, Maxwell dear. Big goon like you, growing about an inch a day, and this midget kid, this crippled little humanoid, he actually *scared* you. Not the kind of scare that makes your knee bones feel like water, more the kind of scare where you go whoa! I don't understand this, I don't get it, what's going on?

Like calling me "earthling." Which by itself is pretty weird, right? I already mentioned a few of the names I've been called, but until the robot boy showed up, nobody had ever called me *earthling,* and so I'm lying on my mattress there in the great down under, and it comes to me that he's right, I *am* an earthling, we're all of us earthlings, but we don't call each other earthling. No need. Because it's the same thing that in this country we're all Americans, but we don't go around to people and say, "Excuse me, American, can you tell me how to get to the nearest 7 Eleven?"

So I'm thinking about that for a while, lying there in the cellar dark, and pretty soon the down under starts to get small, like the walls are shrinking, and I go up the bulkhead stairs into the back yard and find a place where I can check it out.

There's this one scraggly tree behind the little freak's house, right? Like a stick in the ground with a few wimped-out branches. And there he is, hardly any bigger now than he was in day care, and he's standing there waving his crutch up at the tree.

I kind of slide over to the chain-link fence, get a better angle on the scene. What's he *doing* whacking at that crummy tree? Trying to jump up and hit this branch with his little crutch, and he's mad, hopping mad. Only he can't really jump, he just makes this jumping kind of motion. His feet never leave the ground.

Then what he does, he throws down the crutch and he gets down on his hands and knees and crawls back to his house. If you didn't know, you would think he was like a kindergarten creeper who forgot how to walk, he's that small. And he crawls real good, better than he can walk. Before you know it, he's dragging this wagon out from under the steps.

Rusty red thing, one of those old American Flyer models. Anyhow, the little freak is tugging it backwards, a few inches at a time. Chugging along until he gets that little wagon under the tree. Next thing he picks up his crutch and he climbs in the wagon and he stands up and he's whacking at the tree again.

By now I've figured out that there's something stuck up in the branches and he wants to get it down. This small, bright-colored thing, looks like a piece of folded paper. Whatever it is, that paper thing, he wants it real bad, but even with the wagon there's no way he can reach it. No way.

So I go over there to his back yard, trying to be really quiet, but I'm no good at sneaking up, not with these humongous feet, and he turns and faces me with that crutch raised up like he's ready to hit a grand slam on my head.

He wants to say something, you can tell that much, but he's so mad, he's all huffed up and the noise he makes, it could be from a dog or something, and he sounds like he can hardly breathe.

What I do, I keep out of range of that crutch and just reach up and pick the paper thing right out of the tree. Except it's not a paper thing. It's a plastic bird, light as a feather. I have to hold it real careful or it might break, that's how flimsy it is.

I go, "You want this back or what?"

The little freak is staring at me bug-eyed, and he goes, "Oh, it talks."

I give him the bird-thing. "What is it, like a model airplane or something?"

You can tell he's real happy to have the bird-thing back, and his face isn't quite so fierce. He sits down in the wagon, and he goes, "This is an ornithopter. An ornithopter is defined as an experimental device propelled by flapping wings. Or you could say that an ornithopter is just a big word for mechanical bird."

That's how he talked, like right out of a dictionary. So smart you can hardly believe it. While he's talking he's winding up the bird-thing. There's this elastic band inside, and he goes, "Observe and be amazed, earthling," and then he lets it go, and you know what? I *am* amazed, because it does fly just like a little bird, flitting up and down and around, higher than I can reach.

I chase after the thing until it boinks against the scrawny tree trunk and I bring it back to him and he winds it up again and makes it fly. We keep doing that, it must be for almost an hour, until finally the elastic breaks. I figure that's it, end of ornithopter, but he says something like, "All mechanical objects require periodic maintenance. We'll schedule installation of a new propulsion unit as soon as the Fair Gwen of Air gets a replacement."

Even though I'm not sure what he means, I go, "That's cool."

"You live around here, earthling?"

"Over there." I point out the house. "In the down under."

He goes, "What?" and I figure it's easier to show him than explain all about Gram and Grim and the room in the cellar, so I pick up the handle to the American Flyer wagon and I tow him over.

It's real easy, he doesn't weigh much and I'm pretty sure I remember looking back and seeing him sitting up in the wagon happy as can be, like he's really enjoying the ride and not embarrassed to have me pulling him around.

But like Freak says later in this book, you can remember anything, whether it happened or not. All I'm really sure of is he never hit me with that crutch.

4.
What Frightened the Fair Gwen

Freak's not in my room for ten minutes before he sets me straight on the Fair Gwen. He's able to hump down the steps by himself, except it makes him sort of out of breath, you can hear him wheezing or I guess you'd call it panting, like a dog does on a hot day. He gets into my room and I close the bulkhead door, and he goes, "Cool. You get to live down here all by yourself?"

"I eat upstairs with Grim and Gram."

Freak works himself up onto the foot of my bed and uses a pillow to make himself comfortable. It's pretty dim down here, only the daylight from one basement window, but it catches him just right and makes his eyes shine. "Gram must be your grandmother," he says. "Grim would be, I suppose, a sobriquet for your grandfather, based on his demeanor."

I go, "Huh?"

Freak grins and pushes back his yellow hair, and he goes, "Pardon my vocabulary. Sobriquet means 'nickname,' and demeanor means 'expression.' I merely postulated that you call your grandfather 'Grim' because he's grim. Postulate means — "

"I know," I say. Which is a lie, except I can guess what he means, figure it out that way. "So how come you call your mom 'Fair Gwen of Air,' is that a nickname?"

Freak is shaking his head. I can see he's trying not to let on that he's laughing inside. "Guinevere," he finally says, catching his breath. "The Fair Guinevere, from the legend of King Arthur. You know about King Arthur, right?"

I shrug. The only King Arthur I know is the brand of flour Gram uses, and if I say that I'll *really* sound like a butthead.

He goes, "My mom's name is Gwen, so sometimes I call her the Fair Guinevere or the Fair Gwen. King Arthur was the first king of England, way back when there were still dragons and monsters in the world. Arthur was this wimpy little kid, an orphan, and there was this magic sword stuck in a big stone, okay? The old king had died, and whoever could pull the sword from the stone proved he was the next king. All these big tough dudes came from all over to yank at the sword and they couldn't budge it. One day this wimpy little kid tried it when nobody was looking and the sword slipped out like it was stuck in butter."

"So he was the king, this little kid?"

Freak nods, he's really into this story, and he's

making shapes in the air with his hands. This is the first time for me, hearing Freak really talk, and right away I know one thing: When he's talking, you can't take your eyes off of him. His hands are moving, and it's like he's really seeing it, this story about an old king.

"Arthur's magical sword is called Excalibur, and the Fair Guinevere is this pretty girl who becomes his queen. 'Fair' in those days meant the same as 'beautiful' does now. Anyhow, Arthur got bored just sitting around, so he invited all the knights of England to come live in the castle. They all ate supper at this round table, which is why they were called the Knights of the Round Table. Every now and then King Arthur would send them off on a special secret mission, which in the old days they called a 'quest.' They had to slay dragons and monsters and evil knights. I assume you know what a knight wears into battle?"

I think so, but I like hearing Freak talk, so I go, "Better tell me," and that's when I find out why he's so interested in some clanky old knights.

Because Freak really lights up and he goes, "The knights were like the first human version of robots. They wore this metal armor to protect them and make them invincible. When I get my stuff unpacked I'll show you the pictures. It's pretty amazing, really, that hundreds of years before they had computers they were already attempting to exceed the design limitations of the human body."

I go, "Huh?" and Freak sort of chuckles to himself, like he expected me to go "Huh?" and he says, "The design limitations of the human body. You know, like we're not bullet-proof and we can't crush rocks with our bare hands, and if we touch a hot stove we get burned. King Arthur wanted to *improve* his men, so he made them armor-plated. Then he programmed them to go out and do these quests, slay the dragons and so on, which is sort of how they program robots right now."

I go, "I thought there weren't any real robots. Just in the movies."

Boy does that make his eyes blaze. Like whoa! talk about laser beams! He's like *fuming,* so upset he can hardly talk.

Finally he gets control of himself and he goes, "I suppose I must make allowances for your ignorance. On the subject of robots you are clearly misinformed. Robots are not just in the movies. Robotics, the science of designing and building functional robots, is a *huge* industry. There are *thousands* of robot units presently in use. *Millions* of them. They don't look like the robots you see in movies, of course, because they're designed according to function. Many robotic devices are in fact sophisticated assembly units, machines that put together cars and trucks and computers. For instance, the space shuttle has a robot arm."

"Right," I say. "I saw that on TV."

Freak sighs and rolls his eyes. "Ah, yes," he says. "Television, the opiate of the massives."

For about the eleventh time I go, "Huh?"

"Opiate, a drug," he says. "Massive, that means large and heavy. Thus television is the drug of fat heads. Opiate of the massives."

"You don't have a TV?"

"Of course I have a television," he says. "How else could I watch *Star Trek*? Matter of fact, I watch *tons* of tube, but I also read tons of books so I can figure out what's true and what's fake, which isn't always easy. Books are like truth serum — if you don't read, you can't figure out what's real."

This time I don't say *huh* because then I might have to explain how I'm an L.D., and reading books is the last thing I want to do, right after trimming my toenails with a lawn mower, gargling nails, and eating worms for breakfast. Of course Freak has probably already guessed I'm a learning disabled, because he's had a look around my room and it isn't exactly the public library.

"I'll lend you some of my books," he says.

"Cool," I say, like it's just what I've been waiting for, another chance to prove I'm a butthead.

Then we both hear it at the same time, this voice calling his name and sounding real worried.

"The Fair Gwen," he says. "I gotta beam out of here."

I go up and open the bulkhead door and his

mother is in the back yard and she's looking at the little red wagon. She catches sight of me coming up out of the down under and it's like somebody shot her. Like she's scared out of her mind. "Kevin?" she says. "I'm looking for a little boy."

Freak is huffing and puffing as he humps himself up the steps, and the Fair Gwen grabs Freak and puts him in the wagon and I swear, she almost *runs* home, like if she doesn't get away quick something really bad is going to happen. Freak is in the wagon and he's trying to look back at me, trying to shrug his shoulders and let me know he doesn't understand what got into the Fair Gwen, but *I* know.

It's pretty simple, really. She's scared of me.

5.
Spitting Image

There's a place I go inside my head sometimes. It's cool and dim in there and you float like a cloud — no, you *are* a cloud, the kind you see in the sky on a windy day, the way they keep changing shape except you can't really *see* it changing? It just sort of happens, and suddenly you realize the cloud that looks like a big hand with fat fingers now looks like a catcher's mitt, or a big soft TV set? Like that.

Anyhow, I went there right after the Fair Gwen ran off with that look on her face, like: What was he *doing* with my poor little boy, stealing him away in the wagon?

What I do is lie on the floor under my bed, where you can just barely see the bedsprings and stuff because it's so dark, and before long I'm somewhere else, sort of floating, and it's so cool and empty in there, you don't have to think about anything. You're nothing, you're nobody, nothing matters, you're not even there. *Time out*.

Except this time I can't stay as long as I'd like

because Gram is knocking on the door. Going, "Maxwell? Max, are you there? Please answer me, dear, it's important."

Yeah, right. But I wedge out from under the bed — there's getting to be less and less room under there — and I dust myself off and open the door. There's no lock, but Gram has this thing about waiting until I say come in, she makes a big deal about not intruding.

"Maxwell," she says, and she takes a little step inside the room and you can tell she'd rather not be here, she makes this face because the place is dark and messy and probably it smells like my socks or whatever. "Max, dear, I'm sorry to bother you — you know I *never* come into the basement — but I just got a call from Gwen Avery and I think it's important."

Uh-oh, I'm thinking. Now the Fair Gwen is calling up my Gram, probably to report a great hulking beast that lives in the cellar, and I close up inside, waiting for the worst.

"She called to say how sorry she was," Gram is saying.

"Huh?"

"I guess she came to pick up her little boy, is that right? You and Kevin were making friends?"

Making friends. What a wet idea *that* is, but Gram gets her feelings hurt pretty easy, so I don't actually say that. What I say is, "Yeah, I guess so."

Gram is uneasy, I can see her eyes flitting nervously around the room, like she's crossing the border into a really foreign country. This is as good a place as any to mention that even though Gram is my grandmother, she doesn't *look* like a granny, she looks more like a mother because she was, as she always says, "a mere child myself" when my real mother was born.

"Well, uhm, I get the impression poor Gwen wasn't expecting to see you looking so big, and now she thinks she's offended you. Does that make any sense?"

"I guess so. You know her, huh?"

"Oh my yes," says Gram. "Gwen was a good friend of your mother's. They were both pregnant at the same time. Then later on you and little Kevin went to the same day care, did you know that?"

I give a shrug because I don't really like Gram to know how much I remember about way back then.

Gram is saying, "She said — she especially wanted me to tell you this, Max — she said she's delighted that you and Kevin are going to be friends. That's the word she used — delighted. And she's inviting you to supper."

First thing, without thinking, I say, "Do I have to?"

Gram reaches out and she puts her hand on my shoulder, real light and feathery, you can feel how nervous she is just to touch me, and how it makes her uncomfortable to have to look up at me, because did I mention I'm a lot bigger than Gram? Bigger than Grim, too? Bigger than most people? It's true.

Gram says, "She feels bad about how she treated you, Maxwell, dear, and she wants to make it up to you. You don't *have* to go, but it would be the right thing to do."

"It was no big deal," I say. "She just ran away is all. I guess I scared her."

"It wasn't you," Gram says.

"No? Then who was it scared her?"

Now she's got her tongue stuck, and you can see her swallowing in her throat, like her mouth is dry. "I'll just leave that to Gwen," she says. "She's quite a remarkable young woman, you know. Raising that poor boy all on her own."

"He's not a poor boy," I say. "You should hear him talk. I think the rest of him is so small because his brain is so big."

"Yes," says Gram. "Well well."

Gram is always saying that, well well, like it means something, which I guess it does to her. Anyhow, I agree to have supper with Freak and his mom, even though the idea of it makes me feel tensed up, like there is a hand inside my stomach and the hand is, you know, making a fist.

It turns out to be not so bad. The Fair Gwen, right away she's beaming at me, bouncing around the kitchen and talking a mile a minute, so fast the words kind of smoosh together.

"SodidSusanexcusemeyourgrandmothermentionyourmomandIwerepalsthatis . . . untilshe gotmarriedexcusemeInever . . . *could* abide thatmanIalwaysthoughthewascrazyand . . . scary isitokaytosaythatyou . . . won'tbeoffended?"

It's like this delay while I sort it out, and then I go, "Yeah, Gram told me," and the stuff about her knowing my father and thinking he was sick in the head, I decide no comment is the way to go.

"You were the cutest little baby," Gwen says. "I remember like it was yesterday. We were all of us living over in the tenements in those days, because the rent was so cheap and we were all just starting out."

Freak is on the floor, digging through the packing boxes for pots and pans and stuff, he's almost inside this box, all you can see is his funny little rear end sticking out. You'd think he was maybe two years old, that's how small he is, until you notice where his leg brace makes a lump in his pants.

From inside the box he goes, "Hey, Gwen, leave the guy alone, huh? You're going spastic."

"Am I?" Gwen asks. She's at the counter, going through drawers and looking for spoons or whatever. "Sorry, Max. That is, I'm sorry we got off on the wrong foot. It's just, you know . . ."

Freak's head pops out of the box and he's got this wicked know-it-all grin. "What she means is, you're a spitting image of your old man."

Gwen says, "Kevin, please," and her voice is

real small, like she's embarrassed.

"Yeah," I say. "Everybody says that."

"They do?"

I shrug. Is it really such a big deal for a boy to look like his father? Which is typical butthead thinking, because of course it's a big deal, if your father happens to be in prison. Which everybody in town knows about, it's not like there's any secret about what he did or why he's there, except everybody *acts* like it should be a secret, and the bigger I grow and the more I look like my old man, the worse it gets.

"You really knew him?" I say. "I mean him and my mom when they were together?"

"Not very well," Gwen says. She's looking for a knife to slice open a pack of hot dogs. "I never saw much of your mom after they got married. He made it . . . difficult for your mother to have any friends."

There's a knife on the table and I pick it up and hand it to the Fair Gwen. She doesn't flinch away and I decide she's okay, she's really pretty cool.

"So," Freak is saying. "When do we eat? My fuel cells are depleted."

Supper is great. The Fair Gwen makes this really tasty potato salad with spices and stuff, way better than the mushy stuff Gram makes, and we have hot dogs fried in a pan with the buns toasted up butter-crisp just the way I like, and two kinds of relish and three kinds of mustard, and red onions cut up real small.

We sit out in the back yard eating from paper plates, and Freak tells robot stories that are so strange and funny I'm laughing like a maniac and then I'm choking and Freak is pounding me on the back.

"Expel the object!" Freak shouts. "Regurgitate, you big moron!" and he gives me another thump and I cough up this yucky mess, but I'm still laughing so hard my nose is running.

What a goon, except it really *is* funny, me trying to sneeze a hot dog through my nose, and we're both laughing like total morons.

"This is great," Gwen says, looking at Freak and me. "I'm so glad we decided to move back, you know? I feel like we're all getting a fresh start."

It's time to go home, Gram gets nervous if I'm not back before dark. Everything seems really great, just like Gwen says, except when I lie down on my bed it hits me, boom, and I'm crying like a baby. And the really weird thing is, I'm happy.

6.
Close Encounter of the Turd Kind

Fourth of July, right? Everybody goes nuts. The dads are getting drunk and having their cookouts, and the moms are trying to keep all the brats from blowing their precious little pinkies off with cherry bombs, and the kids are running wild through the back yards. It's like no rules apply, and that makes everything real *edgy,* if you know what I mean, like let's have a blast and who cares what happens.

Don't get the wrong idea. I *love* the Fourth. It's just that people tend to get all choked up about firecracker holidays, and they don't see what's *really* going on, which like I say is the dads swilling beer and acting numb, that's the basic formula.

Not that Grim ever swills anything stronger than root beer. No way. The poison never crossed his lips, he likes to say, even though I've seen a picture of him in the army and that sure *looks* like a bottle of beer in his hand, and he's got that same wacked-by-a-hammer grin that dudes always get when they're drinking.

Anyhow, this is the first year I get to go to the fireworks without Grim and Gram, which I've never understood, because it's right down by the millpond where I've been allowed to go for years, so why should it make a difference just because about a million people show up to watch the rockets' red glare over that smelly pond?

The deal this year is that I get to go with Freak, which Gram thinks is a good idea because she's afraid he'll get crushed or something, she actually thinks people are going to *step* on him, which just goes to show how brainless she can be sometimes, and scared of everything. I mean nobody steps on little kids down there, so why should they step on Freak?

Turns out the thing to worry about is not kidstompers, but beer swillers, like I mentioned before. Because Freak and I are still a couple of blocks from the pond, just kind of easing our way along, when these punks start mouthing off.

"Hey you! Mutt and Jeff! Frankenstein and Igor! Don't look around, I'm talkin' to you, boneheads. What is this, a freak show?"

I know that voice. Tony D., they call him Blade, he's at least seventeen and he's already been to juvy court three, four times. I heard he cut a guy with a razor, he almost died, and everybody says the best way to handle Tony D.

and his gang is, you avoid them. Cross the street, hide, whatever it takes.

"Yeah you," he goes, and he's doing his hippity walk, strutting along, he's got these fancy cool cowboy boots with metal toes. "Yeah, Andre the giant and the dwarf, hold on a sec, I want a word with you."

Only the way he talks, he goes ah wanna woid weecha, except it's bad enough having to listen to the creep, I don't want to have to spell the dumb way he talks. Anyhow, big mistake, we stop and wait for Tony D., alias the bad-news Blade.

"Got any, dudes?" he asks, pretending like he's friendly. He's a couple feet away, but you can smell the beer on his breath. Also it smells like he ate something dead, for instance road kill, but maybe that's my imagination.

"Pay attention," Tony D. says. "I asked did you got any."

Freak, his chest is all puffed out and his chin looks hard and he's looking right up at Tony D., and he says, "Got any what?"

Tony D. has his hands on his hips and his punkster pals are trying to get closer, working through the crowd. He leans over Freak and he says, "Boomers, you little freak. M80s. Maybe a rack of cherry bombs, is that what's making a lump in your pocket, huh?"

Freak starts to hump himself away, trying to walk faster than he really can, which makes his leg brace bump against the ground. "Come along, Maxwell," he says over his shoulder. "Ignore the cretin."

Blade goes, "Hey what?" and he moves right in front of Freak. "Want to say that again, little freak man?"

Freak says, "Cretin. C-R-E-T-I-N. Defined as one who suffers from mental deficiency."

Hearing how little tiny Freak is dissing the fearsome Tony D., alias Blade, I can't help it, I laugh out loud. Tony D. is looking up at me and he's showing his white teeth, I swear they've been sharpened to look like vampire teeth, and I go, "Uh-oh," and start to get real cold inside. Real icy, because I can see that Blade is trying to make up his mind, is he going to fight me, or is he just going to kill me quick?

Just then I hear the whoop of a siren and like a miracle this cop car comes out of nowhere, heading for the millpond, and Blade takes one look and he and his punksters are out of there, burning rubber in their Reeboks.

Freak goes, "Whew! That was a close encounter of the turd kind," and it takes me a second to get the joke, but then I'm laughing, amazed he can be so cool about it, like it was no big deal that Tony D. was after us.

"You *can* take him, right?" he asks a couple minutes later.

I go, "Are you kidding? You can't just fight Blade, you have to fight his gang, too."

"You mean you *couldn't* take him and I was giving him lip?"

"That's about the size of it."

Freak goes, "Oh my *gawwwwwwd*!" and he's shrieking and laughing and whooping it up so loud that everybody is looking at us like we're total goons, which isn't far from the truth.

Freak hasn't got his crutch tonight, just the leg brace, and he's laughing so hard he falls down. Not that he has far to go. Anyhow, I pick him up and I'm amazed how light he is. Like it's *nothing* for me to lift him, and maybe that's where I get the idea. Because later, when we're down by the pond and the first of the rockets is streaking up, up, up, Freak is making a fuss because he can't see. There are so many people crowded around, all he can see are feet and knees, and people are lifting their little kids up to see the fireworks explode like hot pink flowers in the sky, and so I just sort of reach down without thinking and pick up Freak and set him on my shoulders.

He's kind of trembly up there until he grabs hold of my hair to steady himself, and then the first really big rocket whams off, a humongous *thud*! I can feel in my stomach, and Freak is shouting, "Awwww *right*!" and I know it's okay, he's not flipped out because I picked him up and put him on my shoulders like he was a little kid instead of possibly the smartest human being in the whole world.

"Magnesium!" he shouts as the white sparkles glitter down over the pond. "Potassium chlorate!" as the shells go womp-womp-womp and everybody goes oooooooh. "Potassium nitrate! Sulphur! Aluminum!" And after a burst of hot red fire in the sky, Freak tugs my hair and screams, "Copper! That's copper powder combusting with oxygen!" And when the fire blossoms are flashing blue he goes, "Good old strontium nitrate!" and I'm thinking whoa! is there anything this little dude *doesn't* know?

At the end, like always, they have a thing they call the "grand finale," when they just go nuts and light off everything at once and it sounds like World War III, whizzing and banging and popping, and there's so much hot stuff falling from the sky you can hear it sizzling in the pond. Freak keeps on shouting out the names of chemicals and elements, until the last spark dies in that scummy pond and the crowd cheers and then everybody tries to leave at once, like a bunch of morons.

7.
Walking High Above the World

You ever notice how the smell of gunpowder makes you thirsty? Because after the fireworks I'm aiming us for where the food carts are parked along the street, thinking about an ice-cold lemonade, how *clean* it will taste, and for a moment I almost forget that Freak is riding on my shoulders.

"Amazing perspective up here," he's saying. "This is what you see all the time."

"I'm not *that* big," I say. "This way you're like two feet taller than me."

"Cool," he says. "I love it."

We're working our way through the crowd and we're almost to the food carts when Freak tugs on my hair. "Cretin at two o'clock," he says, real urgent. "Two more at three o'clock."

I go, "Huh? What?"

"The Blade and his gang," Freak hisses. "They've locked on to us. Their trajectory is converging. Go to the left," he says. "Make it quick, if you want to live!"

Too bad I'm a little confused about rights and lefts. If I don't think about it I know, but if I have to think about it quick my mind goes blank. Right? Left? What does it all *mean*?

"Left!" Freak says, and he kicks me with his little foot, like he's digging into a horse and it clicks in my head. Go that way! Follow the feet! "Faster," Freak is saying, and he's urging me on, it's lucky for me the little dude doesn't have any spurs, but I don't care, I just want to get clear of Blade.

"Warp factor nine!" Freak is shouting. "More speed, o mighty beast!"

Now I'm running at a full gallop, weaving through the crowd, and I don't even need to look back, all I have to do is follow the way Freak is kicking his feet, steering me. I'm pretty sure we're getting away until this punk comes out of nowhere, he's one of Blade's gang and he's got this big ugly grin.

"Over here! Tony! Got 'em cornered!"

"What do I do?" I say to Freak.

He goes, "I'm thinking, I'm thinking!"

I can hear Blade before I can see him. Hear his wicked laugh, so mean and dirty it makes my stomach freeze up and my knees feel squishy.

"You! The freak! You and that giant retard, I'll cut you down to size. Dice and slice, baby! Freak show time!"

And now I can see him, see that pointed white grin and his eyes so dark and cruel, and he's swaggering through the crowd, he's got us surrounded with punks, everywhere I turn there's another mean face trying to look as tough as Tony D.

In a small voice I say, "Tell me what to do," and Freak pats me on the shoulder and says, "Just give me a nanosecond to process the alternatives."

"Slice and dice!" That's Blade, and he's reaching into his back pocket.

"Make it quick," I hiss, and then Freak is kicking my right shoulder and I turn that way and he's saying "Go! Go!" and I run right over this punk, he's so surprised he loses his bubble gum and he tries to grab my leg but I kick free and I'm running right and then left, running blind and just letting Freak decide which way we should go because he must have a plan, a dude as smart as that.

Which I'm right about, he *does* have a plan. Only the plan is to run out into the smelly millpond and drown us both.

"Go on!" he's shouting from up above my head. "Trust me, we'll be okay!"

Blade is shouting, too, and I can hear his feet pitter-pattering behind me. Catching up.

"Warp speed!" Freak is shouting, and he's kicking with both feet now, which means go straight. "Head for the H_2O!"

The pond is right ahead of me, and I'm sort of running along the edge, crunching over the bottles and cans and candy wrappers, and then

I hear this zingy sound and I just know that Blade is swinging a knife, cutting the air right behind us, and there's nowhere to go but into the pond, like Freak wants me to.

I almost lose it right there, taking that first step, because it's a gunky pond and the mud is really oozy and deep and it sucks right up to my knees. But I'm so scared of getting cut by Tony D., so scared he might *bite* me with those wicked teeth, I just keep going. There's this great ugly *sucking* sound as my feet come back up out of the mud and I stretch out as far as my legs will go and I take another step and I just keep going.

I'm going so fast that the water is up to my chest before Freak gets my attention, he's tugging at my hair with both hands. "Whoa!" he's saying, "slow up, we did it."

The mud is up around my knees and it's real hard to turn around. Finally I get so I'm facing back at the shore and there's Blade, just his head above the water, and he looks all white and scared. "Help!" he's blubbering, choking on that dirty water, and then his punksters are splashing in to rescue him. Man, they can hardly get him loose, the way he's stuck deep in that mud, and before they drag him to shore they're all covered with slime and mud. They're gasping like fish, almost too tired to cuss us out, but that doesn't last.

Blade is covered with mud right up to his neck, which on him looks natural. He turns to his gang, who look as slimy as he does. "Get some rocks, it's target-practice time!"

"What do we do now?" I ask, because the mud is still sucking me down. It's over my knees now, and the water is right up under my arms and even Freak's feet are getting wet.

"Wait," Freak says. "The cavalry is coming, can't you hear that bugle?"

I'm listening, but I can't hear anything except for Blade and his gang, and how they're scrambling around trying to find some rocks to heave at us.

I can see Blade rearing back to throw, and the first one misses us.

"Can you move?" Freak says.

"I don't think so."

It's true. The mud is up over my knees, and I'm locked in place. I can't even fall down, that's how stiff it is. I'm like a big fence post, and everybody knows a fence post makes a good target.

More splashes as the rocks fall short. At first they're throwing stuff that's too heavy. Pretty soon they smarten up, and Blade says, "Smaller rocks! Get me smaller rocks!" and I know in my heart we're doomed.

Then up above me there's this really loud, high-pitched screech. Freak has his fingers in his mouth and he's whistling. Real shrill and shivery and so loud it almost hurts my ears. And then I see what Freak has been seeing all along, a cop car cruising real slow along the road around the pond, which is what they always do after the fireworks.

Freak is whistling and the cop car spotlight comes beaming around the pond until it settles on us. I'm blinking because the light is so bright, and Freak is making a fuss and waving his arms and we hear the metal megaphone sound of a cop voice ordering us not to move. Like we could even if we wanted!

It's hard to see in the glare of the spotlight, but Freak tells me that Blade and his punks are running away. Like snakes on sneakers, Freak says.

"Officers!" Freak is shouting into the white light. "We request assistance!"

They finally have to use ropes to pull me out of there. Freak won't let go, he stays right where he is on top of my shoulders even when this cop in a boat tries to lift him off, and then we're up on the bank of the pond and everybody is being real nice and giving us blankets and Cokes and saying they know all about Tony D., they'll keep an eye on him, don't you worry.

"Okay, boys, you'd better give us your names and we'll call your mothers," this one cop is saying, and there's this other guy who is looking at me funny and he says, "Hey, isn't that Kenny Kane's boy? Must be. Old Killer Kane, is he still inside?"

Freak is still holding tight to my shoulders and when they ask him for his name, he says, "We're

Freak the Mighty, that's who we are. We're nine feet tall, in case you haven't noticed."

That's how it started, really, how we got to be Freak the Mighty, slaying dragons and fools and walking high above the world.

8.
Dinosaur Brain

It turned out to be a cool summer.

I figured we'd get in trouble for running into the pond. It looked bad for a while when the cops drove us home and I got out all soaking wet and covered with gook, and when Grim was hosing me down he had this really pruney look on his face, like he was smelling something bad, but the cops made out like I was a hero or something, rescuing the poor crippled midget kid. So Grim listens to the cops and then he gives me this weird look, like, *imagine my surprise,* and he goes in the house and then Gram comes running out in her nightgown with this big fluffy towel and she really makes a fuss.

Me rescuing Freak. What a joke, right? Except that's how it must have looked from a distance, because they never knew it was Freak who rescued me — or his genius brain and my big dumb body.

Gram is there rubbing me with the towel and her hands are shaking and she's saying, "Oh, I saw those blue lights and I thought the worst," and Grim is behind her looking at me real intense and shaking his head, and he's saying, "Who'd a thunk it, Mabel," which is some kind of joke because Gram's name isn't Mabel.

Anyhow, they take me inside and the first thing Gram does is give me a bowl of ice cream, and Grim, he keeps shaking his head and he goes, "What this young man needs is a cup of coffee. Real coffee," and then he gets busy putting the filter in the machine and measuring out the coffee and standing by while it drips through, and he's got this stern look like he's thinking deep thoughts. By the time I polish off the ice cream, Grim is handing me coffee in a china cup, from the set they never use.

He gives me that cup like it's a really big deal, maybe because I'm not allowed to drink coffee yet, and he's so Grim-like and serious I open my mouth to say what's the big deal, you really think this is my first cup of coffee (yeah, right!), and something happens and the words come out: "Thank you, sir," and it's like I'm *possessed* or something, I've no idea where the things I'm saying are coming from, or why.

I go, "Thanks for the towel, Gram. And the ice cream. Could I have sugar in the coffee? Two teaspoons, please," and Grim claps his hands together and he says, "Of course you can, son," and it's like *whoa!* because he never calls me that. Always Max or Maxwell or "that boy."

Next thing he's clearing his throat and coughing into his fist and Gram is looking at the two of us and she gets this Gram-like glow, like this is how it's *supposed* to be, the way things always happen on *The Wonder Years,* with the family getting all gooey and sentimental about some numb thing the bratty kid did while he's having all his wonderful years or whatever.

Gram says, "I want you to promise me something, Maxwell dear. Promise me you'll keep away from the hoodlum boy and his awful friends. Nobody got hurt this time, but I shudder to think what *might* have happened."

And Grim, bless his pointed little head, he goes, "Maxwell can handle himself, can't you, uh, Max?"

Right. *Uh, Max.* Not son. Which is okay by me.

"I can run," I say to Gram. "I see Tony D., that's what I'll do."

"Good boy," Gram says. "I thought, because you're so much bigger than he is . . . well, you just do that, dear. You run away."

"He's not running away," Grim says, real impatient. "He's taking evasive action. Avoiding a confrontation. That's a very different thing, right, Max?"

I nod and drink my coffee without slurping and decide it's better not to mention that Tony D. carries a knife and he's probably got guns, too, because then Gram would only worry and she's such a clunker when she's worried.

Like I said, it turns out to be a pretty cool summer. Usually what I do is just hang around and look at my comic books and watch the tube, or go shopping with Gram if she really makes a fuss. I hate the beach because the beach is stupid, the cool crowd looking sleek and tanned and aren't-we-gorgeous?, and because if you saw me lying on a blanket you'd go, hey, why is that albino walrus wearing sunglasses?

So mostly I just vegetate in the basement and pick my navel, to quote Grim, Mr. Belly Button Lint himself.

Freak changes all that. Each and every morning the little dude humps himself over and he bangs on the bulkhead, wonka-wonka-wonka, he may be small but he sure is noisy. "Get outta bed, you lazy beast! There are fair maidens to rescue! Dragons to slay!" which is what he says every single morning, exactly the same thing, until it's like he's this alarm clock and as soon as I hear the wonka-wonka-wonka of him beating the bulkhead, I know what's coming next: fair maidens and dragons, and Freak with that wake-up-the-world grin of his, going, "Hurry up with the cereal, how can you eat that much, you big ox, come on, let's *do* something," he's so full of eveready energy you can practically hear his brain humming, and he never can sit still.

"Ants in the pants," I say one morning when

he's ready to yank the cereal bowl off the table, he's in such a hurry to *do* something, and he goes, "What?" and I go, "You must have ants in your pants," and he gets this funny look and he goes, "That's what the Fair Gwen always says, did she tell you to say that?" and I shake my head and finish the cereal real slow and Freak goes, "For your information there are two thousand two hundred and forty-seven known subspecies of hymenopteran insects, Latin name *Formicidae,* and *none* of them are in my pants."

Which cracks me up, even though I don't understand a word he's saying.

"I propose a quest," he says. "We shall journey far to the East and see what lies there."

By now I know what a quest is because Freak has explained the whole deal, how it started with King Arthur trying to keep all his knights busy by making them do things that proved how strong and brave and smart they were, or sometimes how totally numb, because how else can you explain dudes running around inside big clunky tin cans and praying all the time? Which I don't mention to Freak because he's very sensitive about knights and quests and secret meanings. Like how a dragon isn't really just a big slimy fire-breathing monster, it's a symbol of nature or something.

"A dragon is fear of the natural world," Freak says. "An archetype of the unknown."

I go, "What's an archy-type?" and Freak sighs

and shakes his head and reaches into his knapsack for his dictionary.

This is true. He really *does* keep a dictionary in his knapsack, it's his favorite book, and he pulls it out like Arnold Schwarzenegger pulling out a machine gun or something, that's the fierce look he gets with a book in his hands.

"Go on," he says, making me take the book, "look it up." And now I wish I hadn't said anything about this archetype dude because I *hate* looking up stuff in his stupid dictionary.

"Start with A," he says.

"I know that."

"A-R," he says. "Just go along the A's until you come to A-R."

Yeah, right. Easy for a genius to use the dictionary, since he already knows how to spell the words. And R's never look like backward E's to Freak, which is the way they look to me sometimes, unless I really squint and think about it.

"Careful," he says. "You'll bite off your tongue and then we'll have to waste the day at the emergency room, getting it reattached. Microsurgery is *such* a bore, didn't anybody ever tell you that?"

"Huh?" I say, but I do close my mouth so my tongue doesn't stick out. I'm still looking in the dictionary for "archetype" and I'm looking for words that are underlined with red ink, because that's what Freak does the first time he looks up a word, he makes a line under it, and you'd be amazed how many are underlined, there are whole *pages* like that, where he's looked up every single word.

Finally he spells out all the letters for me, and I find the stupid word.

"There's nothing about dragons here," I say, squinting hard at the stuff under the word. "It just says 'pattern.' So what is it, a sewing type of thing?"

Freak has this disgusted look and he takes the dictionary and he goes, "You're hopeless. Pattern is the first definition. I was referring to the *second* definition, which is much more interesting. 'A universal symbol or idea in the psyche, expressed in dreams or dreamlike images.' "

Like that helps, right? I'm getting bored with the dictionary, so I pretend to understand and Freak finally gives up and he shakes his head and goes, "I don't know why I bother. Dinosaurs had brains the size of peanuts and they ruled the earth for a hundred million years."

9.
Life Is Dangerous

So out we go. It's a habit by now, Freak riding up high on my shoulders and using his little feet to steer me if I forget where we're going. Not that we always know. Freak likes to make things up as he goes along. You think you're just walking down this ordinary sidewalk and really you're crossing this dangerous bridge, the kind made of vines that hangs high up in the air over a deep canyon, and when Freak makes it up it seems so real, you're afraid to look down or you'll get dizzy and fall off the sidewalk.

"Don't ever look down," he says. "Just keep your eyes closed." And then he puts his hands over my eyes and tells me to keep walking straight. "One foot," he says. "Now the next."

I'm fighting to keep my balance, and his hands are making me dizzy.

"One more step," Freak says. "Steady. Steady. Now lift up your hoof — I mean your foot. There, we made it!" And he takes his hands away and I see we've crossed the street.

"Go East," he says when I get to the end of the block. "That way, mighty steed! Yonder lies the East!"

I go, "How do you know which way is East?" And then something is glinting in my eye and Freak is showing me this little compass.

"The Official Cub Scout Compass?"

"That's a clever disguise so you don't know how valuable it is," he says. "This is actually a rare and valuable artifact passed down for generations. Lancelot used it, so did Sir Gawain, and for a time the Black Knight kept it on a chain next to his heart."

I go, "So the Black Knight was a Cub Scout, huh?" and Freak laughs and says, "That way. We go to the East on a secret mission."

We walk for miles. Way beyond the pond and the playground and the school, and for a while we're going through this really ritzy neighborhood of big white houses and blue swimming pools. Freak keeps saying stuff like, "That's the Castle of Avarice," and, "Yonder lies the Bloated Moat," and when we go under trees he'll say, "Proceed with caution," or, "All clear," depending on how low the branches come down.

"We must be East," I say. "Have we got to yonder yet?" because my stupid feet are getting sore, but Freak pats me on the head and says, "Yonder always lies over the next horizon. You could look it up if you don't believe me."

"Oh, I believe you."

On and on, block after block, through all these

neighborhoods that Freak says are really secret kingdoms. I'll bet we've gone ten miles at least, because my legs think it's a hundred, and even as light as Freak is, he's starting to feel heavy.

"We're almost there," he says. "Turn at the end of the block."

"Where is it we're going?"

"You'll see," he says, "and you *will* be amazed."

Ahead there's this busy intersection, cars whizzing by, and it all seems sort of familiar.

"Can we stop for a Coke?" I say. "Grim gave me a dollar, big deal, but we can split it."

Freak goes, "Then that shall be your reward, faithful steed — tinted sucrose and bubbles of air. Onward! Onward to the Fortress!"

It turns out the Fortress looks like part of a hospital, which it is. The regular hospital is around in front and there's this new building added on out back. MEDICAL RESEARCH, it says over the door, and I know because I made Freak spell it out.

"Does that mean they do experiments and stuff?"

Freak says, "Indeed they do."

"What kind of experiments?" I ask.

"Can you keep a secret?" he says. "Do you swear on your honor?"

"Sure. On my honor."

Freak is really excited, he's shifting around on my shoulders so much, I'm afraid he'll fall off.

"That's not good enough," he says. "You need to swear by blood."

"You mean like cut myself?"

"Well, no," he says, and you can tell he's thinking about it real hard. "An actual incision is not necessary. It's the same thing if you just spit on your hand."

"Huh?"

"Saliva is like blood without the red," he says. "Do as I say, spit in your hand."

So I spit in my hand, just a little drop, but Freak says it doesn't matter how much, a single molecule would work, because it's the principle of the thing. "Now put your hand over your heart," he says.

I put my hand over my heart.

"Now swear on your heart that the data you are about to receive will be divulged to no one."

"I swear."

Freak bends down and he's got his hand cupped around my ear and he's whispering: "Inside the research building is a secret laboratory called The Experimental Bionics Unit. The unit's mission is to develop a new form of bionic robot for human modification."

"What's that?" I say.

"Shhh! Speak of this to no one, but at some future time as yet undetermined, I will enter that lab and become the first bionically improved human."

"I still don't know what it means," I say.

"Bionics. And please don't make me look it up in the dictionary."

"Bionics," Freak says. "That's the science of designing replacement parts for the human body."

"You mean like mechanical arms and legs?"

"That's ancient history," Freak says. "The Bionics Unit is building a whole new body just my size."

"Yeah? What'll it look like? A robot?"

"A human robot," Freak says. "Also it will look a lot like me, only enlarged and improved."

"Yeah, right," I say. "Let's go home, my feet are tired."

Freak tugs hard at my hair. "True!" he says, with his voice getting high and excited. "I've been in there, in the special unit! I have to go every few months for tests. They've taken my measurements, analyzed my blood and metabolic rates. They've monitored my cardiac rhythms and my respiratory functions. I've already been X-rayed and CAT-scanned and sonogrammed. They're fitting me for a bionic transplant, I'm going to be the first."

I can tell he really means it. This isn't a pretend quest, or making houses into castles or swimming pools into moats. This is why we came here, so Freak could show me where he's been. The place is important to him. I understand this much, even if I still don't understand about bionics or what it means to be a human robot.

"Will it hurt?" I ask. "Getting your parts replaced?"

Freak doesn't answer for a while and then he says in his stern, smart voice, "Sure it will hurt. But so what? Pain is just a state of mind. You can think your way out of anything, even pain."

I'm pretty worried about the whole deal, and I go, "But why do you want to be the first? Can't someone else be first? Isn't it dangerous?"

"Life is dangerous," Freak says, and you can tell he's thought a lot about this. After a while he kicks me with his little feet and says, "Home."

10.
Rats or Worse

One thing that happened over the summer, I grew even more.

Grim takes a look at me one day and he goes, "All that walking you do, it must be stretching out your legs. And carrying poor Kevin around, that seems to be putting real muscle on you."

"He's not that heavy. And anyhow it's not fair everybody always says 'Poor Kevin,' just because he didn't grow."

Grim gives me this long, sorrowful look and then he clears his throat and says, "You're quite right, he *is* a rather remarkable boy."

"He's memorized almost the whole dictionary. You can ask him anything and he knows what it means."

"You don't say," Grim says, and he has this smug look like maybe Freak is lying and a total goon like me would never get it, and I want to tell him he's wrong about Freak and the dictionary, but instead I just shut my face and go down under.

Grim, he's okay sometimes, like when Tony D. chased us into the pond, but most of the time he thinks he knows everything, which he doesn't. And if you don't believe me, look under "grim" in the dictionary, it sure doesn't say "a smart grown-up." No way.

So I'm hanging out down under, listening to some of my thrash tapes on the fake Walkman I got last Christmas, when Freak pops up on the side of my bed. Because of the headphones and the volume being pumped up to mega-decibel I never hear him come in, he's just suddenly *there*, like whoa! and I'll bet I jumped about a foot.

Freak rolls his eyes and goes, "Ah, music, how it calms the savage beast."

"How'd you get here?"

"Would you believe teleportation? No? Then I came down through the bulkhead door like always. And like always, I have a quest in mind."

Right away I go, "My feet hurt."

"We don't have to leave the neighborhood."

"Cool. What kind of quest is this?"

Freak grins. "A treasure hunt. Except we don't really have to hunt because I already know where the treasure is."

"Where?"

"Underground," he says. "Specifically, in the sewer."

"Yeah, right," I say and sit back down on the bed. Freak is looking at me sideways and I can tell he's not telling me everything, which he almost never does, not all at once.

"Truth," he says. "The treasure is hidden in a storm drain. This has been confirmed by visual observation."

"Treasure in a storm drain? You mean like gold and diamonds kind of stuff?"

"Possibly," he says, acting mysterious. "Anything is possible."

The deal is, we have to wait until night, so no one can see us messing with the storm drain. Not just night, Freak says, we need to do it at exactly three in the morning.

"Optimum darkness occurs at oh-three-hundred hours," he says, looking at the new watch his mom gave him, the kind that tells you what time it is in Tokyo, just in case you're wondering. "We must dress in black and cover our faces with soot."

For the next couple of hours we try to find soot, but it turns out you need a fireplace for soot, or at least a chimney, so Freak finally decides that my idea about using regular dirt will have to do.

"I've got black dungarees," I say, "but no black shirts. Can I just wear a dirty shirt?"

Freak makes a face and says, "What a *disgusting* idea. Don't worry about the shirt, I'll get you one. Can you manage black socks?"

You ever notice how long it takes for things to happen when you know they're *supposed* to happen? My fake Walkman has a built-in alarm, and I set it for two in the morning and wear the headphones to bed, but before you can wake up you have to fall asleep, and I never *do* fall asleep because I keep waiting for the alarm to go off. Which is, I know, typical butthead behavior.

I'm lying awake in the dark on a hot summer night and I'm thinking, *Treasure in the sewer? What kind of quest is this, huh? Is Freak completely making this up or what?*

Meanwhile there's this cricket making this creaky cricket noise that normally is okay, except when you're trying to fall asleep then it's *not* okay, and you want a big can of Raid, send it to Disney World or insect heaven or wherever it is that dead crickets go.

Question: How come Freak knows about this stuff in the storm drain?

Question: How come we have to put dirt on our faces?

Question: How come three in the morning?

Question: How long do crickets live?

Finally I give up on the first three and work on the cricket problem, but the little critter is pretty clever, it stops cricketing whenever I get too close and I never *do* find it and squash it with my shoe, which I swear I am ready to do, even if crickets are supposed to be harmless.

And then after almost forever it gets to be two-thirty and I figure that's close enough, I'll go up and wait under Freak's window like I promised.

There's no moon, the sky is dark and empty,

and the back yards are so lonesome it feels creepy and exciting — the truth is, I've never been out alone at this time of night.

I only fall down a couple of times, which isn't bad considering how hard it is to see. When I get to Freak's bedroom window, he's waiting for me.

"You sound like a car wreck," he says. "Here, you better put on this shirt so you don't glow in the dark."

Out of the window he hands me this silly-feeling shirt.

"Hey wait a minute, this is you mom's blouse!"

"It's black," he says. "That's what counts. The camouflage factor."

"Forget it," I say and give him back the Fair Gwen's blouse.

Freak sighs. "Okay," he says. "Roll around on the ground and darken yourself."

That's easy, and better than wearing some dumb blouse. "What about you?" I ask, when I'm covered with dirt, enough so I want to sneeze.

Freak goes, "Beware the Force, earthling," and he stands up in the window and I can see he's got a Darth Vader costume on, except he's not wearing the mask part. He opens the window all the way and I lift him out and put him on my shoulders.

He goes, "Pledge to me your fealty," and I say, "Huh?" and he says, "Never mind, there's no time to look up 'fealty.' Just promise you'll do what I say."

"I promise."

"Go to the end of the block," he orders. "Attempt to conceal us in the shadows."

That's easy, because the street is one big shadow. It's so dark I can hardly see my feet, or maybe I got some dirt in my eyes, but the point is no one sees us because there's no one to see us. You'd never know anybody lived here, let alone a whole blockful of people, it's like we're on an empty planet or something.

"Was the real Darth Vader as tall as this?" Freak asks, from where he's riding high up on my shoulders.

"I thought it was just a movie."

"You know what I mean. What's that!"

"That" is a cat that runs out from under my feet so out-of-nowhere sudden that my heart goes *wham*.

"Was it a black cat?" Freak wants to know.

"Too dark to tell," I say. "Are we almost there?"

Finally I figure out it's hard to see because the Darth Vader cape is hanging in my eyes, but by then we're at the end of the block and the storm drain is right there by the curb.

"See if you can pull it open," Freak says. He's standing with his arms folded, and the expression on his face — well, he really *does* look like a pint-sized Darth Vader.

I hook my hands in the storm drain grate and

give it a heave but nothing happens.

"I can't budge it."

"Try again," he says with his arms folded, like he's a lord of the universe.

I try again and it's like the grate is Super Glued or something. No way can I pull it up. Freak is tugging at my leg and he goes, "Option Two is now in effect."

He reaches inside his little cape. Out comes a flashlight, one of those small kinds that look sort of like a cigarette lighter, and also a spool of kite string.

"I devised a special retrieval device," Freak says.

"Looks like a bent paper clip on a string," I say, and Freak tells me to shut up and follow orders.

"You hold the string," he says, and then he gets down on his knees and shines the little flashlight through the grate. "Can you see it?" he asks. "Can you?"

I look, but it's hard to see anything and it smells like something died in the storm drain, which come to think of it, it probably did. Rats or worse.

"Down there," Freak says. "The beam is hitting it right now."

"That? That's just a piece of junk."

"Wrong," Freak says, real fierce. "It *looks* like a piece of junk. It may very well contain fabulous wealth. Drop the line down and see if you can hook it."

I'm thinking, boy, what a butthead, rolling in the dirt for this little Darth Vader so he can play pretend games in the middle of the night, but I do what he asks, I drop the hook down, and much to my surprise, it actually hooks into something and when I pull up on the kite string I can see what it is.

"A purse," I say. "Looks like a grotty old purse."

"Careful," Freak says. "Pull it up to the grate so I can grab the strap."

I bring it up an inch at a time, and Darth — excuse me, Freak — manages to get his small hand down through the grate and grab hold of the soggy old purse and then he almost drops it. I yank up on the kite string and we both manage to squeeze the slimy purse up through the bars.

"Whew! Mission accomplished," Freak says.

The old purse is torn and wet, and I don't want to touch it unless I have gloves on.

"Gross," I say. "Somebody must have flushed this down a toilet."

"No way," Freak says. "I saw one of Tony D.'s punks stuff it down there yesterday morning."

"Yeah? They must have stole it."

"No doubt," Freak says, and he opens the clasp and points his little light inside the purse.

By now I know there isn't going to be any treasure, but still this is pretty cool, recovering stuff that Blade's gang ripped off from some little old lady or whatever.

"A wallet," Freak says, and he flips open this cheap-looking wallet, the kind that's made to hold credit cards.

There's no money inside, but there is a plastic ID card, and on the plastic card is a lady's name.

"Loretta Lee," Freak says. "I'll bet you anything she's a damsel in distress."

Which, as it turns out, is almost true. The real deal is that she's a damsel who *causes* distress. Which we find out the very next day.

11. The Damsel of Distress

The address on the ID card is this place on the other side of the millpond. They used to call it the New Tenements, but now everybody mostly calls it the New Testaments, which Gram told me has nothing to do with the Bible.

"People will make their jokes," she says. "Call that place whatever you want, but you are not to set foot over there. Is that clear, Maxwell dear?"

It's not like I *wanted* to go into the Testaments, so it was real easy to keep that promise, and then the day after we pull that soggy purse out of the sewer Freak explains how it's okay to break a promise if you're on a quest.

"There may even be a reward involved," he says.

"The lady won't have much money if she lives in the Testaments," I say. "Poor people live there, and dope fiends."

What we do is go down to the playground and cut over behind that little patch of trees, just in case anybody is looking, and then we can circle around behind the pond. Freak is riding up top, which he almost always does now. That way he doesn't have to wear his leg brace or carry his crutches, and besides, I like how it feels to have a really smart brain on my shoulders, helping me think.

Freak is talking a mile a minute, more stuff about the Round Table and how important quests are, and why knights are bound up with oaths, which is not the same thing as swearing, and I'm trying to listen and not ask questions because if I ask questions, he'll pull out his dictionary.

When we get to the Testaments, though, Freak shuts right up. It's this big, falling-apart place with a bunch of apartments, and it looks sad and smells like fish and sour milk. There're a lot of bikes and toys lying around, mostly bashed up and broken, and the little kids who live there look almost as busted up as the toys. When they see us coming they make these screaming noises and run away, but you can tell they're not really scared, they just want to pretend like we're a monster or something, eek eek.

"Maybe we should reconsider this particular quest," Freak says. He's up there on my shoulders and he's getting fidgety, squirming around.

But we're already outside the apartment door, and I go, "Maybe she really needs that ID card," so it's my fault what happens next.

The door opens before we even ring the bell,

and this hand comes snaking out and reaches for the mailbox and finds this rolled-up newspaper and pulls it back inside. And there's something about the blind way that hand moves that's creepy. Get out of here, I'm thinking.

Then, before I can get my feet moving fast enough to leave, this woman's voice is cussing us out.

"Iggy!" she says. "Iggy, come here and see this!"

Now she's standing in the doorway, this scrawny, yellow-haired woman with small, hard eyes and blurry red lips. She's wearing this ratty old bathrobe and she's smoking this cigarette and squinting at us and making a face.

"Iggy," she says out of the side of her mouth, "come here and tell me is the circus in town or what?"

Next thing there's this big hairy dude in the doorway, he's got a huge beer gut and these giant arms all covered with blue tattoos and he's got a beard that looks like it's made out of red barbed wire.

"Ain't the circus," he says, spitting a big gob on the step. "This here is the carnival."

Freak isn't saying anything, and I want to get out of here, so I go, "Sorry, wrong number," and I'm trying to back away and not fall over a tricycle when the hairy dude comes out the door real quick and gets in my way.

"Not so fast," he says. "Who sent you?"

"I know the big one," the woman is saying.

She's waving her cigarette around and squinting her eyes up and you can tell she's thinking on something, worrying it like a dog with a bone. "I seen him around somewhere. Don't he look familiar, Iggy? Don't he?"

Freak finally says, "Please excuse us, we have the wrong address. We were, uhm, trying to locate a Miss Loretta Lee."

The tattoo dude hears that and he starts to laugh, this fat sound way down in his big belly, and he goes, "You hear that, Loretta? This an old flame of yours or what?" Then he reaches up and pokes me in the chest hard enough to make me catch my breath, and he says, "Cat got your tongue, kid? What is this, a Siamese-twin act?"

All I can think to say is, "Oops," because we have the right address after all. The squinty woman in the robe is Loretta Lee, and even more important, Iggy is Iggy Lee, and I feel like a total butthead because I've heard of Iggy Lee, he's the boss of The Panheads, this bad-news motorcycle gang.

"We found your purse!" Freak blurts out, and he tosses down the purse and Iggy Lee catches it with one hand and he gives Loretta this secret look, like he's going to have some fun here.

"You better come inside," he says, looking up at Freak. "You and Frankenstein."

"Sorry," Freak says, and his voice is chattery high. "We'll have to decline your kind invitation because we, uhm, we have to leave now."

Loretta flicks her cigarette butt at my feet and she says, "Iggy says come inside, you better do it."

So we go inside. I have to take Freak off my shoulders so we can get in the door and that's when Loretta looks at me real hard and she says, "I know that one. It's like a flash from the past, Iggy. You know him?"

Iggy isn't paying any attention to her, he's pointing at this ratty chair and he says, "Sit down, it makes me nervous looking up."

Loretta comes around and she says, "Don't be making Iggy nervous. Not this early in the day. Last dude made him nervous, they had to — "

"Shut up, Loretta," Iggy says in this real quiet voice. "I'm thinking. You're right, he *does* look familiar."

I'm sitting in this chair, which feels like it might bust apart, and Freak is right next to me and I can see he's trying to stand straight but it's not easy because he's all bent up inside.

"Names," Iggy says.

Freak clears his throat and tries to make his voice sound deep and more grown up. "We're sorry to disturb you, but we have to go home now. It's a matter of some urgency."

Iggy reaches out and he flicks his fingers at Freak's nose, *whack*. I can tell it hurts, but Freak doesn't say anything, he just tenses up.

Iggy goes, "I ask a question, you better answer, get it? Names. I want your names."

Freak tells his name and then mine and Iggy

reaches down and pats him on the head. "Very good," he says. "Now that wasn't hard, was it? Next question, where'd you get Loretta's purse?"

Freak tells him we found it in the storm drain. He doesn't mention us dressing up all in black, or the Darth Vader costume, or anything about knights or quests.

"Next question," Iggy says. "Where's the money?"

Loretta coughs on her new cigarette and says, "But Iggy, there wasn't any money," and he goes, "Shut up, Loretta," and she coughs again and shuts up, you can tell she's afraid of Iggy, the way she holds herself tight whenever he says anything.

Freak goes, "I've got two dollars in change, you can have it but we have to go home now."

Iggy gives him this look like he's thinking seriously about throwing up and he says, "What is it with you, you've gotta go home? We're having a nice little talk here, don't spoil it."

All of a sudden Loretta jumps up and she goes, "Iggy! Iggy! I've got it! Kenny Kane! Remember Kenny Kane?"

For a second I think he's going to hit her, and then he relaxes and really looks at me and his eyes go wide and he nods and says, "Sure. That's it. Kenny Kane. You're right, he's a ringer for old Killer Kane. Must be his kid, huh? Sure it is."

Loretta looks real happy that she finally figured it out and she runs into the kitchen and kicks some stuff out of the way and pulls open the refrigerator and we can hear her laughing and saying, "I *knew* it, I just *knew* it."

When she comes back in she's got two cans of Bud and she pops them both and gives one to Iggy. "Breakfast of champions," she says. "What a flash, huh? You remember that time old Kenny — "

"Shut up, Loretta!" Iggy says, then he chugs the Bud and squashes the can in his fist and he drops it right on the floor. Which is the first time I notice all the other crushed cans, they're everywhere, the whole place is like a trash can or a big ashtray or something.

Meanwhile Freak is giving me this look like he has no idea what's going on, and that look scares me more than Iggy Lee and all his tattoos.

"I've got him, too," Loretta says, snapping her fingers. "The midget or dwarf or whatever he is. He must be Gwen's kid, you remember Gwen? Stuck-up Gwen?"

"No," Iggy says, and his eyes are burning into me. "Never heard of Gwen."

Loretta goes, "Doesn't matter. What a flash this is. Kenny Kane. Time flies, huh, Ig? I can remember when these two were *born*. And then, what was it, a couple years later Kenny does his thing and he's in the yard, right? Doing time."

Iggy says, "That he is. I know a guy knows him inside." He gives me this creepy look and he says, "You go up there to visit the old man, you tell him Iggy says hello, okay?"

"I doubt he even *knows* his father, Ig. He was only a little kid when it happened. Right?"

I don't say anything and Freak is looking at me like he's never seen me before and then Iggy says, "Killer Kane. What a tough hombre *he* was."

Loretta says, "I heard he seen the light in there. He's got religion, is that true?"

"I don't know."

Iggy snorts and he says, "He don't know. You don't know much, do you?"

I shake my head.

Loretta says, "He's some kinda retard, Ig. He don't even know how big and strong he is, I'll bet." She pokes Iggy or tickles him and in this strange giggly voice she says, "Whyn't you find out? Find out if he's as strong as he looks?"

Iggy scowls and he goes, "Give me a break, Loretta." He gives me this long look and then he hooks his thumb at the door and says, "Show time is over, boys. Get out of here, the both of you."

Loretta says, "But, Iggy, we could have some fun."

"You're the retard, Loretta," Iggy says. "What if Killer Kane hears I was messing with his kid? No thank you."

"He's in for life," she says. "What's the harm?"

"Life ain't life, how many times I tell you that?"

Loretta is squinting at him and she goes, "Are you serious? He's getting out someday?" and Iggy looks at me and tells her to shut up again.

Finally we get to the door and that's when Loretta wants to rub Freak on the head. Real hard, with her knuckles.

"This is for luck," she says to Iggy. "It's good luck, rubbing a dwarf on the head."

Freak is trying to duck away and he says, "I'm not a dwarf and I'm not good luck."

So Loretta gives up on rubbing his head and she stands up straight and folds her arms and says, "Hey, midget man? I know all about you. Your old man was a magician, did you know that?"

Freak is scuttling around behind me, keeping out of her way, but when she says that, I can tell he wants to know about his father, if maybe he really *was* a magician.

"Yeah," Loretta says. "Right after you was born. He *must* be a magician, because as soon as he heard the magic words 'birth defect,' he disappeared."

A second later Iggy shoves us out the door.

12.
Killer Kane, Killer Kane, Had a Kid Who Got No Brain

I feel real bad for Freak, because he hates it when people try to rub his head for luck, but I don't say a word, I just run us home, thumping the short way back around the pond, and my big feet never even trip me up because I'm on automatic, I'm this running machine.

"Whoa!" Freak says when we get to his house. "Now *that* was an adventure, huh?"

"An evil dude like Iggy Lee, we were lucky to get out of there alive."

Freak goes, "No way, that was all talk."

Yeah, right. The real deal is that I was scared the whole time I was there, and so was Freak, even if he won't admit it now.

"That stuff about my father was true," Freak says, studying his fingernails and acting real cool again. "The Fair Gwen won't talk about it. All she says is, 'He made his decision and I made mine.' But I know he ran away because of me. And you know what?"

"What?"

"Good riddance to bad rubbish."

For some reason that really gets me laughing. Something about the way he says it, or maybe it's all that nervous stuff left over from the New Testaments. Whatever, I'm rolling on the ground like a moron and Freak is strutting around and saying stuff like, "Loretta my Queen, wouldst thou accept my hand in marriage?" and, "Sir Iggy, wouldst thou do us all a big favor and fall upon thy sword?" And I'm laughing so hard I can hardly breathe.

Everything is pretty much okay after that. One thing we don't do, though, we don't talk about my father, good old Killer Kane. Which is fine by me.

School.

For the last week or so it's like getting jabbed with a little needle every time I hear that word. Gram is trying to pretend how excited she is I'm finally in the eighth grade, like this is a really big deal. Which is a joke, because the only reason I got passed from seventh grade is because they figured this way the big butthead can be — quote — someone *else's* problem, thank God, we've had quite enough of Maxwell Kane — unquote.

Gram takes me out to the mall to get new clothes, which is about as much fun as going to the dentist, except maybe worse because at least at the dentist you're mostly just in a chair with the door closed, where at the mall with Gram it's like hello, world, here I am, take a good look.

This girl at the shoe store, she's got a little smirk and she goes, "Thirteen triple E? Do they make shoes that big?" and Gram goes, "I'm quite sure they do, dear, you go ask the manager." And then she looks at me and she goes, "Maxwell, this is *not* major surgery, so you will please, as a special favor to me, wipe that wounded look off your face and try to be polite."

Yeah, right. The manager, when he comes out with these Brand-X running shoes, he wants to help me take off my old shoes, like he's pretty sure I can't do it by myself, but I give him this look and he backs off and lets me do it myself.

"I wish you'd tie those laces, dear," Gram says when I'm squishing around in the new shoes.

"That's the fashion," the manager says with this heh-heh-heh laugh. "Actually, they're designed that way. You don't *need* to lace up."

Just to prove what a jerk he is, I tie up the laces and that makes Gram happy. Which is funny sometimes, how little it takes to make her happy, except you can't really figure what until you've already done it. Does that make any sense?

Finally we escape from the mall and I've got enough new clothes to last me, as Grim points out, a week or so.

"You could just keep letting down his cuffs,"

Grim says. "Except they don't have cuffs now, what am I thinking?"

"I think he looks quite handsome," Gram says. "Maxwell, please turn around. And keep your shirttail tucked in."

"Ah, leave him alone," Grim says. "He's not a fashion model."

"I just can't get over it," Gram says. "Our little Maxwell is growing up."

"Growing is right," Grim says. "The boy is certainly growing."

The deal is, Freak and I get to be in the same classes. He made the Fair Gwen go in and see all these people at the school, because I wasn't supposed to be in the smart classes, no way, and finally they all agreed it would be good for Freak, having someone to help him get around.

Gram acts kind of worried about it and she doesn't want to sign the papers, like she thinks the L.D. class has done me a lot of good or something, and being in the genius class is just going to make me slower and dumber than ever. But one night I come up the cellar stairs real quiet and Grim is saying, "Let's give it a try, nothing else has worked, maybe what he needs is a friend, that's the one thing he's never had with all those special teachers." And the next morning she signs the papers, and when we get to school the first day, Freak helps me find my name on the list and it's true, we're in all the same classes.

At first all the other kids are so into looking

cool and acting cool and showing off their new outfits, they hardly notice us in the hall, Freak riding high on my shoulders, or the deal where his desk is always right next to mine. That wears off, though, and by the time we leave math, which is just passing out the textbooks and a bunch of numbers chalked on the blackboard, you can hear the whispers in the hall.

Like, hey, who's the midget? And, there goes Mad Max; and, excuse me while I barf; and, look what escaped from the freak show; and, oh, my *gawd* that's *disgusting*.

"Maxwell Kane?"

This is from Mrs. Donelli, the English teacher, she's new to the school, and when I nod and raise my pencil, she goes, "Maxwell, will you please stand up and tell the class something about your summer?"

Which, if she wasn't new to the school, she'd know better, because getting up in the class and saying stuff is not something I do.

"Maxwell," she goes, "is there a problem?"

By now there's a lot of noise and kids are shouting stuff like, "Forget it, Mrs. Donelli, his brain is in his tail!"

"Ask him to count, he can paw the ground!"

"Maxi Pad! Maxi Pad! Ask him quick about his dad!"

"Killer Kane! Killer Kane! Had a kid who got no brain!"

Mrs. Donelli has this look like she stepped in something and she can't get it off her shoe. The shouting and singing goes on and on, and pretty soon some of the kids are throwing stuff at us, pencils and erasers and wadded-up paper, and it's like Mrs. Donelli has no idea what to do about it, the room is out of control.

Then Freak climbs up on his desk, which makes him about as big as a normal person standing up, and he starts shouting at the top of his lungs.

"Order!" he shouts. "Order in the court! Let justice be heard!"

For some reason, maybe because he looks so fierce with his jaw sticking out and his little fists all balled up and the way he's stamping his crooked little feet, everybody shuts up and there's this spooky silence.

Finally Mrs. Donelli says, "You must be Kevin, is that right?"

Freak has this look, he's still acting really fierce, and he goes, "Sometimes, I am."

"Sometimes? What does that mean?"

"It means sometimes I'm *more* than Kevin."

"Oh," says Mrs. Donelli, and you can tell she has no idea what he's talking about, but she thinks it's important to let him talk. "So, Kevin," she says, "can you give us all an example?"

Next thing I know, Freak has his hands on my head and he's getting himself on my shoulders and he's tugging at me in a way that I know means "stand up," and so I do it, I stand right up in class and I can see Mrs. Donelli's eyes getting bigger and bigger.

I'm standing there with Freak high above me and it feels right, it makes me feel strong and smart.

"How's *this* for an example?" Freak is saying. "Sometimes we're nine feet tall, and strong enough to walk through walls. Sometimes we fight gangs. Sometimes we find treasure. Sometimes we slay dragons and drink from the Holy Grail!"

Mrs. Donelli is backing up to her desk and she says, "Oh, my, that's very interesting, I'm sure, but could you both just sit down?"

But Freak is riding me like he's the jockey and I'm the horse, he's steering me around the class room, showing off. He's raising his fist and punching it in the air and going, "Freak the Mighty! Freak the Mighty!" and pretty soon he's got all the other kids chanting, "Freak the Mighty! Freak the Mighty! Freak the Mighty!" even though they don't know what he's talking about, or what it means.

I'm standing up straight, as tall as I can, and I'm marching exactly like he wants me to, right and left, backwards and forwards, and it's like music or something, like I don't even have to think about it, I just do it, and all those kids chanting our name, and Mrs. Donelli has no idea what's going on, she's definitely flipped out and more or less hiding behind her desk.

The whole class is raising their fists in the air and chanting: "Freak the Mighty! Freak the Mighty! Freak the Mighty!"

I can't explain why, but it was really pretty cool.

Anyhow, that's how Freak and I get sent to the principal's office the first time together.

Mrs. Addison, she's the principal, she takes one look at us waiting outside her office, and she goes, "What have we here?"

"I'm afraid there has been a slight misunderstanding," Freak says. "If you'd be so good as to allow me to explain."

Mrs. Addison is this really serious-acting black woman with tight gray hair in a bun and these suits that make her look like she works in a bank or something. She has this funny little smile like she's sucking on a lemon and it quick turns sweet, and then she goes, "By all means. Let's hear what you have to say. Convince me."

I can't really remember what Freak said, except that he used so many big words, she had to keep looking stuff up in his dictionary, which she seemed to get a real kick out of, but the important thing is, whatever Freak told her, she fell for it.

13. American Chop Suey

I used to think all that spooky stuff about Friday the Thirteenth was just a pile of baloney. But now I'm getting my own personal introduction to what can happen. It's October, and so far things have been going pretty good, better than I ever expected. Me and Freak are like this unit, and even Mrs. Donelli says she is starting to get used to us, which is her way of admitting that Freak is about twice as smart as she is, and for sure he's read more books.

She keeps saying stuff like, "Kevin, we *know* you know the answer, because you *always* know the answer, so wouldn't it be nice if someone else got a chance? For instance, your friend Maxwell?"

Freak goes, "He knows the answer, Mrs. Donelli."

"Yes, Kevin, and I'm sure you're correct because you're *always* correct, but for a change I'd really like to hear Maxwell speak for himself. Maxwell? Maxwell Kane?"

This is dumb because what does it matter if I know the answer? If I don't know, then Freak will tell me and he'll say it in a way I can understand, which is a lot better than Mrs. Donelli can do. So what I do, I just shrug and smile and wait, because I know she'll get tired of asking and move on to the next. As a matter of fact I *do* know the answer — the reason Johnny Tremain got mad and hateful is because he burned his hand in a stupid accident — and I know about that because Freak has been showing me how to read a whole book and for some reason it all makes sense, where before it was just a bunch of words I didn't care about.

My reading skills tutor, Mr. Meehan, he says stuff like, "Max, the tests have always shown that you're not dyslexic or disabled, and this proves it. As you know, heh heh, my personal opinion has always been that you're lazy and stubborn and you didn't *want* to learn. So if hanging out with Kevin somehow improves your attitude and your skills, that's great. Keep up the good work."

It was Mr. Meehan who had a word with Mrs. Donelli, and that's why she finally gave up on trying to make me talk in class, and instead she waits until study hall, where she asks me the same questions alone and I tell her the answers. She still doesn't get it, though, because she always goes, "But, Maxwell, if you can speak to me, then you can speak to your classmates, right?"

Wrong. Big difference. I can't explain what it is, except that my mouth shuts up when there's more than one or two people, and a whole classroom full, forget it.

"Okay, you're shy about public speaking, but how does that apply to writing down the answers? If you can read, then you can write, right?"

Wrong again. The reading stuff Freak helped me figure out by showing how words are just voices on paper. Writing down the words is a whole different story. No matter what Freak says, writing the stuff down is not like talking, and my hand feels so huge and clumsy, it's like the pencil is a piece of spaghetti or something and it keeps slipping away.

Mrs. Donelli says okay for now, she's satisfied I can read, but we'll really have to work on this writing thing, won't we, Maxwell, and when she says that, I just nod and look away, because inside I'm thinking, forget it, no way.

Like Freak says, reading is just a way of listening, and I could always listen, but writing is like talking, and that's a whole other ball game.

Anyhow, what happens first on Friday the Thirteenth, we're in homeroom when this note comes from the principal's office:

Maxwell Kane, your presence is requested.

Gulp.

So Freak and I get up to go and the teacher

says, "No, Kevin, you stay here. Mrs. Addison was very specific. Maxwell is to go alone."

Freak starts to smart-mouth her, then he changes his mind and he nudges me and whispers, "Just give 'em name, rank, and serial number. Deny everything. You aren't back by ten hundred hours, we'll organize a search-and-rescue mission."

He offers to lend me his dictionary, in case I want to try out any big words on Mrs. Addison, but I'm already so worried about being called in alone, all I can think is they're going to put me back in the learning disabled class. I've already decided I'll run away if they do that, I'll go live in the woods somewhere and jump out and scare people. Anyhow, I don't take Freak's dictionary along because my hands are trembly and I might drop it, or Mrs. Addison might ask me a word and I'll forget how to look it up and prove I'm still a butthead goon.

Mrs. Addison is waiting outside her office, like she does, and she's trying to smile but she's not really a smiling kind of person and I can tell this is serious, whatever it is.

Like maybe somebody died.

I go, "Gram! Is Gram okay?"

"Yes, yes, everybody is fine. Come in and sit down, Maxwell. And please try to relax."

Yeah, right.

Mrs. Addison is sitting there in her big chair and she's looking up at the ceiling and then she's looking at the floor, and at her hands, and finally she gets around to looking at me. "This is rather difficult, Maxwell. I don't know where to begin. First, let me say we're all very pleased with your progress. It's nothing short of miraculous, and it almost convinces me you knew how to read at your level all along and were for some reason keeping it a secret."

I'm not really hearing what she's saying because there's like this little bird fluttering around inside my chest, and it makes me blurt out: "You're putting me back in L.D., right?"

Mrs. Addison comes over and pats me on the shoulder. I can tell it makes her nervous, touching me, but she does it anyway, and she goes, "No, no. Nothing like that. This has nothing to do with school, Maxwell. This is a personal situation."

"Because if I have to go back in the L.D. class, I won't. I just won't. I'll run away. I will, I will."

"Maxwell, this is *not* about your class work, or even about school. This is about your, uhm, father."

My, uhm, father. Which makes me wish all of a sudden I'd done something wrong and Mrs. Addison was just giving me detention.

She takes a deep breath and folds her hands together like she's praying and she says, "A request has been forwarded to me from the parole board. A request from your father. Maxwell, your father wants to know if — "

"I don't want to hear it!"

I jump up and cover my ears, holding my

hands real tight. "Don't want to hear it! Don't want to hear it! Don't! Don't! Don't!"

What happens when you go nuts in the principal's office, she calls in the school nurse, and the two of them are trying to hug me and calm me down, and it's like I'm back in day care or something.

"Maxwell?" Mrs. Addison is saying. She's trying to pry my hands away from my ears. "Maxwell, please forget about it, okay? Forget I said it. You don't have to do anything you don't want to do, okay? And I'll make sure of that, I promise. I swear on my honor, he can't make you do anything you don't want to do. I'm going to make that *very* clear to the parole board, and to his lawyer. Very clear indeed."

Finally I take my hands off my ears, which wasn't really working because I could still hear everything they said, and big surprise, I'm sitting in the corner of the room, down on the floor with my knees all hunched up, and I don't even remember how I got here.

It's like I blanked out or something, and the nurse is giving me this cup of water, and the weird thing is she's crying.

"I'm sorry," I say. "I didn't mean to hurt you."

"You didn't," she says. "I cry easy, don't you worry about it."

I do worry about it, though, because if she's crying, I must have hit her and I don't remember it. Which, if you think about it, is *really* scary.

Who knows what I might do and then not remember it?

The worst thing happens later, in the cafeteria.

Freak has this thing about American chop suey. He *loves* the stuff. The gooier the better. You'd never believe a person so small could eat so much, and when he holds up his plate, he always says, "Please, sir, more gruel," and I always say, "It's American chop suey, not gruel, I looked up gruel, remember?" and he always goes, "I beg of you, sir, more gruel!" and so finally I go up to get him another helping.

When I come back, something is wrong. Freak's face is all red and swollen up and he's making this huk-huk-huk noise. He can't talk, all he can do is look at me and try to say something with his eyes and then I'm running to get the nurse.

"Quick. He can't breathe! He can't breathe!"

Then she's running as fast as me and she's yelling for someone to call an ambulance.

Back in the cafeteria, Freak is turning purple. The nurse grabs him and she's got this plastic thing she shoves into his mouth and his eyes are closed up tight and one of his legs is kicking.

I don't know what to do so I start hopping up and down in one place, and when the kids keep crowding around I push them back, and the next thing Freak's face is starting to look pink instead of purple and he's breathing okay.

Right about then the ambulance comes, I never even heard the siren, and Freak is trying to talk in this croaky voice as they put him on the stretcher. "I'm okay," he keeps saying. "Really, I'm okay, I just want to go home."

The deal is, once they call the ambulance, you have to go to the hospital and get checked out, that's a rule. I keep trying to get into the back of the ambulance with him, but they won't let me. Finally Mrs. Addison has to come out and pull me away until the ambulance leaves with just the light going and not the siren.

"You've had quite a day, haven't you?" she says, walking me back into the school.

"It's not me who had quite a day," I say. "Kevin is the one. All he did was try and eat his lunch."

Mrs. Addison gives me this look, and then she goes, "You're going to be okay, Maxwell Kane. I'm sure of it now."

She's okay for a principal, but for some reason I still can't make her understand that it's not me who had a really bad Friday the Thirteenth.

And I swear on the dictionary, if Freak ever tries to eat American chop suey again, I'll dump it on his head or something.

14. Cross My Heart and Hope to Die

Gram lets me stay home the next day because Freak is getting out of the hospital, and I'm right on the front step when the Fair Gwen pulls up in her car. Freak is riding in the back, you can barely see him in the window, and he's got this big grin that makes me feel like everything is going to be okay, the way everybody keeps saying.

I go, "Is it okay if I carry him inside?" and the Fair Gwen says, "Of course."

"He has to rest," she says. "He stays in the house until I say different, is that understood?"

In his room, Freak is right away ordering me around, bring me this and go do that, and you'd never guess he's been sick.

"A minor incident," he says. "Easily corrected by biogenic intervention."

"You mean that robot stuff?"

Freak goes, "Ssssh! The Fair Gwen must not know of the plan. The very idea strikes fear into her heart."

"Well it *is* pretty scary," I say, "getting an operation to give you a whole new body."

"I'm not scared," Freak says. "I'm looking forward to it."

"So when does it happen?"

Freak gets this faraway look and he says, "I'm not sure. Dr. Spivak, she's my doctor, she says maybe a year or two."

"But how come you need a new body?" I ask. "How come you can't just stay like you are?"

Freak shakes his head, like he knows I'm not smart enough to understand. "No one stays like they are," he says. "Everybody is always changing. My problem is, I'm growing on the inside but not the outside."

He doesn't want to talk about it anymore, which is fine with me. And in another couple of days, everything is back to normal and we're going to school like always, and everything is going real good until Christmas vacation when, if you'll excuse the expression, all hell breaks loose.

I'm in the down under, trying to get the stupid wrapping paper to cover the stupid presents I got for Gram and Grim, when this shouting starts upstairs.

Understand, Grim *never* yells at Gram, not that I can ever remember, and Gram, well, the worst thing she ever does is cry when she's mad. But *somebody* sure is yelling up there, and so I sneak up the stairs and I don't even have to put my ear to the door, that's how loud it is.

"Over my dead body you will!"

That's Gram yelling, and her voice is big and full of tears. Grim's voice isn't nearly as loud, and I open the door a crack to hear whatever it is that's made Gram so mad at him.

"I have an obligation," he's saying. "A man has to protect his family."

"Not with a gun!" Gram yells. "Not in this house! I won't have it! Oh, I can't stand it. How could they do this to us? How *could* they!"

"He fooled 'em," Grim is saying. "Just like he fooled Annie. Just like he fooled us once upon a time. Never again, though. That man tries to set foot in this house, I aim to shoot him."

"No guns," Gram says. "You don't know about guns."

"Of course I do. I was in the army, wasn't I?"

"That was thirty years ago! I know what will happen, don't you think I've dreamt about it for the last eight years? He'll come in here and he'll take that gun away from you, and then *he'll* do the shooting."

By now I've figured out who they're talking about, and I guess you have, too. None other than *Him*. Killer Kane, my father.

"Maybe they won't let him out," Gram is saying. "If they do, they'll give us protection."

"Sure they will," Grim says. "Just like they protected our Annie."

Next thing, Gram is crying, and you can tell Grim is trying to make her feel better, going,

"There, there, my dear. I know, I know. There, there."

A while later, I hear the cellar stairs creaking. It's Grim, and he knocks on my door.

"Come on in."

Grim comes inside and for once he doesn't tell me what a rat hole I'm living in, or how it smells like a locker room because I forgot to put my socks in the hamper. He sits on the edge of the bed and folds his hands together. I never think about how old he is because he never acts old, but tonight he's all white and bent and his skin is saggy. He's about a thousand years old, and he says, "I guess you heard the ruckus? Your gramma gets so upset, bless her heart. Can't abide the idea of violence. Can't say I blame her."

"Did he escape?" I ask. "Is that what happened?"

Grim shakes his head. "He's up for parole."

"That's dumb. That's *so* dumb."

Grim goes, "You hit the nail on the head, son. What I did do, just so you know, I went into court and made it so he won't be allowed within a mile of this house. If he *does* try to come here, they'll send him back to prison, the judge promised me that much."

I say, "Maybe you *should* get a gun."

Grim doesn't say anything for quite a while, and then he goes, "Maybe I will, maybe I won't. I can't tell your gramma about it, though, and it breaks my heart to lie to her. That's one thing we've never done."

"I won't tell."

Grim is quiet again, and then he stands up from my bed and in this real old, tired voice he says, "Everything is going to be okay, Max. I'll make sure of it. But for the next few days I want you to stay in the house. Promise me you'll do that?"

"Cross my heart," I say. "Cross my heart and hope to die."

15.
What Came Down the Chimney

Christmas Eve is real quiet. Like Freak says, "You could hear a mouse fart." Which, even if it is a stupid joke, makes Grim smile and shake his head.

Freak and the Fair Gwen have supper with us, and we're all trying to pretend like everything is normal, and nobody says a word about Killer Kane getting out of prison. The Fair Gwen is wearing this dark red silky blouse and a long black skirt that almost touches the floor, and her waist is so small, she looks like one of those Christmas ornaments, the kind that makes a tingle-bell sound when the branches move.

Freak is all dressed up, too, he's wearing this tweedy new suit jacket that has patches on the elbows and Grim says all he needs is a pipe and he'll look like quite the professor.

"No tobacco," Freak says. "Nicotine is a toxic waste of time."

"Just the pipe," Grim insists. "You don't have to smoke it."

"Don't get him started on bad habits," Gram says. "Maxwell, pass the mint sauce."

Mint sauce is one of Gram's specialties, and you'd be amazed how it improves everything, which is why I've been keeping it close by. Anyhow, the food is the best, you can't beat Gram for Christmas or Thanksgiving or birthdays, and we all eat until we're fit to bust, except the Fair Gwen makes sure Freak doesn't eat too fast.

"You'd think I was starving him," the Fair Gwen says.

"Please, sir, more gruel," he says, holding up his plate and making a funny face where his tongue sticks out sideways, and Gram laughs so hard, she has a coughing fit, which makes us all shut up.

After supper we sit around like you do, admiring the tree and talking about how lucky we are not to be homeless, and Grim starts telling these old stories about when he was a kid and they got lumps of coal in their stockings.

"If we were lucky, we got an apple core," he says, "or a few orange rinds."

"Now, Arthur," Gram says. "You never got a lump of coal in your life."

"You're right. We never even *got* a lump of coal, can you imagine? My father couldn't afford coal, so he'd write the word 'coal' on a piece of paper and put it in our stockings and we'd *pretend* it was a lump of coal, that's how poor we were."

The Fair Gwen is laughing to herself and shaking her head.

Gram says, "How can you tell such lies on Christmas Eve?"

"I'm telling tales, my dear, not lies. Lies are mean things, and tales are meant to entertain."

And so we all sit there acting polite and listening to Grim make up stuff no one would ever in a million years believe, and all of us have a cup of hot chocolate and a piece of Russell Stover candy right out of the box, and then it's time to pass around a few of the presents.

Gram has this rule that you can open one on Christmas Eve and you save the rest for morning. Which can be tough, deciding what to open first. Grim always starts it off because, like he says, he's really a kid at heart and he can't stand to wait.

From Gram he gets this wooly sweater that buttons up the front and he acts surprised, even though he's got about a hundred just like it already. Then Gram opens her present from me, which is a bracelet made of shells from beaches around the world, and she right away puts it on and says it's just what she wanted. Which is so like Gram — if you gave her an old beer can she'd act pleased and say it was just what she wanted.

Then Freak opens his present from me and even before he gets the paper all the way off, he gives me this thumbs-up and says, "Cool." It's a gizmo that looks like a jackknife, but really it's a whole bunch of little screwdrivers and wrenches and even a little magnifying glass. I'm pretty sure Freak can invent stuff with it if he feels like it.

Gram gives the Fair Gwen this scarf that just happens to match her blouse, and everybody goes ooh and ahh, and then I finally decide what present to open. Right away you'd know it was something Freak did, because the box isn't square, it's pointed at the top like a pyramid, and instead of regular wrapping paper, he's got Sunday comics taped all over it, and it's driving me nuts trying to figure out what would fit inside a pyramid-shaped box.

Freak seems like he's just as excited as me, even though he already knows what he put inside. "Take off all the paper first," he says. "There's a special way to open it."

Real careful, I peel off all the paper, and the thing is, it's not a pyramid-shaped box he bought somewhere, he *made* it. You can see where he cut out the pieces of cardboard and taped them all together, and written on the sides of the pyramid are these little signs and arrows.

"Follow the arrows," he says.

The arrows point all over the place and I have to keep turning the pyramid around, until finally I get to this sign that says:

PRESS HERE AND BE AMAZED

"Go on," Freak says. "It's not an explosive device, silly — it won't blow up in your face."

I press the spot on the pyramid and all of a

sudden, all four sides fold down at the same time and I'm looking inside the pyramid and, just like Freak promised, I'm amazed.

"The young man is a genius," Grim is saying. "And I don't use that word lightly."

Grim is right about that, because Freak has the whole thing rigged with these elastic bands and paper clips, which is what made the sides unfold all at the same time, and inside is this little platform and on the platform is a book. Not a normal book, like you buy in the store, but a book he made himself, you can tell that right away. It looks so special, I'm afraid to pick it up or I might ruin it.

"What I did was take all my favorite words," Freak says, "and put them in alphabetical order."

"Like a dictionary?"

"Exactly," Freak says, "but different, because this is *my* dictionary. Go on and look inside."

I open up the book the way he asks, and the pages smell like a ballpoint pen. It starts with A, just like a regular dictionary, but as Freak said, it's different.

A

AARDVARK, a silly-looking creature that eats ants

AARGH, what the aardvark says when it eats ants

ABACUS, a finger-powered computer

ABSCISSA, the horizontal truth

"You don't have to read them all tonight," Freak says. "Save some for tomorrow. I gotta tell you, though, you're gonna flip when you see what I did with the Z's."

This is the best, getting Freak's dictionary. Everything else is extra.

I figure it will take forever to fall asleep, because my head is full of stuff. Grim and his written-down lump of coal, the pyramid with the special book inside, and how fat, wet flakes of snow were falling when the Fair Gwen towed Freak home in his American Flyer wagon, and the way he was pretending to boss her by saying, "On Donner! On Dasher! On Guinevere!" and she's telling him to shut up or she'll leave him outside until he turns into a snowman.

Which must be why I'm dreaming about a little snowman who looks like Freak. The snowman keeps saying, "Cool. Cool." And when I wake up, I can feel the cold coming into my bedroom. Which is weird, because it's always warm in the down under, with the furnace right next door.

I think I hear the wind right there in the room.

Except it's not the wind.

Someone breathing.

Someone who rises up darker than night, as big as the room, and puts a giant hand on my face and presses down.

"Don't say a word, boy," he whispers. "Not a sound."

I try to move, try to shrink myself back into

the bed, but the hand follows me down. The hand is so hard and strong I can't move, and it feels like my heart has stopped beating, it's waiting to see what will happen next.

"I came back," he says. "Like I promised."

16.
A Chip off the Old Block

Once on the TV this dude hypnotized a lobster. Maybe you saw it. He touches a lobster and it freezes, it can't move. That's sort of what happens to me when his hand clamps over my mouth. Like I'm paralyzed and my head is empty and all there is in the world is that big hand and this cool breath like the wind.

"So this is where the geezers stuck you, huh?" he whispers. "Down in the basement, out of sight, out of mind?"

I still can't see his face, he's this huge shape in the room.

"Everything changes now," he says. "It's time I got to know my own son, who had his mind poisoned against me."

He makes me sit up and shushes me to make sure I won't make any noise. Making noise is the last thing I want to do, because I don't know whether or not Grim ever bought that gun he mentioned, or what might happen to him if he tries to use it. Gram's bad dream about Grim getting shot with his own gun seems pretty real right now, and I don't want to be the one to make it come true.

"I know what they told you," he says. "It's all a big lie, you understand? I never killed anybody, and that's the truth, so help me God."

By now I'm sitting up on the bed and he's making me put on my clothes and the weird thing is, none of this is a surprise. Somehow I always knew this would happen, that he would come for me, in the night, that I would wake up to find him there, filling the room, and that I'd feel empty.

I'm so weak, I can hardly put my shoes on. Like when you wake up and your arm is still asleep and you can't hardly make it move? That's what I feel like all over — numb and prickly and as light as a balloon. Like my hands might float up in the air if I let them.

"This'll be an adventure," he says. "You're going to have the time of your life, boy. Okay, we're leaving, and not a peep out of you."

The bulkhead door is open, and you can see the stars. Some people think the stars look close enough to touch, but Freak says the sky is like a photograph from a billion years ago, it's just some old movie they're showing up there and lots of those stars have switched off by now. They're already dead, and what we're seeing is the rerun. Which makes sense if you think about it. Someday the rerun will come to an end and you'll see all the stars start to flick off, like a billion little flames blown out by the wind.

"This way," he says. "Quiet as a mouse."

There's snow on the ground. Not a lot, enough to cover the ground. I can tell how cold the air is, but I can't feel it, even without a jacket, which I didn't have time to put on. The cold doesn't matter. Nothing does, really, not Grim and Gram or the old stars in the sky, or Freak and the Fair Gwen. They're all just make-believe, this dream I was having for a long time, and now I'm awake again and he's still filling the room somehow, even though we're outside.

The lights are out at Freak's house, and I'm thinking: *The stars clicked off* and I don't even know why I'm thinking that, it's like a dead voice in my head or something.

We're under a streetlight when he says, "Let me look at you."

He's got these big eyebrows that make it hard to see his eyes and that's fine, I don't want to see them, looking at those eyes is *asking* to have a bad dream.

"My, my," he says, checking me out. "Will you look at this? It's like I'm looking at an old picture of myself. You really *are* a chip off the old block, you know that?"

I don't say anything, and he reaches out and touches my face real gentle, as if he'd never hurt a fly. "I say, boy, do you know that? Answer me now."

"Yes, sir," I say. "Everybody says so."

"Christmas Eve," he says. "You know how many Christmas Eves I've been deprived of my own blood kin? Now is that fair, to do that to a man? Lock him up for a crime he never did?"

He's waiting for me to answer, and I say, "No, sir, not fair."

"That's over and done now," he says. "We're starting fresh. Just you and me, boy, that's how it was meant to be."

I'm standing there under the streetlight and it's amazing how quiet it is. Like everybody went away or died. The quiet is almost as big as he is. He's as tall as me, only wider everywhere, and for some reason, maybe because we're not far from Freak's house, I'm thinking this weird thought: *He doesn't need a suit of armor.*

No, and he doesn't need a horse, or a lance, or a pledge to the king, or the love of a fair lady. He doesn't need anything except what he is. He's everything all rolled into one, and no one can ever beat him, not even the brave Lancelot.

He's squinting around, his eyebrows are furrowed shadows, and he says, "You know what I think of when I see a neighborhood like this? Hamsters, is what I think. That's how these people live, like hamsters in cages. They have their little wheels to run on and that's what they do for the whole of their lives, they run and get nowhere. They just spin."

I stand there.

"They poisoned you against me, I know that," he says. "Give it time, you'll see the truth."

He starts walking fast and I walk with him, like my feet already know where to go. We're cutting through the side streets and heading down to the pond, all cold and white and frozen. Tomorrow morning a bunch of kids will take their new sleds and skates out there, and probably lose their new mittens and scarfs and get yelled at by their moms and dads, but tonight the pond is as empty as the moon, as empty as my head.

Once a car goes by real slow around the pond, and I've got this strange feeling there's no one at the wheel.

He hooks his finger in my shirt collar and makes me duck down until the car goes by.

The car passes and you can't see through the dark windows and you can hear the snow crunching under the tires, squeaky and frozen.

"We're invisible," he says, making me stand up. "Now now, isn't that a kick in the pants?"

My feet already know where we're going. The New Testaments. There're a few lights on in the old buildings, and you can see some of the windows are cracked, it looks like a knife cut against the light, and he's saying, "You know about Mary and Joseph, how they sought shelter in Bethlehem, and how the baby Jesus was born in a manger?"

I try to nod and the funny thing is, even though I'm not cold, my teeth are chattering, so it's like the rest of me is freezing but my head hasn't noticed.

"That's what we're doing, seeking shelter," he says. "Except this isn't exactly a manger we're going to."

"No, sir," I say. "It sure isn't."

He touches me real soft on the back of the neck and says, "I didn't ask you a question, boy. Rule number one, don't sass your old man."

I make sure my mouth stays shut. We're coming up on the Testaments and they look almost pretty with the new snow coating the roofs and making the yards clean and white and soft. You can see where an old bike handlebar is coming up through the snow, and shapes of other things left out, and even the old car up on blocks looks new, like it might take off into the air without any wheels.

I know where we're going, even though he doesn't tell me.

The door opens before we get there, and Loretta Lee is standing in the light and she's saying, "Iggy! Come look what the cat dragged in."

He says, "Say hello to my boy, Loretta. Ain't he a chip off the old block?"

Then we're inside, and Iggy is there bolting the door behind us and closing the shades, and Loretta, she's wearing this real slinky red dress that looks like it might fall off if she sneezed, she's saying, "Mission accomplished, hey Kenny? I knew you could do it, if anybody could."

Iggy says, "Watch your mouth, Loretta."

"I do believe you've been drinking," my father

says. "Has she been drinking, Iggy? I thought I made myself clear."

"Hey, it's Christmas Eve," Iggy says, and he sounds real nervous. "A little punch, what can it hurt?"

"A little punch," Loretta says, and her voice is slurpy. "That's all."

She's wearing these fake eyelashes and they're coming loose, so her eyes look almost as blurry as her red mouth. I know because she keeps flapping her eyes at me and smiling so I can see where the lipstick got on her teeth.

Iggy says, "She's okay, Kenny, you got my word."

"Oh *right*," Loretta says. "Turned over a new leaf, Preacher Kane turned over a new leaf so there's no booze for *anybody* on Christmas Eve, even in our own house where a man is his castle."

"Oh, shut it," Iggy says, and he makes Loretta sit down on the busted couch, where she kind of leans over and waves at me, wink wink.

"Bring me and my boy some food," my father says. "We've been out in the cold for eight long years and we're hungry, aren't we, son?"

"Yes, sir," I say.

Iggy goes out into the kitchen to fry up some hamburgers and we sit there waiting, not saying anything. Loretta is snuggled up on the couch, passed out with this dreamy look on her face.

I eat that greasy hamburger, even though I can hardly stand to swallow, and Iggy is fussing around like it's such a big deal, having Kenny Kane in the house, and it's hard to believe he's the same Iggy who is boss of The Panheads, this motorcycle gang that strikes fear into the hearts of everybody, including the cops.

Then Loretta wakes up and stretches like a cat, yawning so you can practically see right down her throat, and she says, "I guess I needed that." Then she giggles, hiding her mouth. "I guess I need a lot of things."

My father wipes his mouth with this folded-up paper napkin and he ignores her and looks at Iggy and says, "You ever do time, you could be a cook."

Iggy gives this nervous heh heh heh, like wouldn't that be fun, being a cook in prison. He says, "Any time you want, I'll show you that place I told you about."

My father stands up. "Now is good," he says. He looks right at me. "Come on, boy."

17.
By All That's Holy

There's a back alley between the tenement buildings, you can't see it from the road, and Iggy takes us along the alley to this other place. You can tell how the door has been busted in and the lock broke, and we go into the dark hallway.

The lights come on and the first thing I notice is the perfume an old lady wears, and the smell of cats.

"It ain't much, but the old bat who lives here took the Greyhound to visit her sister for the holiday," Iggy says. He's trying to smile.

The little room is warm and close-feeling, and the furniture is real old and saggy. There's a big old TV with a doily on the top, and an empty goldfish bowl, and piles of newspapers tied up neat with string, and a Bible on this little table by the TV. Also there's this trick picture of Jesus on the wall, where his eyes keep following you, and you go cross-eyed looking at it.

"Ain't much worth taking," Iggy says.

My father is looking around, making sure the

curtains are closed. "You think I'd steal from an old woman?" he says.

Iggy shakes his head. "I sure don't."

"Never you mind," my father says. "This will do in a pinch, until we get started."

"I better get back to Loretta."

"You do that."

My father watches the door shut behind Iggy and he doesn't say anything. I'm just standing there in the middle of the room because I don't know what he wants me to do.

"Make yourself comfy, boy," he finally says. "I'm going to check we have a back way out."

I'm looking at the door we came in by, just looking, when all of a sudden he's there behind me, and I feel the cool air of him on the back of my neck.

"You wouldn't light out on me now, would you?"

"No, sir, I wouldn't."

"Sit down," he says. "We need to talk, man to man."

I sit down in this old-lady chair that's so soft, I almost sink through to the floor and I'm wondering what happened to the cats. Maybe she took them with her, to visit her sister. Or maybe Iggy let them out and they can't get back in.

He leans over me and puts his big hands on the arms of the chair and he says, "Now, your grandparents say you're nothing but a dysfunctional retard, but no kin of mine is a retard, and that's a fact. So first thing, you've got to start acting smart. Use your head. We've got a situation going here, boy, so the way to handle it, you just do exactly what I say, no matter what. Understood?"

"Yes, sir."

His hand shoves through my hair and I can feel how strong he is, even though he doesn't hurt me.

"That's good," he says. "That's real good."

He goes into another room and I can hear a door banging and stuff being moved around and when he comes back, he's got this rope in his hands. "A boy who doesn't know his own father might be dumb enough to run away," he says. "We can't have that, can we?"

"No, sir."

"No, sir, what?"

"No, sir, we can't have that."

What he does is tie up my feet and hands and then he loops the end of the rope around his waist.

"I'm taking sack time while I can," he says. "You're as smart as I think you are, you'll get some shut-eye, too."

He turns out the light and lies down on the floor beside the chair, with just his arm for a pillow, and for a long time I can't tell whether he's asleep or pretending. Then I decide it doesn't matter, if I move, the rope will surely wake him.

It seems like we're frozen inside that room, even though the air is warm and stuffy. The soft chair keeps a hold of me, I'm not strong enough to get up, my feet and hands are getting tingly where they're tied, and pretty soon I can't even keep my eyes open.

I'm half asleep, dreaming a cat is in the other room, mewing for milk, and I'm still thinking about that cat when something tugs me.

He's sitting there in the dark, so I can't see his face, and he says, "Wake up, sleepyhead. I better tell my own son a thing or two he needs to know about his own father. First thing, like I already said, I never killed anybody. I'm big like you're big, so folks assume things they shouldn't. You understand what I'm saying?"

"Yes, sir, I do."

"Good. Now the other thing is the geezers you've been living with all these years. I bet they never gave you the presents I sent you, did they?"

"No, sir, they didn't."

He shakes his head real sorrowful. "That's a crime, not giving a boy presents from his father. I suppose you didn't get the letters I sent? No, if they didn't give over the presents, they likely tore up the letters. Another crime against humanity, that's what *that* is. They hated me from the first sight. On account of my appearance, and because I wasn't good enough for their precious daughter. As if a man should be blamed for how fearsome or cruel he looks, when in fact he's truly a loving person inside. Which I am. I can hardly see a sad movie without crying and I'm not afraid to say so."

There's just enough streetlight coming through the curtains, so I can make out part of his face when he turns it. You can see where there's a wet spot on his cheek, and he brushes it away.

"I've been locked up like an animal," he says. "Every single night I cried myself to sleep and that's a fact. Killer Kane, that's just an unkind nickname they hung on me. You know how kids can be mean in school, mean as animals? It was like that, only these weren't kids, they were adults who should know better, except they're so ignorant and hateful they believe the worst."

His voice is sort of ragged, but you can't help but listen to him, you follow the words up and down like you're riding through mountains and you can't see to either side, all you can see is the road just ahead.

"A great injustice was done to me, boy," he says. "What those people did, they stole my life. They took *years* away from me, might as well have cut out my heart with a knife, that's how it was to lie awake each night and think about the injustice was done to me. They'd blame me for all the wrongs in the world, those people. By which I mean the geezers, *her* folks that always hated me, and of course the police who failed to see the truth of the situation."

He stops to rub away another stream of tears. There's no crying in his voice, you can't hear it there, but sure enough the tears are all over his face, slick and shiny in the pale, pale light.

"I woke up just now worrying that you might wonder why I never did mention her. Your mother. You might still be thinking the wrong way on that, and believe what they told you. You being such a tiny little thing when it happened, how could you know the truth of it?"

He gets up then, and he goes over by the TV set, far enough so the rope is tugging at me. Then he's back and he's got a book in his hands.

"You know what this is, boy?"

"The Bible," I say.

"You can tell that in the dark, can you? That's fine. What I'm going to do, I'm putting my right hand down on this Bible, see?"

"Yes, sir, I see."

"And I'm putting my other hand over my heart, can you see that?"

"Yes, sir, I can."

"That's good, boy. Now listen up. I, Kenneth David Kane, do swear by all that's Holy that I did not murder this boy's mother. And if that isn't the truth, may God strike me dead."

I'm waiting to see if something happens, and nothing does. The room is the same. It smells of old-lady perfume and missing cats, and my hands and feet are still tied by a rope to his waist.

"Satisfied?" he says.

I want to answer him but my throat closes up and my tongue is so dry, I can't hardly open my

18.
Never Trust a Cripple

I'm waiting for something to happen. The whole world except me is asleep and the only sound is him breathing heavy. I'm trying to see through the curtains, out the old lady's window when it finally gets light, but the snow is stuck to the glass and everything is fuzzy, which is pretty much how I feel.

Looking down at him on the floor, how he overflows the rug, I think about that story where a giant falls asleep and is tied up by little people. Not that I do anything. I'm just a blob in the chair with numb hands and numb feet.

Finally what happens, there's a noise from the back and these light skittery footsteps, and then my father comes awake so fast he almost yanks me from the chair.

He's on his feet with this wild look in his eye, and Loretta Lee glides into the room.

"Merry Christmas, boys," she says. She's got this pizza box in her hands, holding it out like a present.

"Where's Iggy?" my father asks.

"Waiting for Santa Claus," Loretta says. "Ain't nothing open this morning, but we got this left over, you're welcome to it."

"Best put that down," he says, and he pulls on the rope and lifts me up. He gives her this cold look. "You go on and get Iggy," he says.

Loretta Lee is wearing this long winter coat, it looks clean and brand-new, so she probably got it for Christmas, but her legs are skinny and bare where her feet go into these old rubber boots. She's smoking this cigarette and squinting through the smoke at my father, like she's trying to figure out what he's thinking.

"Why can't you be nice, Kenny?" she says. "We had some good times in the old days, remember?"

"The old days are over," he says. "That the best you can do for us, leftover pizza?"

"Hey, pizza is good for you," she says. "It has vitamins and stuff."

"I still want to see Iggy."

Loretta takes a drag on her cigarette and she's got this crooked smile. Her eyes keep flicking at me and the way I'm roped up, but mostly she's looking at him. "Ig'll be up soon," she says. "He had himself a tough night."

"I have business with him, Loretta," he says. "Important business."

"I'm sure," she says, and she turns in her boots and leaves through the back.

The pizza box is sitting there on the table, but

my father says we can't eat anything touched by her dirty hands, so he walks me out into that dark little kitchen and he unties me and we go through the cupboards and find mostly boxes of prunes and old cereal. There's nothing in the refrigerator that hasn't already gone bad, so I eat a bowl of cornflakes with water and I'm so hungry, it almost tastes good.

"This is what they call a temporary situation," he says. "I know a way we can live like kings if we play our cards right." He stops for a while and squints at me, like he wants to see inside my head. "We'll be heading for warmer weather. That agreeable with you, boy?"

"Yes, sir, it is."

He seems real thoughtful. "I had a lot of time to plan this out. A lot of time to study people, figure what makes them tick. First thing, we'll get a bus, one of those RV things, a real big one, because it's important to look impressive. Put a name up on the side: The Reverend Kenneth David Kane. Or it might be we'll go with another name, just to be on the safe side. Did you guess I was a man of God, boy, could you tell that by looking at me?"

"Yes, sir," I say. "I mean, no, sir."

"What's that mean, boy?"

"I don't know, sir."

He reaches out and tussles at my hair. "You'll learn," he says. "You'll be standing out in front of the bus in a real nice suit. What you do is collect money in a basket. You won't have to steal it because folks will give to a man of God, and what they love to hear about is a bad man who has redeemed himself. I learned how to preach the word to a lot of illiterate convicts, but they were no more ignorant than a lot of other folk. No, sir. We're going to do just fine."

After I finish the cornflakes, he ties me up again.

"This is just a precaution," he says. "Can't take any chances until you see the light. You want to see the light?"

"Yes, sir, I do."

He's grinning at me and he taps himself on the chest and says, "You're looking at it, boy. I *am* the light, and don't you ever forget it."

He turns on the TV, it hardly comes in at all the screen is so fuzzy, and he keeps switching channels and he's cussing out the old lady for having such a crummy TV. All that's on is Christmas stuff and cartoons and what he wants is the news, to see if we're on it.

"I bet they haven't even missed you," he says. "Kept you down in that cellar like an animal, how would they know?"

We're sitting there waiting for Iggy when the blue lights start flashing bright against the curtains. He quick grabs me by the neck and shoves me down to the floor and we both lie there. The blue lights go by real slow, you can see them shining all around the room.

"Might be someone else they're looking for,"

he says. "A place like this, it could be anybody. Still, you can't be too careful."

When the lights stop flashing, he crawls to the window and looks out.

"There's nothing dumber than a dumb cop," he says. "If they were so smart, they wouldn't be working on Christmas day, would they?"

"No, sir," I say.

"You hush up, boy, and let me think."

I'm lying there on the floor tied up when Iggy sneaks in through the back. I know it's him by the draggy way he walks, and the heavy boots.

"Kenny!" he's whispering. "You there?"

" 'Course I'm here," he says. "Show yourself."

Iggy comes into the room and his eyes are darting around. At first he's surprised to see me trussed up, then he shrugs and doesn't look at me anymore. "Close call," he says. "You see that cop car?"

"I saw it."

"They come right up to my door looking for the boy," he says. "I said, come back with a search warrant, you want to see what I keep under my bed, but I let 'em have a good look from the door, satisfy 'em you weren't there."

"They believe you?"

"Who knows with cops?"

Then my father is sort of drooping his arm around Iggy and giving him a squeeze, and you can see the cold, scared look in Iggy's little eyes, and that wet mouth of his inside his beard. "You turn on me, did you?" my father says. "That how they just happen to come to your place, of all the places in this town?"

Iggy laughs real nervous. "It was that crippled midget kid," he says. "They had him out in the car. It must have been him, Loretta saw him peeking up over the seat."

Freak.

"What midget kid?" my father asks. "You think I'll fall for that?"

Iggy points at me and says, "Ask him does he have a midget friend. The two of 'em stole Loretta's purse, that's how come they know this place. That's the God's honest truth, Kenny."

My father kneels down and looks at me up close. His face doesn't show anything. "Well?" he says. "What's your story?"

"We didn't steal it," I say. "We just brought it back."

"Oh," my father says. "Now *that's* an interesting story. I *like* that story."

Iggy is talking fast, like he can't wait to get rid of the words and leave. "The crippled-up kid belongs to Gwen. Remember Gwen? Her and your wife were pals, that's what Loretta says."

My father puts his hand on Iggy and shoves him down into the old lady's chair. "Never mind about her. It doesn't matter how the cops got onto you, all that matters is they *did*. And now what do we do about it?"

Iggy is scratching at his beard and he starts to

say something and my father says, "Shut up and let me think."

Iggy shuts up. Every now and then he sneaks a look at me like he's trying to tell me something with his eyes, but I can't figure out what.

After a while my father says, "First thing, get me a firearm. Something small but functional. Next thing is transportation. I don't care what, as long as it runs. Can you do that for me?"

Iggy says he can, no problem.

"Then do it," my father says. "The quicker the better."

Iggy leaves, walking backward out of the room. My father lifts me up by the rope and says, "I know you have more sense than to waste your time stealing pocketbooks with a cripple kid. You can't trust a cripple, but I guess you know that now, don't you?"

He shakes the rope.

"Yes, sir, I do."

19.
Into the Black Down Under

We have to leave the old lady's place because you never know, the cops might come knocking on each door.

"They're like bugs," my father says. "They're not too smart, but there's lots of them and they keep at it."

On the other side of the alley is this boarded-up building, it used to be part of the Testaments until a fire burned it out, and my father decides we'll hide there until Iggy gets a car for us.

He reaches out and pulls off a big piece of plywood with one hand. The screechy noise the nails make sounds like a cat fight, and the next thing there's a real cat, a black one, that leaps out from behind the plywood. My father jumps so hard, he yanks me to the ground and I bump my head.

"Dumb animal," he says. "Get up now, that's just a scratch, a little blood never hurt a man."

It doesn't hurt, and anyhow I sort of like the

taste of salt in my mouth, it makes me feel awake.

"Get in there," he says and then he's pulling me through this old burned-out window and we're inside the building.

Everything is black and wet and dripping except for where snow has come down through holes in the roof. Most of the inside walls are gone, and you can see where the center beam was chewed by the fire. All the old pipes and wires are hanging down, and everywhere underfoot is broken glass the color of smoke.

"I used to wonder exactly what Hell looked like," he says. "Now I know."

He finds a place where the stairs go down into the basement and he pulls away the boards and planks. "You should feel right at home," he says. "Cooped up like you were in that cellar hole."

It's so dark he has to use a cigarette lighter, and the flame is so puny, you still can't see to the bottom of the stairs. "You go first," he says. "We can't have both of us on the same step. It might break."

The steps are made of thick wood, but slick and punky soft where the water has been dripping all these years, and I can feel how it sags under my feet. There's a rail that's hard to grab with my hands tied, and the way he's holding up the lighter you might as well keep your eyes closed because it's that dark, you can't see a thing.

I slip and start to fall, and then he's pulling back on the rope and I'm hanging there in the middle of the air with my feet skittering and he's going, "Easy does it, boy. We'll take this one step at a time."

Finally we get to the bottom. There's a little slant of light coming through this narrow cellar window, enough so we can feel our way around all the burned junk that has fallen through the floor.

"The accommodations could be better," he says. "I'll grant you that. Soon as Iggy fixes things, we'll be on our way."

He ties my feet back up and loops the rope tight around this old busted-up boiler that's tipped over, so I can't move or see what's behind me.

"Understand you can't be trusted quite yet," he says. "Once we get on the road, things will be different. You'll get smarter, every mile we put between us and this place."

He rips a piece off my shirt and ties it on my mouth so I can't be shouting, he says, and wake up the neighborhood. He rubs his hand through my hair again, real gentle. I'm pretty sure there's this sweet smile on his face, although it's so dim you can't be sure. "You just sit tight here a minute," he says. "I have to see a man about a car."

Then he's gliding away, and I hold myself still in case this is a trick and he's really sneaking up behind me to see if I can get my hands loose. Which I can't, they're numb and bloated from the rope cutting into my wrists, and finally I stop trying and just sit there letting my eyes open up in the dark.

I can barely make out that narrow window. Hardly big enough so a cat could slip through, and under it is this big pile of coal slagged up against the foundation wall. Overhead there's creaking with the weight of him moving around, trying to be light on his feet.

I'm listening to him up there and trying to see out that little window when something moves against the light.

I'm pretty sure there's a scratching sound coming from the window, except you can't always believe what you hear in the dark. Then whatever it is goes away and I'm thinking it was probably a cat, or maybe a dog sniffing around. Finally I just keep still, because the more I move, the tighter the rope gets.

Next thing, I hear someone on the steps, these light feet trying to be real quiet, and then a flashlight comes on and this woman's voice says, "You there, kid?"

Loretta Lee.

I can't say anything because of the gag. All I can do is sort of kick around a little, let her know where I am. You can tell by her shaky, thin voice she's scared of the dark. "Kid? Tell me that's you. Oh, Lord Jesus, what am I *doing* down here?"

Then the beam of that flashlight is hitting me right in the eyes, and she's tripping over stuff trying to get to me. First thing she does is pull the gag off, and I take a deep, deep breath that makes my lungs burn.

"It ain't right," she whispers. "Keeping your own kid tied up, it ain't right. He ain't the man I thought I remembered, that's for sure."

I want to say something, but I'm not sure what and anyhow my mouth is too dry. She's put the flashlight on the floor, aiming up so she can try to untie the rope.

"The man is a genius for knots," she says.

I can feel how her hands are shaking as she's fumbling around. Also I can hear the boards creaking overhead but you can't be sure, it might be just the wind.

Loretta goes, "The plan is, Iggy keeps him busy while I get you loose, now isn't that a good plan? There's enough cops up there to start a war, we'll be safe enough we get out of this godforsaken place."

Her hands are pulling at the rope, nervous and quick, but the knots just keep getting tighter. Finally she gets this idea to cut the rope on the ragged edge of the boiler. "I saw this in the movies once," she whispers. "I forget what movie."

She's working the rope against the sharp edge of that old boiler and sure enough, it cuts through. Just the one cut won't do it, though, and she has to do it twice more before my wrists get loose, and I can't really help much because my hands are all numb and swollen.

"Next thing is this piece around your ankles," she says. "I sure can't carry you up out of here. You think you can walk, I get this loose?"

"Yes, ma'am," I say.

That makes her giggle. "My, ain't we got polite all of a sudden," she says. "There, that should about do it."

My feet come loose and I try to stand up and I have to lean some of my weight on her. She goes, "Just a second, Sugar, let me get this flashlight."

She bends over for the flashlight, and then she's making this sound like something is caught in her throat.

Two big hands are squeezing her neck. I see how my father is coming huge out of the dark and he's got his hands around her throat, shoving her back.

"You ignorant creature," he says. "I'll teach you to put your dirty hands on my son."

Loretta can't say anything, she's sinking down to her knees and trying to pull his hands away from her neck, but it's useless, she can't stop him, he's squeezing her dead with his bare hands, and no one can stop him, no one, no one.

20. *Freak the Mighty Strikes Again*

Even a total goon like me knows you can't stop Killer Kane, but I go ahead and try anyhow. My hands are still numbed out and I can hardly walk, so all I can do is sort of fall on top of him and try to shove him loose from her.

I'm going, "Stop! I see you! I see you! Daddy, please please stop, you're killing her!"

He just twitches me away. He's made of iron and steel, he's gritting his teeth and squeezing her neck. You can see the whites of her eyes, and she's not even trying to get away anymore.

I try to get between them and I'm going, "I saw you kill her! I saw you kill Mom! I never forgot, not ever! I know you did it! I *know*!"

It's like I'm trapped underwater or something, so weak and floaty I can't hardly fight him, can't pry his fingers loose from my mother's neck. From Loretta's neck. Because everything is mixed up and he's doing the same thing to Loretta Lee he did to my mom, choking the life out of her, and he's got that same cold killer look because he *wants* her to die, like he wanted Mom to die, and nothing else matters except what he wants.

I'm there in the dark, pushing at him. The light catches her eyes and I can see her looking at me, she's so far away it's like I'm four years old again, peeking out from behind the bedroom door and then running to bang my little fists at him while the light fades from her eyes.

I can't get him loose of her, so all I can do is keep screaming, "I know you killed her! I saw you! I saw you do it! You killed her and I'll never forget, not ever!"

Finally he kind of jerks his head and I can feel him looking at me and then his hands open. Loretta slips away and I can hear her breathing like a broken bird in the cellar dark.

"What?" he says, reaching for me. "What did you say?"

"I saw you do it," I say. "I saw you kill my mother."

"You weren't but four years old," he says, and now his big hands are starting to curl around my neck, except he's holding me soft. I can feel his heart beating, and his cool breath in my face that makes me want to fall asleep. "You can't possibly recall that event," he says. "You think you can, but you can't."

"I can," I say. "I do."

"That's the poison they put in your mind, boy. They brainwashed you into thinking you can remember."

He's pulling me closer, holding me soft by the neck, and now I can feel the pulse in his hands.

"They never talk about it," I say. "They don't have to because I can't ever forget it, no matter how much I try."

"No," he says, and his face is so close, I can feel the heat rising off him. "Impossible, you can't."

"You were wearing your brown corduroy trousers," I say, talking so fast, it makes me shake inside. "And the black T-shirt with no sleeves. I tried to stop you and I couldn't, and you carried me back into my room and put me to bed and told me I was just dreaming. You locked me in that room and I ran to the window and broke it with my hand and started yelling for someone to come and help Mommy."

My father sighs and says, "Lord, I wish you hadn't done that, boy. It cost me years."

"They caught you, Daddy, and they put you away forever except then you fooled them and they let you go."

"I have to clean this up," he says, like he's talking to himself alone. "I have to clean this up and get out of here."

That's when his hands start to tighten hard and fast around my neck. I'm trying to fight him but I'm so small and weak and he's so big and strong, you can't stop him, no one can stop Killer Kane.

He squeezes and squeezes and squeezes.

I'm in this faraway place, falling backwards

real slow and dreamy, when I hear a window breaking. Then a small faraway voice is saying, "Put your hands up, villain!" and I really am falling and the air is coming back into my lungs so fast, it hurts.

I'm lying there all crumpled up sideways. I can see Freak. He's rolled down through the cellar window into the pile of coal, and he's trying to stand up.

"I'm warning you," he says in that fierce bold way he has.

He's got a squirt gun, one of those big blaster models that holds about a gallon of water.

Killer Kane is looking at me, he's looking at Loretta all crumpled and moaning, he's looking at Freak. Then he shakes his head and goes, "I know a real gun when I see it, you little monster."

He makes a move, reaching out. Freak scuttles back a little ways but he can't really run and even if he could, there's no place to go.

"This is your partner in crime?" Killer Kane says to me. "I guess maybe you *are* a retard after all."

Freak is pointing the squirt gun right in his face and he says, "Guess what I got for Christmas, Mr. Kane? Guess right, because your life depends on it."

Killer Kane doesn't say anything, he's just reaching out real slow because he knows that Freak can't get away.

"This squirt gun," Freak says. "And a chemistry set. That's what I got for Christmas."

Killer Kane just looks at the squirt gun. He shakes his head, like who are you kidding?

"Sulfuric acid," Freak says, raising up the gun and sighting along the barrel. "Good old reliable H_2SO_4, an oily, colorless, corrosive liquid used in dyes, paints, explosives, and many chemical experiments."

Killer Kane says, "You're lying, kid, you can't fool me."

That's when Freak squeezes the trigger and sprays him right in the eyes.

Then Killer Kane is screaming in this high, scared voice. His hands are scrubbing at his eyes and it's like that scream wakes me up, because the next thing I know I've got Freak in my arms and I'm running through the dark for the stairs, running as fast as I can on feet I can't even feel.

"Go!" Freak is yelling. "He's right behind you, go!"

I can't look back but I can feel him, feel the icy-cold breath of him on the back of my neck, and the hands reaching blind to grab me and then I'm going up the stairs, just flying.

The steps are breaking under my feet and he's howling in rage behind me, his hands are scrabbling at my ankles and for just a second he has me.

I kick loose and then we're up on the first floor, bursting out of the cellar hole. I can see daylight coming through the boarded-up plywood and I cover Freak with my arms and just dive right through that plywood, *wham.*

The sunlight blinds me and we're skitter-rolling through the clean, cold snow.

Hands are grabbing at me, and I'm fighting to get away.

"Easy!" a voice says. "Take it easy, kid, you're okay!"

Iggy Lee. He's looking down at me with red eyes and you can see where he's been chewing at his beard. I'm sitting there in the snow squinting up at Iggy and all these cops, there must be a million cops, and Freak is laughing like a maniac and saying, "It worked! He fell for it! Soap and vinegar and curry powder! It worked like a charm!"

I don't understand what he's talking about right then, it's only later I figure out there wasn't any real acid in the squirt gun, it was soap and vinegar and curry powder that made Killer Kane think his eyes were burning up — Killer Kane, who is still rubbing frantic at his eyes and begging for help when they put the handcuffs on him and shove him into the back of a police van.

All I've got room to think about is poor Loretta. That's what I'm telling the cops, that she's down there in the cellar. I'm afraid that no one is listening but they must be, because right away they're bringing her up out of the cellar and Iggy is running to her and crying out her name.

"She's still breathing," somebody says.

Then Gram is shoving through the crowd of cops and Grim is right behind her, and Gwen is there, too, and everybody is making a big, sloppy fuss, especially Gram, who's hugging me so tight I can't hardly breathe.

The Fair Gwen is hugging Freak and she's saying, "I told you to stay in that car, didn't I? Didn't I?"

Freak, he's looking over her shoulder at me looking over Gram's shoulder, and he gives me the thumbs-up as she carries him away.

"Freak the Mighty!" he says. "Freak the Mighty strikes again!"

21.
The Accident of Nature

We all of us had to go down to the police station, of course, where they took a bunch of pictures of the bruises on my neck, and then they insisted I needed X rays and so we had to go over to the hospital and get *that* done and then go back to the police station again, which wore on my nerves almost as much as being kidnapped.

Grim, the second time we go to the cops, he's sitting there in this room with me waiting, and he says, "I can't tell you what it felt like, coming up out of the basement and seeing that double track of footprints in the snow. I knew it was him, I just knew in my heart."

He kept insisting that Gram go home, which she finally did, because we were there at the police station for hours more, me telling all about it over and over, until I thought I would faint dead away if just one more person asked me what happened after I woke up in the dark and was stolen from my own bed.

Grim, he just keeps patting me on the arm

and saying, "This is important, Max. Maybe this time they'll lock him up for good."

That's what everybody keeps saying, that this time they've got Killer Kane where they want him, in violation of parole, in violation of a restraining order, abduction of a minor, and two counts of attempted murder, me and the Heroic Biker Babe, which is what the papers took to calling Loretta Lee.

The word is she's hurt pretty bad because he cracked a bone in her neck, but she'll be okay in the long run. Iggy, when I saw him that time in the hospital waiting, he was chewing a hole right through his beard he was so worried, and it made me think he wasn't such a bad dude after all.

It all goes to show, like Grim says, that you can't always judge a book by the cover.

It turns out to be a pretty weird Christmas vacation, as you might imagine, and Gram keeps fussing at me and won't let me sleep in the cellar.

"I don't care if he *is* under lock and key," she says.

Grim, he says please humor the woman, she's worried about to death, and so I sleep upstairs on the foldout and at night Gram keeps checking to see I'm there. Which is a pain, but she can't help herself, and anyhow I'm just as glad not to be alone in the down under.

Freak, well, the Fair Gwen just about threw a fit when she got him home, because of him disobeying a direct order and sneaking away to rescue me, but after a while she calms down and all she does is just look at him and shake her head.

"What am I going to do with you?" she asks.

"Put me up for adoption," he says. "I want to go live with the Waltons."

He means the TV show that keeps repeating, and of course he's teasing her, but the Fair Gwen is not amused.

"No more crazy adventures or dangerous quests, young man. You have to be careful," she keeps saying. "Extra careful."

She means the trouble he has sometimes catching his breath, because of the way his insides keep growing faster than his outside, which hasn't really grown at all.

Freak goes into the medical research place every few months now, which he says is a real pain, not that it actually hurts.

"Dr. Spivak says my unique status as a marvel of genetic aberration makes me an object of intense curiosity," he says in that lofty way of his. "Specialists from the world over are familiar with my case."

"What about the secret operation?" I ask when the Fair Gwen can't hear us. "The one where you'll get a robot body?"

Freak gets this very cool, scientific look on his face, and he always says the same thing: "The bionic research continues, my friend. The work goes on."

I don't know why I keep asking, because it gives me the creeps. You'd think I could be as cool as Freak about the idea, because it's him that's going to get a new bionic body, but just thinking about it makes me want to jump up and run around.

I keep telling Gram that when Freak is in the hospital for his tests I shouldn't have to go to school, because we're like a team, but she won't buy it.

"I know Kevin has been a great help to you," she says. "But you've got a brain of your own, haven't you dear?"

Yeah, right.

The other thing about school that's different after Christmas vacation is how jealous everybody is that we got our pictures in the paper and on the local TV. Mrs. Donelli in English calls us "the dynamic duo" and she put a cutout picture from the paper up on the bulletin board. Wouldn't you know some goon put mustaches on us the very first day.

Freak says he looks cool with a mustache and he can't wait to grow one, and he makes Mrs. Donelli leave the picture up. Me, I'd just as soon forget about the whole thing. I really hate the idea of having to testify at the trial and tell what really happened, but everybody says I have to, if I want him locked up for the rest of his life. Which I do, especially after what he tried to do to poor Loretta, who was only trying to help.

"They can't make you if you don't want to,"

Freak says. "A son doesn't have to testify against his father."

"Grim thinks it will do me good. Plus he's really worried he'll get off again, or fool the jury by quoting from the Bible."

"Grim worries too much," Freak says. "*Everybody* worries too much."

The way it finally turns out with Killer Kane, Freak is right. Because just before the trial is supposed to start, and I've got my fingernails chewed down to the second knuckle, Grim gets this telephone call that makes him punch his fist in the air and go, "Yes! Yes!"

What happened, they made a deal and Killer Kane pled guilty, which means he has to serve out the rest of his original sentence plus ten more years.

"He'll be an old man when he gets out," Grim says. "He'll be older than me."

That should make me happy, but instead I feel really weird and worried, and Grim, who still thinks he knows everything, says I just have to get used to the idea.

"The man is an accident of nature," he says. "All you got from him is your looks and your size. You've got your mother's heart, and that's what counts."

The weird thing I keep thinking about, what if something happens when I get older and I turn out to be another accident of nature?

Grim sees me thinking about that one night just before bed, and he sits on the end of the foldout and he says, "Things will make a lot more sense when you finish growing up, Maxwell. Now sleep tight and don't let the bedbugs bite."

Grim means well, I know that, but sometimes he says the numbest things. Because it's growing up that worries me.

22.
Remembering Is Just an Invention of the Mind

"Spring has sprung," Freak says. "And so are we."

This is the day school gets out, and we're taking the long way home. By now I've been carrying him around on my shoulders for almost a year. We call it walking high, and even if we haven't been going on any dangerous quests lately, so the Fair Gwen won't have to throw a fit, Freak hasn't exactly given up on slaying dragons.

"The world is really and truly green all over," he says. "Do you remember what it used to be like, back in the Ice Age, when the glaciers covered the earth and the saber-toothed tiger roamed the frozen night?"

"Uh, no," I say. "How could I remember that? I wasn't even born."

"Don't be a pinhead," he says. "Remembering is just an invention of the mind."

I go, "What's that supposed to mean?"

"It means that if you want to, you can remember anything, whether it happened or not. Like I can remember what it was like in the Ice Age. I kept trying to invent stuff — the wheel, central heating, indoor plumbing — but the Neanderthals were happy with just a campfire and a fur coat."

If you guessed that Freak has been reading a book about the Ice Age, you're right. He's been seeing a saber-toothed tiger behind every bush, except that so far, all of them have turned out to be stray cats, or once it was this skunk and it's a good thing I can run fast or we'd have to soak in tomato juice, which is the only way to get rid of the stink.

"Inventing electricity would be tough," he says, "without copper wire and magnets, but I could handle inventing a compass — all you have to do is rub the needle. That way everybody could head south and get away from the glaciers."

"First you need to invent a time machine," I say. "So you can go back there and give all the cavemen a hard time about indoor plumbing."

Freak goes, "You don't need a time machine if you know how to remember."

Which is something I'll always remember, him saying that and me trying to figure it out.

Freak's birthday is a couple of days after school gets out, and the Fair Gwen has already made it clear he's not getting a ride on the space shuttle.

"Thirteen is supposed to be extra special," he says. "The least you could do is get my name on the list. Or how about a linear accelerator, just a small one so I can split a few atoms?"

The Fair Gwen goes, "I suppose this means you're going to be an obnoxious teenager."

The deal is, this is really two birthdays for the price of one, because Freak the Mighty is almost a year old.

"Talk about a prodigy," Freak says. "One year old and already he's on his way to ninth grade."

The Fair Gwen just rolls her eyes when we talk like that. Freak says we can't expect her to understand, because you can't *really* get what it means to be Freak the Mighty unless you *are* Freak the Mighty.

Anyhow, the party is just a family affair because Freak isn't supposed to get overexcited, which is like saying the moon isn't supposed to go around the earth.

"Last year I got the ornithopter," he says. "This year, why not a helicopter? A real one, though, you can't expect a teenager to play with toys."

"Why not a jet plane?" the Fair Gwen says.

"Cool," Freaks says. "A Learjet."

What he's really getting, and I've been sworn to secrecy, is this new computer, the one he's been drooling over in his computer magazines. It comes with a modem, which means if he has to stay home for some reason, he can go to school over the telephone. The idea is I'd be there in the classroom with a matching computer. The only problem, I don't know squid about computers.

"You'll learn," the Fair Gwen says. "Kevin will teach you."

"But why would he have to stay home?" I ask her.

We're out in the kitchen and she and Gram are frosting the cakes and Freak is hanging out in the living room, acting like he intends to have a party every day for the rest of his life.

"Maybe he won't have to stay home," the Fair Gwen says, and she and Gram kind of lock eyeballs for a second, that secret code that mothers have. "This is just in case, Max."

"I think maybe he already guessed about the computer," I say. "That's why he's jerking your chain about the space shuttle ride and Learjets."

"I'm not surprised," the Fair Gwen says. "You can't keep anything from Kevin."

Freak hardly touches his supper, he says he's saving his appetite for the cake, and finally we're all done eating except for Grim, who keeps rubbing his belly and rolling his eyes and telling the Fair Gwen what a genius she is with fresh peas and new potatoes and salmon and he'll have just a smidgeon more, thanks, until finally Gram clears her throat and smiles and Grim has to apologize for being such a pig.

The funny thing is, when at last they do bring

out the cake, Freak asks me to flame out the candles while he makes the wish, and then he doesn't even touch his piece, he just sort of pushes it around the plate. I figure he's so excited about getting the new computer that he's lost his appetite. Not that he's letting on he doesn't feel good, he's acting just as wise and smart-mouthed as ever.

"I should have asked for earplugs," he says when we're done singing "Happy Birthday." "You better check the glassware for cracks."

"Hush up," the Fair Gwen says, "or we'll give you another chorus."

When she brings out the computer he acts so surprised and happy, maybe he really *is* surprised. Right away he wants to turn it on and show off what a brain he is, and because it's his birthday we all have to sit there and admire him and go, "Amazing," and "Fantastic," and "Kevin, how did you know that?" and so on.

He's showing Grim how to play 3-D chess, and just watching that makes me dizzy, so after a while I go out to the kitchen and help clean up, which is something *I'm* good at.

"Maxwell never breaks a dish," Gram is saying. "He's very sure-handed for someone so large."

We're almost done putting stuff away and wiping the counter when Grim shouts from the other room.

All he says is, "Kevin!" but we can tell right away that something is wrong.

We run in and Freak is leaning back in his chair making this wheezing sound, panting real fast, and his eyelids are flickering.

"He's having a seizure," Grim says. "Call an ambulance."

The Fair Gwen is already on the phone.

I run out in the street and start waving my arms and jumping up and down so they'll know where to stop, and I keep running back in the house to check on things, but the Fair Gwen says there's nothing we can do except wait.

23.
The Empty Book

They won't let me visit him the first day, and Gram says I'll just have to be patient and let the doctors do their business, but I can't stand just sitting around so I decide to walk over to the hospital, which Grim says is miles and miles, but suit myself.

I know how to get there because Freak and I went yonder that way once so he could show me the medical research building. It's not the same, though, without Freak along to turn the houses into castles and the swimming pools into moats.

All I keep thinking is, what a gyp it is to have to go into the hospital on your birthday.

Finally I get there and I see the Fair Gwen's car in the visitor parking lot, but Grim says I should leave her alone and let her tend to her son, so what I do is go around back to the medical research building and find this stupid little tree I can sit under.

I have that old ornithopter bird with me and

I'm winding it up and flying it around. Figuring maybe Freak will get a chance to look out the window and see it flittering by, that's my plan, and I'm under that puny little tree messing with the bird until this guy mowing the lawn makes me move. So I wander around to the front of the hospital and that's when the Fair Gwen finds me.

"Maxwell!" she says, and she gives me this great big hug. A wet hug, because she's been crying. "Max, we've been looking all over for you. Kevin wants to see you. He's making quite a fuss about it and Dr. Spivak says it's okay, but just for a few minutes."

So the Fair Gwen takes me inside, and I figure we're heading for the medical research building, but instead we go into the regular hospital.

"He's in the ICU," she says.

"So they're taking really good care of him?"

"They're doing their best, Max," she says.

The intensive care unit is this place where there are so many nurses, you can't hardly turn around without bumping into one, which I do as soon as we get there. Every patient gets a room alone, and there's all this electronic gear the Fair Gwen says is called "telemetry," which means when Freak sneezes, the nurses know about it before he can wipe his nose.

I'm not scared at all until I actually go into his room and see how small he looks on the bed. They've got him sitting up with all these tubes going into his arms and up his nose and Dr.

Spivak is guarding him, she won't let me come too close.

"I thought no visitors was the best policy for now," Dr. Spivak says. "But what Kevin wants, Kevin gets."

Dr. Spivak is this small woman with short red hair and a real stern face, and it's like she's mad because Freak wants to see me, or because I'll break some of her precious equipment.

"That will be all," Freak says to her. "You are dismissed."

The thing is, his voice sounds funny. Not just faint and weak, but kind of whistley. Only when I get closer do I see he's got this weird little plastic button stuck in his neck.

"It's called a tracheotomy," he says, holding his finger against the button, which stops the whistling noise. "Standard procedure to facilitate breathing."

"Does it hurt?"

"No way," he says. "I think it's cool. Listen to this."

Then he plays with his finger against the button, making his throat whistle a tune, which he says is the theme from *Star Trek*, although you can hardly recognize it.

"So when do you come home?" I ask.

Freak can't move much the way they've got him set up in the bed, so he sort of shakes his eyes instead of his head. "I'm not coming home," he says. "Not in my present manifestation."

I go, "What?"

"The Bionic Unit is on red alert," he says. "Tonight they'll take me down there for my special operation. The next time you see me, I'll be new and improved."

"I'm scared," I say.

"Don't be a moron," he says. "You're not the one having surgery."

"I still wish they wouldn't."

"Don't argue with me," he says.

I have to lean close to hear him because his voice is so small and whispery.

He goes, "If you argue with me, I'll get upset and they can tell on the telemetry. Then *you'll* get in trouble."

So I just stand there like a lump and don't say anything for a while. I put the ornithopter on the foot of the bed, but I don't think he notices.

"See that book on the table?" he asks.

He can't point, but I see the book on the table.

"Open it," he says.

The book reminds me of the dictionary he gave me for Christmas, except when I open it, all the pages are blank.

"That's for you," he says. "I want you to fill it up with our adventures."

"Huh?"

"Write it down, dummy. I was going to do it, but now it looks like I'll be busy getting used to my new bionic body. It'll probably take me weeks just learning how to walk with long legs."

I put the book down.

"You're the one with the brain," I say. "I'm the long legs."

"Don't get me upset," he warns. "I won't have the time, so you'll have to do it. Just write it all down like you're talking. Put in all the fun we had, the cool things we did. Our adventures."

"But you *know* I can't write, Kevin."

"It's all in your head, Max, everything you can remember. Just tell the story of Freak the Mighty, no big deal."

I pick the book back up but I don't say anything more about how hopeless it is, me trying to write stuff down, because I don't want to set off the telemetry. He does that himself about a minute later when he starts to cough and before I can say anything, the room is swarming with nurses and Dr. Spivak is telling me I have to leave.

"Out this second, young man, and let us do our jobs."

They let me wait outside the ICU with the Fair Gwen, who is just standing there at the window wringing her hands and not saying anything, and then finally they come out and say he's okay, it was just a bad spell, that they have him stabilized.

A while later Gram comes into the hospital and she drives me home. Nobody talks much at supper that night, except when Grim opens his big mouth and says, "Poor Gwen looks like she's in terrible pain."

I go, "Poor Gwen? She's not the one having the special operation."

Grim and Gram just look at each other like they can't believe I'm so dumb, and finally Gram says, "Maxwell, dear, make an effort to eat your vegetables."

That night I put the empty book in the pyramid box for safekeeping, and for good luck.

24. *The Return of Kicker*

The deal is, I'm not supposed to bother anybody at the hospital. Yeah, right, like me being there is going to screw things up. The way everybody is acting around here, you're supposed to shut up and not do anything but wait, which makes me crazy.

So early the next morning when Grim is still snoring loud enough to rattle the windowpanes, I get up and sneak out of the house. The way I figure, I can check on Freak and be back in time for breakfast, no harm done.

It doesn't work out like that, to say the least.

The sun is just coming over the millpond and there's this spooky mist on the water. You can hear all the frogs making a racket under the lily pads and the mosquitoes sound like bullets whizzing by and I have to kind of slap and run until I get clear of that smelly old pond.

Moving fast, like the sun is chasing my heels, I'm running down this long faint shadow of me that stretches out ahead, you can't ever catch up with it.

I'm thinking with my feet, like the rest of me is still asleep.

Not that I'm completely alone. There's this one old guy, he's actually out cutting his lawn, he's got these headlights rigged up on his rider mower, and he's wearing pajamas, too, like it's normal, everybody does it.

When I get to the hospital the streetlights are just starting to click off. The lobby is empty and there's nobody at the desk to tell me I can't be visiting patients at the crack of dawn.

There are plenty of nurses in the ICU, though, and they see me coming. This one woman runs right out from behind the telemetry station and she's got her hands up to her mouth and I'm pretty sure she's trying to shush me, even though I'm not making any noise.

She's not telling me to be quiet, though, she's saying, "Oh, my God, you must be Maxwell," even though she's never seen me before in her life.

I go, "Is Kevin back yet?"

"Oh dear, oh dear," she says.

"Is he going to be okay?"

"Oh dear," she says. "Oh dear."

Now more nurses are coming out of the ICU. One of them is the one I accidentally bumped into yesterday and when she sees me, she goes, "Better page Dr. Spivak, Kevin was her patient."

That's when I notice that some of the nurses

are crying and looking at me strange and all of a sudden I just go nuts.

Just go nuts.

I'm saying, "No way! No way!" and this nurse is trying to throw a hug on me and I push her away.

Then I'm running down the hall and it's like I'm Kicker again, ready to just blast anybody who dares touch me, and I have to keep running, I'm skidding around the corners and bumping into walls and no one can touch me even if they're brave enough to try, I just keep running and running until I get to these glass doors that say MEDICAL RESEARCH.

The doors are locked and it's dark inside.

Behind me people are shouting to call the guards, and I punch my hand right through the glass and I'm inside, skidding over broken glass through the dark, and I keep going until I come to this other set of doors.

NO ADMITTANCE

No glass this time, they're solid so I can't punch through, and I'm kicking and kicking and slamming into the doors, and that's when all the hospital cops catch up with me.

A bunch of them jump on me and I keep going, running around in circles like an accident of nature until finally there are so many of them on me, I can't stand up anymore.

They're putting handcuffs on my wrists and my ankles and they're sitting on me and going, "We'll have to medicate him," and this one cop says, "With what, an elephant gun?"

That's how Dr. Spivak finds me, covered with cops. She's this worried face leaning down. Her eyes are red and blurry and she's saying, "I'm sorry, Maxwell, we did our best. Better let me bandage up that hand, you're bleeding."

"He believed you," I say. "You said you could give him a new body and he believed you."

"What are you talking about?"

"The special operation," I say. "The Bionics Unit."

Dr. Spivak makes the cops let me up and says she'll be responsible, but they leave the handcuffs on me just in case, and the cop who was talking about needing an elephant gun has this nightstick out and he's ready to bop me if I make a move.

Dr. Spivak sighs and says, "Somebody get me a coffee, please," and then she looks at me and goes, "you'd better tell me all about it."

So while she's bandaging up my hand, I tell her about how Freak has been coming to the medical research lab every few months to get fitted for his new bionic body, and Dr. Spivak's face goes soft and she nods to herself and says, "Well, that explains it."

"It was all a lie, wasn't it?" I say. "You were just telling him that so he wouldn't be scared."

"You know better than that, Maxwell. You couldn't lie to Kevin. I tried a little fib on him when he was about seven years old, because I didn't think a child could handle the whole truth, and you know what he did? He looked his disease up in a medical dictionary."

That's when I know she's telling the truth. Freak and his dictionary.

"Kevin knew from a very young age that he wasn't going to have a very long life," she says. "He knew it was just a matter of time."

"So he was lying about getting a robot body?"

Dr. Spivak is shaking her head. "I don't think it was a lie, Maxwell, do you? I think he needed something to hope for and so he invented this rather remarkable fantasy you describe. Everybody needs something to hope for. Don't call it a lie. Kevin wasn't a liar."

"No," I say. "But what happened to him really?"

"I could tell you all the medical terminology," she says. "But what finally happened is his heart just got too big for his body."

There was talk about arresting me for busting up the hospital — the cop with the nightstick was in favor — but finally they released me into the custody of Grim.

On the way home he goes, "Do you want to talk about it?"

"Just leave me alone," I say.

"You got it," he says.

25.
What Loretta Said

That was a year ago.

I hid in the down under for days and days and kept the door closed, which is why I missed the funeral and the Fair Gwen going away. Gram told me about it afterwards, how she couldn't stand to live in the house with Kevin gone, and who could blame her?

Grim threatened to unscrew my bedroom door but he never did, he just kept saying I should come out for Gram's sake, and sometimes *she'd* come down and say I should come out for Grim's sake, and so on and so forth until finally I gave up and came out.

I don't know if this makes sense, but for a long time I felt like I was a balloon and somebody had let the air out of me. I didn't care if I ever got the air back, because what does it really matter if we're all going to die in the end?

That's how down I was feeling, and sorry for myself. Grim tried to tell me it isn't how long you've got that matters, it's what you do with the time you have, but that sounded so lame and puny next to Freak dying that I just didn't want to hear it.

This one day just before school was supposed to start I was moping around the back yard and thinking again how pointless and stupid everything was and Grim comes over and says, "You know what? Most of us go all the way through life and we never have a friend like Kevin. So maybe you should count yourself lucky."

"Yeah, right," I say.

"Suit yourself," he says. "But let's get one thing straight. You're going back to school if I have to hitch a rope to the bumper and drag you there, is that clear?"

So I went and I hated every minute of it, and I especially hated how people kept feeling sorry for me, as if it was me who died.

Finally one time even Tony D. came up to me and said it was a shame what happened, and I could see that he really meant it, and I just blew up and told him if he ever felt sorry for me again, I'd put him headfirst in the millpond and pound him down into the mud like a fence post. So we're enemies again, which is just the way I like it.

Not too long after that — this was winter by then — I saw Loretta Lee in the street. She still had on the neck brace and you could smell booze on her breath, but what do you expect, a miracle just because she lost her head and acted good for a couple of minutes?

Anyhow, Loretta sees me and she says, "Did you hear about Gwen? She's in California and she's got a new boyfriend. His name is Rick and they're crazy about each other, ain't that good news?"

"I guess so."

"Take it from me," she says, "it is. So what are you doing these days?"

"Nothing."

She gives me this long look and she goes, "Nothing is a drag, kid. Think about it."

I thought about it all the way home.

That night I pulled the pyramid box from under the bed and got the empty book out of the pyramid and I'm thinking, who are you kidding, Maxwell Kane, you haven't got a brain, and that's the truth, the whole truth, the unvanquished truth is how Freak would say it.

So I wrote the unvanquished truth stuff down and then kept on going, for months and months, until it was spring again, and the world was really and truly green all over. By the time we got here, which I guess should be the end, I'm feeling okay about remembering things. And now that I've written a book who knows, I might even read a few.

No big deal.

Freak's Dictionary

A

AARDVARK, a silly-looking creature that eats ants

AARGH, what the aardvark says when it eats ants

ABACUS, a finger-powered computer

ABSCISSA, the horizontal truth

ALGORITHM, math with a rock-'n'-rock beat

ALIMENTARY, what Sherlock Holmes said to Dr. Watson about where the food disappeared

ALLEGORY, a peculiar kind of story that's often pretty gory

ARCHETYPE, what Max sees when he dreams of architects

ARITHMETIC, inventing with numbers

ARMOR, a robotlike suit worn by knights of old

B

BIG LIE, ignorance is bliss

BIONIC, a way to improve on the human condition

BLOVIATE, to expel hot air in the form of words

BOATS, shoes big enough to fit Maxwell Kane

BOOK, a four-letter word for truth serum

BRAIN, a muscle that improves with exercise
BUTTHEAD, one who can sneeze a hot dog through his nose

C
CAMOUFLAGE, how a camel blends into the desert
CIGARETTE, something that should be obscene, not smoked
COPACETIC, the Fair Gwen's word for "everything is cool"
CRETIN, another name for Blade
CRITTERS, small, irritating children, also known as rug rats

D
DEMEANOR, the meaner your face, the worse your demeanor
DICTIONARY, a source of knowledge, fun, and rude jokes
DOWN UNDER, a land far away in Maxwell's basement
DYAD, another word for Max and Kevin
DYNE, unit of energy needed to move a gram one centimeter per second per second

E
EDIFICATION, education that tastes good
ERG, a measure of energy equal to one dyne per centimeter
EXCALIBUR, a sword with magic powers

F

FEALTY, loyalty with an "F"

FOLDEROL, Grim's word for nonsense

FOOD, fuel for humans, preferably so-called junk or UFO

FOOZLE, to make a stupid mistake

FORNAX, a cool-sounding constellation

FORMICIDAE, a type of insect never found in Kevin's pants

FURFURACEOUS, covered with dandruff

G

GADZOOKS, what Grim says when surprised

GALAHAD, son of Lancelot, finder of the Holy Grail

GOON, a four-letter word for Max in a bad mood

GRAM, a sweet lady of light

GRIM, a gentleman of the old school, before they tore it down

GRUEL, whatever you want more of

H

HABERDASHER, a person who chases after windblown hats

HAIKU, versification
by the quantum mechanic
means numberless sum

HAMMERHEAD, a know-it-all

HERSTORY, the past, from the female point of view

HIEROGLYPHICS, Max's handwriting

HISTORY, the past, from the male point of view
HOLUS-BOLUS, all at once
HUMAN, an improbable, imperfect creature

I
IAPETUS, a cool-sounding moon that orbits Saturn
ICARUS, a high-flyer, as in "to do an icarus"
ICHTHYOLOGY, the study of icky foods, for instance fish
IDEA, a seed you plant in your head
IGNEOUS, too hot to eat
INCANDESCENT, an excellent idea
INTERGALACTIC, out of this world

J
JABBAWOCKY, the language of Jabba the Hut
JILLION, millions and millions
JITTERBUG, a nervous cockroach
JOCULAR, amusingly athletic
JOCULARITY, a joke made by a jock
JOULE, a measure of energy equal to ten million ergs
JURASSIC, cool, excellent, what the Fair Gwen calls "far-out"

K
KAZOO, a place where weird-sounding musical instruments are kept in cages
KEVIN, a unit of measurement equal to 70 centimeters

KINETICS, the study of small families
KNIGHT, rhymes with bright and fight and right
KONG, another word for falling down

L
LACRIMATION, an emotional display to be avoided
LAGOON, a French gangster
LANCELOT, King Arthur's bravest knight
LEXICOGRAPHY, what Webster invented, Kevin perfected
LIBRARY, where they keep the truth serum, and the magic carpets
LIFTOFF, what happens when you open a book
LIMERICK, a mighty dude called Max,
saved his pal from bad attacks,
then they conquered the world,
with banner unfurled,
and time left over for snacks

M
MAGNESIUM, the white sparkles in skyrockets
MASSIVES, fat heads who assume that television tells the truth
MATH, you have nothing to fear but math itself
MAX, a unit of measurement equal to 190 centimeters and still growing
MEGAPOD, Max's shoe size

MIDGET, a word used by people with small minds
MUCIFEROUS, any disgusting food, as in muciferous tapioca

N
NANOSECOND, one-billionth of a second
NEANDERTHALS, what we all were before plumbing was invented
NICOTINE, a toxic waste of time
NONILLION, millions of septillions

O
OBFUSCATE, a needlessly confusing word for needlessly confusing
OBSTINATE, Kevin when he knows he's right
ODORIFEROUS, sneaker perfume
OLFACTORY, where they manufacture smells
ORNITHOPTER, a big word for mechanical bird

P
PERCIVALE, a knight who saw the Holy Grail
PHYSICS, what matters to energy
POSTULATE, when you presume to assume
POTASSIUM CHLORATE, the womp in a skyrocket
POTASSIUM NITRATE, the bang in a skyrocket
PRIMORDIAL, the good old days
PRIMORDIAL OOZE, boring conversation about the good old days

Q

QUADRILLION, more than a billion, less than a quintillion
QUANTIC, more than enough, as in "quantic amounts of carrots"
QUANTUM, imaginary sums of impossible numbers
QUEST, an adventure in which you have to use your imagination
QUINTILLION, more than a quadrillion, less than a septillion

R

READING, beaming up into books
RELATIVITY, the study of mysterious relatives
ROBOTICS, the science of designing and building robots
ROBOT, a mechanical entity, sometimes endowed with human characteristics
ROUND TABLE, where King Arthur passes out the snack food

S

SAUROPOD, a vegan
SEISMIC, so exciting it makes you vibrate
SEPTILLION, billions of billions
SPASTIC, how the Fair Gwen talks when she's nervous
STRONTIUM NITRATE, the blue in a sky-rocket

T

TELEMETRY, how to make nurses jump every time you sneeze
TELEVISION, the opiate of the massives
TELLURIAN, another word for earthling
TIME MACHINE, your imagination
TRACHEOTOMY, a unique method of whistling the *Star Trek* theme
TROGLODYTE, one who hates books
TUBILIFEROUS, splendid, close to perfect

U

UFOLOGY, see under food; the study of the Unidentified Frying Objects
UNICORN, a horse who makes a point

V

VAMOOSE, what you say to a moose when you want it to leave
VANQUISH, to defeat in battle, preferably with dragons
VEGAN, a human sauropod
VISCOUS, a thick, vicious liquid

W

WATT, a measure of electricity equal to one joule per second
WRITING, talking on paper

X

XYLOID, another word for blockhead

Y

YONDER, a place that always lies over the next horizon

Z

ZAG, what you do after you zig
ZED, a Z in England
ZEST, the zing in an orange
ZIG, what you do before you zag
ZING, what you taste when you bite into an orange
ZIT, adolescent eruption, not to be confused with teenage volcano
ZOO, an eighth-grade English class

Max the Mighty

*Thanks to Kathryn Lasky,
who pointed me in the right direction.*

1. The Whole Weird World

My name is Maxwell Kane and the thing you should know about me is this: even though I'm a big dude with a face like the moon and ears that stick out like radar scoops and humongous feet like the abdominal snowman, inside I'm a real weenie. A yellow-bellied sapsucker. A gigantic wuss. A coward.

I'll do just about anything to avoid a fight. I'm scared if I hit somebody, they might stay hurt forever, or worse. And then they'd haul me off to prison and everybody would say what did you expect, the boy is a bad apple just like his jailbird father.

Okay, maybe I am a little weird, but if you really think about it *everybody* is weird. That's the truth, and if you don't believe it then maybe you better listen up while I tell you about me and the

Bookworm and what happened when the whole weird world was out to get us.

It started like this. One day after school gets out I'm kind of moping along, minding my own business. Taking the long way home because there's nothing to do when I get there, so why hurry? I'm making sure not to step on any cracks and my brain is telling me don't be such a moron, it doesn't matter about cracks in the sidewalk. But my feet won't listen and they keep being careful, because you never know about cracks, do you?

Get a life, my brain says.

That's when I hear the girl screaming. She's not saying anything, just screaming so loud it puts a shiver in my bones. It makes me freeze up and not move and wish I could be invisible, or at least small. It makes me wish I could turn my ears off like you switch off a radio, and not hear anything. Most of all I want to run away and hide somewhere safe.

Because you can tell from the scream that somebody wants to hurt her.

2.
A Girl Called Worm

The girl keeps screaming and my brain is going, *Mind your own business. Somebody else can help her, not you.*

But there isn't anybody else and the screaming doesn't stop and before I know it my stupid feet start running over the cracks in the sidewalk, taking me closer and closer to trouble.

When I get to the corner of the block, I see this gang-banger messing around in the middle of the street. He's strutting around with his hands behind his back and he's got this sneering expression like he knows a really funny joke and you'll never get it.

"Keep screaming," he says. "Nobody cares."

The scream is coming from this skinny red-haired girl who's maybe eleven or twelve years old. She's got bright green eyes and freckles and her clothes are about two sizes too big and she's screaming bloody murder even though nobody's touching her.

"You big creep!" shouts the red-haired girl. "Lunk head! Bug brain! Give it back!"

"Louder," the gang-banger says. "I can't hear you."

Then he catches sight of me, and his grin gets wider and wider. "What do you know," he says. "Dinosaur boy to the rescue. I thought I felt the ground shaking."

Before I can stop my mouth from saying something stupid it goes, "Huh?"

The gang-banger loves it. "Huh?" he says. "Is that dinosaur talk for 'I'm retarded'?"

That's when I notice the skinny red-haired girl is staring at me. It's not a friendly kind of stare — she probably thinks I'm one of the gang-bangers, or maybe a retard like he says.

I go, "Leave her alone."

"Take it easy, Maxi Pad. We're just having a little fun," the gang-banger says. "You got a problem with that?"

The girl shakes her fist at him and goes, "Give it back or else."

The gang-banger looks at her puny little fist and smirks. "Oooh," he goes. "You gonna hit me?" Then he dances around, taunting her, and I see he's got hold of this small green backpack. A girl's backpack, for carrying school stuff.

"Give it back to her," I say.

He crosses his eyes and makes an oink-oink noise. "Pig boy," he says. "You better go home to Granny."

I try to grab it but he darts away, his teeth flashing white because he's having such a good time. "Moron Max," he laughs. "You're scaring me."

The red-haired girl makes a move but she can't touch him.

"Bookworm, bookworm, ugly little bookworm," he chants.

"Shut up!" she says. She's so mad her eyes look like they're full of green electricity.

"Worm girl!" the gang-banger cackles. "Whattaya have in here, worm food? Is that it?"

He opens up her backpack and roots around inside with this totally mean look on his face. Then he goes, "Whoa! What have we here?"

He pulls out a couple of paperback books and tosses them over his shoulder. Pages scatter and blow away like white leaves.

"Oh, you're real tough," the girl says. "You can beat up a book. I bet you never even *read* a book."

Then the gang-banger whistles and pulls something else out of the backpack. A hard plastic helmet with a light on the front, like miners wear so they can see in the dark.

"Don't you dare touch that!" the girl shouts. Then she goes mental and tries to grab the miner's helmet.

He grins and ducks away. "Finders keepers!" he shouts. "Losers weepers!"

But Worm isn't weeping, she's going nuts. Jumping up and trying to grab the helmet. He keeps dancing away, laughing in her face.

I wait my chance, and when he isn't looking I get behind him and lift the helmet off his head.

"Hey!" he bellows.

But I hold the miner's helmet up high and he can't reach it.

"Gimme that," he says, "or I'll punch your lights out."

"Try it."

The gang-banger curls up his fists and sets up on his feet like a boxer and for a moment I think he really is going to punch me. Then he looks at the girl and he looks at me and he spits on the ground by my feet.

"Who cares about your stupid junk," he says, and saunters away like he couldn't care less. Like he's the coolest dude in the whole wide world because he ripped up a book and scared an eleven-year-old girl.

The girl has eyes like green laser beams and this fierce look on her freckled face, like she thinks I'm the enemy, too.

I go, "Here," and give her the helmet.

The way she holds it in her hands, you know it means something special.

"What's it for?" I ask.

"None of your business," she says. And then she hugs the scratched-up old helmet to her chest and runs away, her thick red hair flying up like it wants to wave good-bye.

My brain didn't know it yet, but that's when trouble really started, the day I met a girl called Worm.

3.
Back to the Dark Down Under

The first thing I do when I get back to the down under is backflop on my bed and stare up at the ceiling while my brain goes, *You idiot, now the gang-bangers will be after you. You're toast, you moron, toast!*

The down under is this room in the basement, with cheesy paneling and an old rug that smells like low tide. Not that I'm complaining. The down under is my very own place, my hidey-hole from the big bad world. My grandmother wants me to move upstairs, into the light of day, she says, but I tried that for a while and thanks but no thanks. If things get really bad I can still crawl under the bed and just veg out until my brain starts working again.

There's all kinds of books and games and junk lying around, but I'm not really in the mood. All I want to do is stare up at the ceiling and try to figure out why a scrawny girl would make such a big deal out of an old miner's helmet. I mean, she really went ballistic over it, right? Totally bonkers.

"Maxwell! Are you there?"

That's Gram, who raised me ever since my mom died. She's calling down from the cellar stairs like she always does. Just checking to see I'm not doing something stupid, like making my own firecrackers, which I don't do anymore since we had that small explosion. Really small, but I guess it sounded pretty bad from upstairs.

"Supper's almost ready!" she calls out in her cheery grandma voice. "Your favorite, spaghetti and meatballs!"

That hasn't been my favorite for about five years, but I haven't got the heart to tell Gram because she tries so hard. She and Grim are old and out of it — they're my grandparents, my mother's people — but they're okay most of the time. Grim still has this way of looking at me sideways, like he can't believe his poor dead daughter gave birth to this huge beast of a boy. Monster Max, the thing in the cellar. But mostly he's a pretty neat old dude, if you don't mind hearing stories about the war for the umpteenth time, and how when he was a lad the grass was greener and the air was cleaner and nobody wore T-shirts with rude words on them.

No bad T-shirts back then, I say, just those yellow stars they pinned on six million people who got sent to the gas chambers. And he'll shake his head and say I give up, the boy reads too many books. Like he's been testing me and I passed. Because once upon a time I couldn't read worth beans, and like he says my brain is now this big sponge that soaks stuff up, and he's still kind of surprised I'm not as stupid as I used to be.

Of course, if Grim knew I'd been messing around with a gang-banger, he'd figure I really *was* retarded after all.

The next time I see Worm is on the bus. Normally I walk home from school, but that day the whole junior high went on this field trip to the Museum of Science, where they've got a lot of neat stuff like a giant see-through model of the human intestine, and robots that talk like R2D2, and this really excellent planetarium where they can make the stars look like dragons breathing fire in the sky.

The bus is super crowded, so I never notice Worm until we're almost home. She's all scrunched up in one of the seats way down in the back, reading this paperback book. A thick one, too. All around her the other kids are going mental and making faces out the window and yelling goony stuff, but she never takes her nose out of that book.

When the bus driver finally comes to her stop he opens the door and waits, like he knows what happens next. The really strange thing is, Worm gets up from her seat but she never stops reading. She walks down the aisle with the book up close to her eyes and she doesn't look anywhere else, not even at her feet to see where she's going. Like nothing is going to stop her reading, not even for as long as it takes to get off the bus.

She keeps reading even when some of the other kids make fun of her. "*Book*worm, *book*worm, ugly little *book*worm."

Worm acts like she doesn't even hear them. As far as she's concerned she's not even there, she's walking inside her book and nobody can touch her.

Because of what happened when I saved her miner's helmet, I'm figuring she'll at least glance at me when she goes by, but she doesn't even notice me. Which if you know how big I am is like not noticing an elephant in your living room.

Weird. Definitely weird.

Even when she's off the bus she doesn't stop reading. She walks away from the bus stop, heading for the crummy end of town, but she never takes her nose out of that book.

"Hey, Frankenstein, what are you looking at?"

"Nothing," I say, but everybody laughs.

They go: "Max and Bookworm sitting in a tree, K-I-S-S-I-N-G!"

But they're wrong, because I'm not going gooey for any girl.

No way.

4.
You Know Who

The next day I'm hanging around the park. It's not much of a park. Just this sloping-down grass place by the old millpond, with a statue of a guy on a horse. Some Civil War general, and he's pointing his sword at the pond like he's going to chase the ducks away. The whole statue is this rusted green color except for his hat, which is white where the birds are always crapping on it.

I'm sitting on this bench by the edge of the pond, tossing pebbles into the water and thinking it's a good thing it's Saturday, because it's way too nice for school. Sometimes I like to stare at the way the sun glitters on the water, these jagged bits of light that float like diamonds or something, and if you look at it long enough you feel sort of hypnotized. Like somebody has cast a spell and when you wake up the world will be changed into a better place.

So I'm sitting there kind of zoned and not really thinking about anything when a familiar voice says, "I heard they call you Freak the Mighty."

I look around and there she is. The Bookworm. Sitting on the bench and staring at me with these really intense green eyes. Eyes so hot and bright you can almost feel the heat.

"Freak the Mighty was two people," I tell her. "Kevin and me."

"Who's Kevin?" she asks.

And so I tell her about my best friend Kevin Avery, a three-foot-high kid with a brain like Einstein, and how the other kids called him Freak because he had leg braces and this crummy disease that meant he couldn't grow. How I used to act so dumb that everyone, including me, thought I didn't have a brain, until Kevin showed me how to think. And how the two of us became Freak the Mighty and went on a lot of cool adventures, slaying dragons and fools and walking high above the world.

"Cool," she says. "So where is he now, your little friend Kevin? Did he move away or something?"

I don't really want to talk about it, but there's something about the way Worm listens that makes it okay. "He died," I tell her. "Last year."

She just sits there for a while, thinking about it. Then she goes, "What a crummy deal."

"Yeah," I say. "It was."

"So," she goes, "now you're Max the Mighty."

For some reason that makes my ears burn hot. "I'm just Max," I tell her. "Just plain Max."

Worm has this sort of smile on her face, like she knows a secret about me, and she's about to say what it is when a worried voice calls out.

"Rachel! Leave the nice man alone!"

I turn and see this woman perched on a bench nearby. She looks real nervous, like she's going to leap up any second and scream for the cops. Like because I'm big and goofy looking I might be a pervert or something.

But before I can get really steamed up I notice the woman looks familiar. She looks a lot like Worm, only older and sadder.

"Rachel!" the woman says.

Worm goes, "It's okay, Mom. He's from school."

The woman gets up from the bench and comes over. She's wearing this long, old-fashioned black dress and she's got this stiff-legged way of walking, like her feet are hurting and she doesn't want them to touch the ground.

When she gets closer I notice these dark bruises under her eyes, and right away I know there's something scaring her and it's not just me.

"I'm sorry, sir," she says, in a low sweet voice that's even sadder than her eyes. "I thought you were a stranger."

She's calling me "sir" like I'm a grown-up, and that makes me feel a little weird. I sort of like it and don't like it at the same time. The trouble with looking like a grown-up is the older I get the more I look like my father. Looking like your father is okay unless dear old Dad happens to be Killer Kane and he's in prison for murdering your mother. Which means people look at me and think maybe I'll grow up to be just like him, or worse.

Worm goes, "We'll be safe here, Mom."

She thinks because I got the gang-banger to leave her alone I can make her safe all the time. What a joke. If she knew what a sapsucker I really am she'd get a head start and never stop running.

"Safe?" I ask. "Safe from what?"

"Never mind that, Rachel," her mom says. "We mustn't involve this young man in our troubles."

But her mom sits down, too. The three of us together on the bench like we're waiting for a bus. Which is sort of strange but okay.

It's quiet for a while, and then Worm pipes up, "You know what that pond reminds me of? *The Wind in the Willows*. Remember how Daddy used to read me that story?"

"I remember," her mom says, kind of wistful.

Worm roots around inside her backpack until she finds a dog-eared copy of the book. She flips through the pages but you can tell she's practically got the thing memorized, she's read it so many times. "Remember how Mole and Badger and Rat like to row around in their little boat? And Mr. Toad is always acting so grand and getting into trouble?" Her voice is going higher, like talking about the story is making her feel like a little kid again. She turns to me and says, "Remember?"

"Um . . . not exactly," I say.

"You never read *The Wind in the Willows*?"

I go, "Um, I saw the cartoon version. On TV." Which sounds so lame, having to admit you never read a really famous book.

I'm expecting Worm to give me a hard time, but she doesn't. Instead she says, "We don't even *have* a TV. You Know Who won't let us."

"Huh?" I say.

"My creepy stepfather. He hates TV even more than he hates books. My real dad loves TV *and* books."

"Rachel!" her mom says, like a warning.

"Well, he does," Worm insists. "My real dad is always sending me stuff to read. He calls me his little bookworm."

Her mom stands up and takes a deep breath. "Come along," she says, taking Worm by the hand. "We have to keep moving."

I'm wondering why they have to keep moving when suddenly this old black station wagon screeches to a halt in the street behind us. No, not a station wagon exactly, it's an old Cadillac hearse, the kind that isn't used for funerals anymore. The motor is smoking and drippy streaks of rust make it look like the hearse is bleeding from the inside.

Suddenly the door flies open and out pops this tall skinny dude with a floppy black hat and a long black coat and black shoes — everything black.

It's the Undertaker. And he's coming to get us.

5.
The Undertaker

They call him the Undertaker because he dresses in black and drives this ratty old hearse. I've seen him on street corners and downtown, waving this Bible around and telling people to give him money because he knows the Truth with a capital "T." Only he never quotes from the Good Book like a real preacher, he just acts like he'll thump you on the head if you don't fork over some cash.

Some people like to egg him on and get him really shouting, but I always steer clear. He is just another angry nutbar ranting about the world gone wrong. A street crazy with a mean streak.

You see a guy like that, you never think he might have a wife and child at home.

"Don't you run from me!" he's shouting. Only he's the one doing the running. Coming right at us, waving his arms. With the long black coat and his cold dark eyes he looks like some kind of crazy black bird flapping his wings.

"Run from me and you run from the Lord!" he snarls.

He's staring furious hard at Worm's mom. She's not looking at him, or me, or even at her daughter. She's looking straight down at the ground like she hopes it will open up and swallow her.

"You hear me?" the man in black shouts. "You hear!?"

"I wasn't running," she explains in this strange dead voice. "We just went for a walk."

I look over at Worm. She's kind of curled up on the bench, hugging her knees. Her eyes are open but you can tell she's not seeing anything on the outside.

I reach out to tap her on the shoulder, to get her attention, and that's when the man in black screams: *"Don't touch that girl!"* Spit flies out of his mouth, he's so angry. His face is white and tight, like a skull without enough skin. "Rachel! Get away from that man this instant!"

Worm won't look at me. She moves slow-footed to where her mom waits.

The Undertaker has planted himself in front of me, like a stake driven into the ground. "What did they tell you?" he demands. "Speak to me, you big oaf!"

I don't know what to say so I decide to stand up instead. The man in black watches me get a lot bigger and taller than he is, and he takes a few steps back, like he doesn't want my shadow to touch him.

I'm still trying to think of what to do next when Worm's mother comes to life. "You win, Martin," she says to the man in black. "Come along, Rachel. Let's go home."

Worm follows her mom to the old hearse. Then just before she gets inside she breaks away and runs back to me and grabs hold of my jacket.

"Rachel! Get back here!"

Worm whispers, "Don't forget," and then she turns and runs back to the hearse. A moment later they speed away, tires screeching.

I'm standing there like the biggest dork in the world when I realize that Worm hid something in my jacket pocket.

6.
Run for Your Life

The lump in my pocket is a book. *The Wind in the Willows*, the worn-out old copy Worm had in her backpack. I open up the cover and see where she's written her name and address on the inside, with the instructions RETURN OR ELSE.

Don't forget. So that's what she meant.

Just my luck. I'm sitting on a park bench minding my own business and now I'm supposed to return a book to a weird girl who's in trouble. I figure that's why Worm put the book in my pocket, so I'd follow her home and be Max the Mighty and save her from her creepy stepdad and leap over tall buildings in a single bound like Superman.

Yeah right.

But even though I'm a weenie, something way inside thinks maybe I *should* return the book and make sure Worm and her mom are okay. That's when my brain says, *Don't be a doughnut — you want to return the book, put it in the mail.*

But the rest of me is thinking I've got to do something, even if it scares me.

Because the Undertaker is always spouting about punishing sinners, and how only he knows what is true, the Truth with a capital "T." What a load of baloney. A man who'd do that to his own family, treat them like dirtballs, he wouldn't know the truth if it bit him on the butt.

The address inside the book is in the projects. That's a place where people don't have enough money, and half the stuff that should be inside the houses is left outside, like old baby strollers, and busted furniture, and cheesy toys that always look sad in the rain. The wrong side of the tracks, like Gram says, except they took out the railroad tracks before I was born, so now it's just the wrong side of town.

Anyhow, I'm trudging along, looking out for cracks in the sidewalk because now I need good luck more than ever. And the more I think about how the Undertaker treats his family, the more it burns me. Cracking his voice like a whip and talking to Worm like she was nothing special, just a thing to be yelled at.

Part of me wants to stop and go back to the millpond and forget about the girl and her mom, but I keep going. Like my brain has switched off and I'm this lumbering beast with feet as big as shoe boxes.

After a while I get to her neighborhood. The buildings kind of lean the wrong way and the shadows are long and spooky. The street signs have been torn down or sprayed over, and I'm trying to figure out which way to go when the shouting starts.

The Undertaker and Rachel's mom. The woman's voice is high and sharp and angry, but you can tell she's scared, too. The Undertaker, well, it makes me feel kind of sick in my stomach because he sounds so cruel and hateful.

I'm like a dinosaur with a second brain in its tail, except the extra brain is in my feet and they're making me follow the terrible dark noise. Follow it through the gloomy shadows that live in the alley, and past the filled-to-the-brim Dumpster, and around by the rusty chain-link fence.

It's still daytime, but the old buildings are so close together it might as well be night. I keep on going and the whole time I've got this feeling like I'm on an elevator going down too fast but I can't get off and any second it's going to hit bottom.

The angry voices are getting louder.

"Keep your hands off that child!"

"Shut up, woman! Shut your mouth or I'll break it!"

"Leave her alone or I'll call the police! And this time I'll tell them the truth!"

They're fighting about the Worm, I can feel that

in my bones. And then I come around the corner of the old tenement building and see the old hearse parked in the street. There's a light coming from the basement apartment. The kind of apartment where the entrance is under the front stoop and there's iron bars on the windows.

The Undertaker is shouting, "I will punish that child as the Lord sees fit!"

And then her mother goes, "You've never even read that Bible! You're not a real preacher, you're a fake!"

And then *smack* comes the noise of a hand slapping hard against a face and then the sound of a woman sobbing. "This can't go on," the woman whimpers. "Martin, please stop. Don't do it, please."

"Quit your blubbering!"

But the woman keeps crying. Crying from deep inside, like her world has cracked open and all the good is leaking out. It's a sound I remember from a long, long time ago, when my father made my own mother cry, and that's why my feet won't let me run away.

I'm not really thinking about what happens next but I want to stop that terrible sad crying and that's why I go down the steps to the front door. Thinking maybe if I ring the bell they'll stop fighting. Dingdong and everything gets better. But there isn't any doorbell and before I can make a fist and knock, the woman cries out, "No! No!"

and then something falls to the floor and everything gets very quiet.

The silence makes me wish I was a thousand miles away. And when I look into the room through the bars on the window, I see a terrible thing. A thing so horrible it feels like my heart has stuck to my ribs and won't ever beat again.

Rachel's mom is lying on the floor, blocking a bedroom door with her body. Her eyes are black and bruised and her nose is bloody and she's not moving.

The Undertaker yanks her arms and pulls her away from the door. He's about to open it. There's a cruel look on his pale white face, and his eyes are cold and gleaming and his angry hands are reaching out.

Ker-wham!

That's when I come crashing through the front door and knock it off the hinges and slam it flat on the floor.

"You!" he screams. But he sees the look in my eyes and how big I am and he backs away.

Rachel's mom moans and raises her head and when she sees me through her swollen eyes she almost smiles.

"Get away from that door!" the Undertaker shouts.

That makes me want to open the door, and I do.

The first thing I see is a light shining on a book. Worm is sitting in a corner with her knees up, in the dark. She's got the old miner's helmet on her head and the light is aimed at this book she's reading.

She knows I'm there but she won't look at me. She's all shut up inside.

When I get my mouth working, it says, "Come on. You have to get out of here. We have to call the police."

Worm just keeps reading her book like the book will save her. Like her stepfather can't touch her as long as her miner's light is shining.

But that won't stop him. Nothing will stop him except getting her away from him, so I grab her backpack, scoop her up in my arms and carry her out of the room.

When I get clear of her bedroom the Undertaker takes a run at me, then pulls up. "She's mine!" he screams. "Give her to me!"

I decide I'd rather die than do what he wants.

Rachel's mom has crawled up from the floor. It's hard for her to talk, but she looks at me and says, "You've got to get her away from here. Please. Take her away!"

Worm has her face hard against my chest and she won't look at her mother.

"Run away!" her mother urges. "Do it! Go!"

And that's how I became a desperate criminal and kidnapper, wanted by the law.

7.
Heading for Home

When you get in trouble, head for home. That's the first thing that comes into my head after me and Worm get clear of the alley. The Undertaker doesn't follow us, which sort of surprises me. Somebody takes away his stepdaughter and he just lets her go?

Of course he's got his hands full, after what he did to his poor wife.

Worm lets me carry her out of the basement apartment, but then she wants to walk on her own. When I ask if she's okay, she doesn't say a word but she reaches out and takes my hand.

"Grim and Gram will know what to do," I promise her.

We can hear sirens wee-ooing in the distance and I'm thinking they'll be putting the cuffs on the Undertaker so he can't hurt anybody else. I don't even want to think about what will happen to Worm, or what she should do until he's locked up in jail and can't hurt her anymore.

We're cutting across the backyards, heading for home because Gram will make everything okay somehow. Hey, after dealing with a big doughnut brain like me, helping an eleven-year-old girl should be easy, right?

Wrong, because when we come up to the back of the house, there are blue lights flashing through the windows. Cop cars in the street. Something in my brain goes "uh-oh."

I put my finger to my lips and Worm nods and doesn't make a sound.

There's a row of thick hedges that runs close to one side of the house, between our yard and the neighbors. I used to hide in there when I was little — after my mom died, but before Kevin moved next door. I'd hide myself in the hedges and pretend I was far away inside the forest where it was green and cool and the good smell of leaves and earth made me feel safe. Grim and Gram knew about the secret hedge place, but they never let on.

I'm way too big to hide in there now, but if I crouch real low and keep my head down I can still look around to the front yard without being seen. And what I see there just about blows my mind.

The Undertaker. He's with the cops but he's not in handcuffs. He's acting all weepy and upset and he's telling the police the biggest bunch of lies you ever heard.

"He was after Rachel. Menacing her! And when my wife tried to stop him, he hit her."

It never happened that way, but he sounds like he believes it. He wipes his eyes and sniffles a bit and says, "You've got to catch him and lock him away before he does my girl any harm."

The cops don't say much, except they tell the Undertaker to stay back. By now the front door has opened and Grim and Gram have come out on the steps. The blue lights make them look pale and old.

"What happened?" Gram asks, real worried. "Is it Max? Did something happen to Max?"

One of the cops says, "Is your grandson home, ma'am? We'd like a word with him."

The Undertaker hears that and goes nuts. "A word!" he shouts. "The boy assaulted my wife and ran off with our girl! Arrest him!"

Grim kind of staggers and grabs hold of Gram and then they're holding each other up and looking sick. Grim says, "Impossible! There must be some kind of mistake. Max wouldn't hurt a soul."

The other cop pipes up and says, "Maybe he doesn't know his own strength, sir. Have you seen him in the last few hours?"

Gram's voice is shaking. "He went down to the millpond," she says. "To the park. He goes there almost every day."

The Undertaker charges up behind the cops, waving his hat around. "See!" he shouts. "I told you! He followed us home from the park! Just like I said!"

Grim straightens up and goes, "You'd better tell us what happened, officer."

The cop doesn't look too happy about it, but he clears his throat and goes, "This man says a youth fitting Maxwell's description broke into their apartment and ran off with an eleven-year-old girl. While trying to stop him, the girl's mother received several blows to the face."

"And the woman told you Max attacked her?" Grim asks.

"She agrees with her husband," the cop says with a shrug.

Grim's voice gets stronger. "Then it wasn't our Max. Couldn't have been."

The other cop goes, "I'm afraid Maxwell was seen leaving the scene of the crime, carrying the girl. There's really nobody else who fits the description, sir. I mean, a boy that big. The door was broken down, knocked right off the hinges."

Gram has a quiet kind of voice but I hear her clear as a bell. "Listen to me, you people. There has been a mistake. Max will be home any minute, and he can explain for himself."

Inside I'm going, *Good for you, Gram*. And I'm thinking maybe I should come out and tell everybody what really happened, and how the

Undertaker is a total liar. Why shouldn't they believe me instead of him?

Then Gram says something that makes my heart drop down into my shoes.

"It wasn't Max who broke down the door and kidnapped the girl," Gram says. "Our boy would never do such a thing. I assume you're taking fingerprints?"

The cops both nod.

"Good," says Gram, like everything is settled. "That will prove it isn't our grandson."

Fingerprints. Mine will be all over the door I busted down. And besides, I really did break in and run off with Worm. That part is true.

The Undertaker is wiping his eyes with his floppy black hat. "Poor Rachel," he sobs. "My little girl."

"We'll find her," one of the cops tells him. "Maxwell Kane is too big to hide."

The other cop pats him on the back and says, "You'll get your daughter back. I promise."

Worm moans and goes, "I knew it. Nobody can stop him."

That's when I decide there's only one right thing to do.

Run away with Worm to a place where the Undertaker can't find her.

8.
Maxwell Kane Is Too Big to Hide

The last time I ran away from home I was five years old and took my teddy bear along for company. Now I'm fourteen and I've got a real live eleven-year-old girl hanging on to my hand like she's afraid I'll disappear.

We're cutting through the backstreets, away from the flashing blue lights, trying to stay out of sight.

"I knew that would happen," Worm says. "He can make my mom say anything. It happened before. They were fighting, you know, like tonight? And somebody called the cops. But when the cops got there, my mom said it was all her fault."

"So what do we do now?" I ask.

"I want to find my real dad," Worm announces. "He'll know what to do."

Actually, that makes sense. Let him be the one

to protect her, he's probably a whole lot braver and smarter than I am.

I go, "So where's your real dad? Does he live nearby?"

Worm shakes her head. "Montana," she says. "In a place called Chivalry."

Great. Wonderful. Geography isn't my best subject, but I know Montana is at least a thousand miles from here, maybe more. So whatever hope it gave me, that all comes crashing down.

"You could phone him," I say.

But Worm shakes her head. "He hasn't got a phone. I've got to see him, okay? It's important." She sounds like she's holding back tears.

I go, "Okay, okay. Take it easy. We'll find your dad, I promise."

The truth of it is, I feel like crying, too. Running out on Grim and Gram is about the worst thing I've ever done. It makes me feel like there's mice fighting inside my stomach and butterflies flitting around inside my head. Maybe I really am stupid, but I can't see anything else to do but somehow get all the way to Montana and let Worm's father fix everything.

More than anything I wish my friend Kevin were here — he'd have a plan. A really cool plan with lots of adventure in it.

"We could take a bus," Worm says. "Buses go to Montana, right?"

"I guess so."

I'm thinking she could go on her own, she doesn't need me to ride on a bus, right? And then I think: What would Kevin do if he were here? He'd figure she was a damsel in distress, and it was our job to keep her safe. No problemo, he'd say. Freak the Mighty to the rescue. All for one and one for all.

Except now it's just me.

"Please?" Worm says.

"Okay, we'll take a bus to Montana and find your real dad."

Thinking about going that far from home makes me kind of sick and dizzy and excited all at the same time. Also I'm wishing the sun would hurry up and go down because something that cop said bothers me. *Maxwell Kane is too big to hide.* And he's right, it's not like I can blend in, or shrink myself down to normal size. All they have to do is be on the lookout for a moon-faced goon with size seventeen shoes. Besides, just about everybody in town knows me by sight.

So we're stumbling along, with me nervous and worried and not paying attention to where I'm going, and that's when I crash right into the trash can. *Wham!* Stuff flies all over the street. Bottles and garbage and old newspapers and a ratty bundle of clothes.

"Wait a minute," Worm says, checking out the old clothes. She picks out a suit coat with holes in the elbows, and an old tie with stripes, and one of those hats like gangsters wear in the movies.

"This is exactly what you need," she says, her eyes going bright. "A disguise."

Ten minutes later we're heading for the bus station. I'm wearing the old suit coat and a fat tie like Grim wears to church on Sunday and a gangster hat pulled down so the brim hides part of my big fat face.

Worm has the idea to smear my cheeks with dirt so it looks like whiskers.

"There you are," she says, dusting the dirt from her hands. "All grown-up."

"No way."

"This'll work," she insists. "I read it in *The Adventures of Huckleberry Finn*. When Huck got in really bad trouble he'd put on a disguise. One time he had to dress up like a girl. You can pretend to be an adult."

"I guess." Already I'm getting the idea that it's easier to go along with her than argue. But I look about as much like a grown-up as a brontosaurus butt.

"We'll need money," Worm reminds me.

I've still got the twenty dollars Grim gave me for my birthday, stuck in the secret compartment in my wallet, and Worm has five dollars in a plastic purse in her backpack, and we figure that'll buy us tickets as far as the next state at least. I'm not thinking about what happens after that, or how we'll really get to Montana, which might as well be as far away as the moon. I'm mostly worried about what happens right now, this very minute.

We're a block from the bus station when the Worm goes, "Uh-oh."

She's spotted a cop car coming into the town square. No lights flashing, but they head straight for the bus station like they're expecting to find us there.

Of course. The first place they'd look, right? And I'm heading right for it.

What a moron.

The cops get out of the car and go to the ticket window. So in another minute they'll figure out we haven't got there yet, and they'll wait to grab us.

Maxwell Kane is too big to hide.

What he really meant was, Maxwell Kane is too stupid to get away.

Maybe they're right and I really am a doughnut brain. And then again, maybe I'm not.

"This way," I whisper to Worm.

We cut away from the town square, down the alleys that go by the big warehouses, out to the place where the interstate highway ramp heads west.

"What are we going to do?" Worm wants to know.

"We're going to break the law," I tell her. And then I do something I promised Gram I'd never do.

I stick out my thumb to hitch us a ride.

9.
The Prairie Schooner

There's nothing colder than wind on the highway. The gusts kick up from cars and trucks that zoom by like we're invisible. Drivers looking straight ahead, making sure their eyes don't see us.

I'm thinking this is a really stupid idea, trying to hitch a ride, when Worm nudges me and says, "You can go home now if you want."

I go, "Huh?"

She won't look at me because her eyes are red and she doesn't want me to see her crying. "It isn't fair, making you come with me. I'm the one who has to run away from You Know Who."

She means her stepfather, with all his lies about what really happened to her mom, and what he might do to Worm if she stays. My brain hears her talking and goes, *Do it, doughnut head. Go home. Tell the truth and see what happens.*

My brain is really stupid sometimes, because

only a crudball creep would leave an eleven-year-old girl all alone in the world, running away from a bad-news dude like the Undertaker. Besides, once we find her real father he can take over and make things right, so it's not like I'm running away forever.

That's what I tell myself, and I'm trying real hard to believe it.

Guys who brag about how cool it is to hitchhike are a bunch of liars. In the first place, you have to stand there like roadkill while dirt blows up in your face. Also your feet ache and your nose fills with the stink of smelly motors and hot tires, and you keep smiling and waving your stupid thumb but nobody stops.

Worm is fidgeting around and acting worried. Her face is so pale you could count every freckle, and her eyes look nervous and scared.

"You got a book in there, right?" I say, pointing at her backpack. "Go ahead and read it. Let me worry about getting a ride."

It's like she was waiting for permission. About two seconds later she's got her nose in a book called *A Wrinkle in Time*. You'd think she was in a library instead of hanging around beside a highway. You can tell she's really good at reading no matter where she is or what's happening around her. There's this look on her face like she's not there at all, she's gone wherever the book takes her.

Me, every time a truck goes by and smacks me in the face with a gust of stinky wind, it makes me feel dumber and dumber. Great idea, hitching a ride. Right up there with making firecrackers in the basement, or that time I put orange soda in the goldfish bowl so the fish could have a drink.

Finally I get so desperate, I decide to try praying, even though it's probably against the rules.

Dear Lord, I'm praying, *if You'll just make somebody stop and pick us up, I promise to be good and pray for more important things, like ending wars and feeding all the hungry people and saving the planet and stuff. Your immediate servant, Maxwell T. Kane.*

It probably doesn't count as a miracle, but when I open my eyes, this old school bus is pulling over into the breakdown lane, kicking up a cloud of dust.

"Hey, cool!" Worm says, looking up from her book.

When the dust clears I see it isn't a school bus exactly. Like maybe it used to be a school bus until somebody painted it over with splotches of bright colors. Ziggy stripes of yellow and zaggy patches of pink and another color that looks like the inside of a ripe cantaloupe. It has curtains on the windows and a big chrome air horn and a name in drippy purple paint on the side:

THE PRAIRIE SCHOONER

I figure anybody who'd paint an old bus like that is probably insane, or at least dangerously wacko. I'm going to tell Worm to forget it, we'll wait for another ride, but it's too late, she's already running for the door.

I catch up with her just as she's scrambling up the steps into the bus. "Hang on!" I'm panting. "Wait a sec!"

I look up to where the driver sits. He's this old dude with silvery white hair braided into long pigtails and a huge lumpy nose and not much chin. He's got a big wide smile and a Santa Claus fat belly, and he's wearing a Hawaiian shirt that hurts my eyes, it's that bright. But the strangest thing of all is his eyeglasses. The lenses are as big around as coffee cups, and so thick his eyes look like they're coming at you through telescopes.

"Howdy doody!" the old dude says. "Welcome aboard. Have a seat and rest your feet!"

The door whacks shut behind me and we're moving. He hits the horn and the loud noise almost stops my heart. I'm staggering, trying to hold on as the bus speeds up and Worm is looking around and going, "I guess you live here, huh?"

"Home sweet home!" the driver says, and gives his horn another blast.

The inside of the bus does look like home, in a funny way.

The old passenger seats have been ripped out and in the front part of the bus there's a couple of old couches bolted to the floor. In the back is a stove and a sink and one of those little refrigerators, and beyond that a couple of bunk beds built against the wall.

I'm trying to take it all in and keep my balance at the same time. Meanwhile Worm settles down on the old couch and acts like everything is normal.

The bus swerves and I fall onto the couch, next to Worm. The driver hits the horn again and shouts, "Make way! Coming through!" Then he's looking at me in the rearview mirror, and he says, "I'm the Dippy Hippie, pleased to meet you!"

I go, "Huh?"

"They call me the Dippy Hippie," he explains. "Dip for short."

I'm thinking maybe we should use made-up names, but before I can think of any, Worm looks up from her book and goes, "I'm Rachel and this is Max the Mighty."

"Rachel and Max," Dip says. "Groovy!"

He's got both hands on the big steering wheel and he's keeping the bus square in the middle of the slow lane. You can tell he's a good driver, even if he is halfway blind, and there's something in his voice that makes me think maybe he's not so strange after all.

"Where you folks headed?" he asks. "Anyplace special?"

"Um," I say, because I'm not sure if it's a secret or not.

"Chivalry," Worm pipes up. "That's in Montana."

"Montana, huh?" Dip nods to himself. "I'm headed in that general direction, more or less. We'll see where the highway takes us. Make yourselves at home. If you're hungry, there's food in the refrigerator. Help yourself."

Food sounds good, so I make me and the Worm a couple of bologna sandwiches with plenty of mustard. I've got no problem finishing mine, but before Worm gets halfway done her head is nodding and her eyelids are fluttering and then she kind of slumps over against me, fast asleep.

She's hugging *A Wrinkle in Time* to her chest and breathing deep and quiet and she looks so peaceful it makes me feel sleepy, too.

The next thing I know the bus has stopped moving and it's dark out.

"Rest stop," a voice explains softly. "All that snoring back there, I figured I'd better catch a few winks before I nodded off at the wheel."

Dip is lying on the other couch. He's got his hands behind his head and I can't tell where he's looking because there's no lights on, just a few stars shining in through the windshield.

"You want to tell me about it?" he asks, real quiet.

I don't know what to say, so I make up some lame story about how we missed the Greyhound bus and decided to try hitching a ride.

"Uh-huh," Dip says. "Rachel is your sister, is that it?"

"Not exactly," I say.

He doesn't say anything for a while and then he sits up and I can see him looking at us. Looking at how the Worm is sleeping so sound and comfortable on that old couch. Like she was safe in her own home. Dip nods to himself and then he says, "Fact is, I'm grateful for the company. Big bus like this doesn't feel right empty."

"It's real nice," I say, looking around. And it is nice, even if it's old and sort of shabby.

"I'm a retired schoolteacher," Dip says. "Me and the wife been planning to take off and see the world, like we always dreamed of doing but never had the time. Then she passed away all of a sudden. Kind of caught me by surprise, you know? After a while I got tired of feeling sorry for myself, so I finished fixing up the Prairie Schooner and took off. You know what a prairie schooner is, Max?"

"No," I say.

Dip sits up straighter and his voice gets happy again. He tells me how in the old days when the settlers headed out West, some of them rigged sails on their wagons and let the wind blow them onto the prairies. Sailing through fields of green, green grass under a big blue sky and all their lives in front of them, until they found a place and made it home.

"Is that where you're headed?" I ask. "Out to the prairies?"

"Wherever the wind takes me," he says. "That's where I'm going. How's that sound to you?"

"It sounds just fine," I say.

10.
Maxwell vs. the Ants

After resting his eyes for a while, Dip gets back behind the wheel and keeps on driving for hours and hours. Through the windshield the highway looks like a long dark tunnel with a white line disappearing into the darkness. Like we're flying forward in a funny kind of spaceship, and the stars are fireflies in outer space, lighting our way.

I ask Dip where we're going, exactly.

"We're heading for the horizon," he says. "Never look back. Eyes on the future, Max. That's the way to go."

Yeah right. Except when the future is a prison cell.

Worm keeps snoozing, so fast and deep asleep you could set off a cherry bomb and not wake her. I can tell she's dreaming, because sometimes her feet will twitch like she's running and her freckled face looks all squinted up and serious, and she's hanging on to her book so hard it'd take a crowbar to pry it out of her hands.

I got a pretty good idea what she's dreaming about. That no-good lying creep she calls You Know Who.

Sitting there in the dark with the sound of the tires taking us farther and farther away, I'm feeling pretty sorry for myself. Wishing I'd never met the girl called Worm. Because if I didn't know her, I'd probably be hanging out in the down under right this minute, reading my comic books or just lying there thinking about nothing at all. I wouldn't know any of the bad stuff that happened, or if I did, it would just be something I saw in the newspaper, or heard about from Grim and Gram.

But the truth is, I did rescue her crummy old miner's helmet and that made her think I was Max the Mighty. And I did kick down that door and help her get away. So now I'm wanted for assault and kidnapping, and nobody is going to believe me, or a strange red-haired girl who lives inside her books.

"Penny for your thoughts," Dip says. His big magnified eyes are looking at me in the rearview mirror.

"Nothin'," I say. "Just stuff."

Dip keeps that old bus heading into the west until the sun rises behind us, and I never do fall back asleep. My nerves keep sparking and twitching under my skin, like I drank too much of Grim's coffee, or stuffed myself with chocolate bars.

There's a thin kind of light in the sky that reminds me of skim milk, and the clouds look dirty and ragged where the wind is pulling them apart. When all the stars are gone, Dip slaps his hands on the wheel and says, "Anybody feel like breakfast?"

Worm pops up like somebody turned her switch on. "I'm hungry," she says, rubbing her stomach. "So hungry I could eat a house!"

"You mean a horse," I say.

"Ick," she says. "What a disgusting idea."

Then Worm gives me a big "gotcha" smile that makes me wish I'd never thought about how it would be if I'd minded my own business and thrown her stupid book away. She's the one who should be feeling sorry for herself and instead she's trying to make me laugh.

Dip pulls into a rest area and finds a spot way in back, where the tall pine trees hide us from the highway. It's green and thick and real overgrown. Like we're out in the wilderness somewhere, beyond where the road ends.

If I didn't know better I'd think we were all alone.

Dip gets out from behind the wheel real slow, and then he has to stretch and unwind, he says, because his old bones are creaky. "I'm like a rusty door hinge," he says. "Nothing a little tai chi won't fix."

"Tai chi," I say. "Is that what we're having for breakfast?"

It turns out tai chi is this strange-looking exercise Dip does each morning. Sort of like a slow-motion dance he learned from this Chinese guy. First thing Dip does is face the rising sun and bow at the waist, like he's meeting the queen or something. Then he raises up his arms real slow and he turns in a circle, holding his hands out like he's looking through a camera. Next he lifts his right leg and kind of dips down and around like he's going to tie himself in a big knot, except he changes his mind and unties himself real slow, and goes around the other way.

Remember, he's a fat guy in a killer Hawaiian shirt with long white hair done up in funny-looking pigtails. And a humongous nose and eyes that look like they're coming at you out of telescopes.

At first I want to laugh because it seems so funny, a guy like him doing this ancient Chinese dance. But there's something so cool and quiet about the way he's moving, so smooth and clean, that you have to take him seriously. He's holding out his hands and bringing them slowly around like they're the moon and he's the earth. And you can tell he's relaxed and peaceful inside.

You'd never think an old guy like Dip could move so beautiful.

Then I look over and what do you know, there's Worm copying him. She's holding out her hands just like he is, and she's got one foot up, turning slowly around. Her eyes are closed tight and there's this serious kind of look on her face that could almost be a sad kind of smile. The sun makes her red hair look glowy like the dawn, and she seems so quiet and easy with herself she almost looks like a different person, except for the freckles.

After he finishes his Chinese dance, Dip puts together the best breakfast ever. He brings out his little camp stove and sets it on a picnic table and cooks up a whole package of bacon, real slow. So slow my stomach is going nuts by the time he stirs in the scrambled eggs. He's got this brown bread that comes out of a can and he toasts that in the other fry pan and slathers it with butter.

The deal is, you put a chunk of egg and bacon on the bread and eat it that way, so you don't have to dirty any plates.

"You guys know the secret ingredient?" Dip asks.

Me and Worm, we're both chomping down so much all we can do is shake our heads.

"Fresh air," he says. "Fresh air is better than ketchup. Makes your taste buds tingle."

When he sees how hungry I am, Dip opens another can of brown bread, and by the time I put that away, my stomach feels as tight as a drum. Tight but good.

I'm feeling so full I decide to lay down on the grass and just stretch out.

Dumbo idea.

The hot feeling starts around my ankles, and before I have time to sit up, my butt is on fire.

"Help!" I cry. "I'm burning up! Help!"

I'm leaping and thrashing around like a total lunatic, ripping at my clothes.

"Fire ants!" yells Dip. "Rachel, you better get in the bus!"

The reason he wants her to go into the bus is so she won't see me pulling my pants down and dragging my butt across the grass.

I must look like the gooniest goon in the world, but I don't care. All I care about is getting rid of those fire ants.

Most people would die laughing, seeing a huge guy like me drag his bare butt in the grass while he's yipping like a poodle, but Dip, he never cracks a smile. He takes charge and shows me how to shake out my pants and brush off the fire ants, and then he turns around and pretends to study the trees while I get dressed.

It's not until we're all back in the Prairie Schooner that he lets it out. Then all of a sudden he's laughing so hard it sounds like a volcano erupting. His glasses fall off and his nose starts to run and he can't hardly breathe, and just watching him gets me laughing, too.

That finally kicks Worm off, and pretty soon

she's giggling and then laughing and pointing at me and making stupid goony faces and going, "Help! Help! My butt's on fire!" and that makes me laugh even harder.

That's when the cops come, when we're all laughing like total maniacs.

11.
The Man with the Crutch

I figure they'll handcuff me for sure. My stomach kind of sinks into my shoes and I'm just sitting there like a mental moron when Dip opens the door and goes, "Hello, officers. What's the trouble?"

One of the cops stays inside the cruiser. The other cop, a skinny dude with small dark eyes and a little mustache, he gets out and saunters over. He's got his hand on his gun and he's looking at the bus real careful.

"Please step out of the vehicle," he calls up to Dip.

Dip gives us a wink and then he gets out of the bus. Meanwhile Worm has got her nose in her book like nothing is happening, like the cops aren't there at all.

"Be glad to oblige," Dip says to the cop.

He's got his wallet chained to his pants and he pulls it out and shows the cop his driver's license. The cop studies it for a long time and then hands it back.

"We had a report of a car being hijacked," the cop says. "Have you seen any suspicious activity at the rest stop?"

Dip shakes his head and says, "No, sir. We've had the place to ourselves."

"Anyone else in the vehicle, sir?"

Dip goes, "A couple of wild outlaws. Maybe you better lock 'em up."

The cop takes him seriously and starts to pull out his gun. Real quick Dip says, "Just my two grandchildren, officer. I was making a joke."

The cop gives him a look like, *What are you trying to pull, buddy,* and then he relaxes a little and says, "Mind if I take a look?"

Dip shrugs and goes, "Make yourself at home."

The bus creaks as the cop comes inside. He stands there blinking like he's got spots in front of his eyes and then he sees me kind of slumped down on the couch. "What's your name?" he asks.

My mouth is too dry to talk.

"That's Mike," Dip says, coming up behind the cop. "He's a little, uh, shy."

"He a retard?" the cop asks.

Right away Dip says, "We don't use that word, officer."

After that the cop pretty much ignores Dip and

me and crouches down so he's level with Worm. "And what's your name, girlie?"

Worm won't look at him and she won't say anything.

Dip butts in. "That's Sally. Sally and Mike. Keeping their old grandpa company until their mother meets us in Denver."

The cop doesn't say anything, he just stands there and squints at me real hard, like he's seen me before. I give him a goofy look and let a little drool run down from the side of my mouth, like I really am retarded. Finally the cop grunts to himself and turns away.

"We're recommending that vehicles park within sight of the highway," the cop says to Dip. "These isolated rest spots can be dangerous."

"Yes, sir," Dip says. "Have a nice day, sir."

The skinny cop gets back in the cruiser and it glides away with the lights still flashing. Dip waits until it gets back on the highway and then he turns to me. "I figured it was nobody's business, what your real names are," he says.

"Thanks."

Dip grins. "You better wipe the drool off your chin, Max. You're pretty good at playing dumb, huh?"

"I've had some practice," I say.

And that's no lie.

We're about to get back on the highway when Worm goes, "Somebody's hiding in the woods."

Dip puts the brakes on and goes, "What?"

"Right over there," Worm says, pointing out the window.

All I see are bushes and thick pine trees. Then I notice the branches moving like there's something in there that wants to jump out. Probably the wind.

"It's nothing," I tell Worm. "Just your imagination."

Worm makes a face and goes, "No way. I saw something."

I'm still thinking her brain is in her book when all of a sudden the bushes open up and out comes this guy leaning on a crutch. Not a real crutch, but part of a tree branch he's using to hobble along. He's got thick yellow hair that grows down almost to his eyebrows and watery blue eyes and he looks kind of oily, like he needs a shower.

Right behind him is this scrawny-but-pretty-looking woman with eyes that kind of bulge out, like she's always surprised. Her face is a little scratched up and she's wearing a flowered dress that must have gotten dirty when she fell down. She looks scared, like she's afraid something else is going to jump out of the bushes any minute.

Dip sets the brake and gets out of the bus and rushes over to help the guy on the homemade crutch. "Max," he shouts back. "Gimme a hand!"

"You stay here," I say to Worm, but she's already back in her book and pretends not to hear me.

When the woman sees me get out of the bus she kind of cringes, like she's afraid I'll hit her or something. "Don't you worry, Miss," Dip says. "The boy is a gentle giant."

The guy with the crutch is hanging on to Dip for dear life.

"Is it broken?" Dip asks.

"Don't think so," the man with the crutch says. "Just hurts like heck."

That's when I notice the woman in the flowered dress is crying. Her eyes are all dark and circled like a raccoon's and her little nose is twitching. "Frank is in so much pain," she says. "He tried to stop them."

"Stop who?" Dip asks.

"The men who robbed us," the woman says. She's got this high, quick-talking voice, like somebody is pulling a string and making the words rush out. "They took everything and then they beat up my husband."

Frank goes, "I'll be okay." But then his crutch slips and he groans.

We help them into the bus and they collapse on the couch. Dip gets an aspirin from the first aid kit and gives it to Frank with a glass of water. "Thanks, buddy," Frank says. "Sorry to trouble you."

"No trouble," Dip says. "What happened?"

What happened is Frank and his wife, Joanie, were on their way to the West Coast because

Frank had been offered this extremely important job raising money for a hospital, and they got sleepy and decided to pull in and rest until daylight. Only when they were sound asleep these three guys in ski masks ripped open the doors and yanked them out of their car and stole it and all the money they'd saved up.

"We're broke," Frank says with a shrug. "They took everything."

Joanie sticks out her chin and goes, "We'll have to start over. It won't be the first time. We'll find a place to settle, I'll get a job."

Worm puts away her book and stares at Joanie for a while, like she wants to figure her out but she can't quite do it. "The cops were here," Worm finally says to her. "Looking for you."

Joanie pulls back like somebody slapped her. "Looking for me? What are you talking about?"

Dip explains how the police were just here a few minutes ago investigating a reported car hijacking.

"No kidding," Joanie says. "The cops were here?"

Frank looks uncomfortable.

"There's a pay phone right over there," Dip says, pointing. "I'll call 911, you can file a report."

He's digging into his pocket for a quarter when Joanie grabs hold of his arm. "Please," she begs him. "Don't."

Frank, he lays back on the couch and smiles to

himself. "I'm tired of lying," he says. "These are good folks, we can tell them what really happened."

"Frank!" Joanie sounds frightened.

"I don't care," he says. "Let 'em turn me in if they want to."

Dip goes, "What are you saying?"

"It's all my fault," Frank says, real quiet. "You see, the truth is, I'm a wanted man."

12.
Safe Inside Her Book

"Oh, Frank," Joanie says. "You make it sound like you're a criminal!"

Frank, he's propped up on the couch, but he already looks better, like he can't wait to get something off his chest. "The law thinks I am. Call 911 and we'll find out. They'll bust me, guaranteed."

Joanie goes, "It's not fair!"

"Fair has nothing to do with it," Frank says. "The law deals in facts, and the facts are against us."

It turns out that Frank and Joanie worked for this orphanage that specialized in crippled kids. Frank was in charge of the staff, and this guy he hired to keep track of the money was actually stealing it and making it look like Frank signed the checks.

"The guy was smooth," Frank says. "I never knew what was going on until it was too late. I just never believed a man could be so low he'd steal from crippled orphans."

"You mean disabled," Dip reminds him. "Not crippled."

"Disabled in the crippled sense," Frank says. "Polio and leprosy and such."

Dip gets this funny look and goes, "I thought they had a cure for polio. And leprosy."

Frank waves his hand and says, "There are a few tragic exceptions, I'm afraid. It doesn't matter now. Facts are facts. The money was stolen and the orphanage was shut down. And it was my fault. I should have known better."

"I see," Dip says.

Then Frank looks Dip straight in the eye and says, "Go ahead. Make that call. I wouldn't blame you."

Dip looks at Frank and he looks at me and Worm, and you can tell he's got a lot on his mind. Finally he goes, "Live and let live, eh? What say we all forget our troubles for the moment and get back on the road?"

Frank lets out a sigh and goes, "I knew you were okay."

Joanie jumps up and gives Dip a big hug and says, "Thank you! Thank you!"

Her eyes are a little wet from holding back tears, but by the time we're back up to speed, Joanie is already making herself at home. She spots the little refrigerator and goes, "Hey, Dip! You got anything to eat? I'm starved!"

And that's how Frank and Joanie joined our little family, and helped good old Dip fill up his empty bus.

Worm goes back to her books. She's got a bunch of paperbacks in her backpack and she tells me she's done with *A Wrinkle in Time* for now and she's into these stories called The Earthsea Trilogy. They're all about sorcerers, and dragons who can talk if you know their secret language, and a lot of other cool stuff that happened a long time ago.

"Magic ruled the world," Worm says, not looking up.

Which makes me think of the times when me and Kevin turned ourselves into Freak the Mighty and we made up our own kind of magic. Once when we were walking along an ordinary street — just dull normal houses and barking dogs — Kevin had me convinced we were crossing a moat into a big castle.

Thinking about that makes me miss Kevin so bad, it hurts inside my chest, and then all of a sudden I'm missing Gram and Grim. I'm even missing my stupid bedroom with the saggy mattress. I'm missing my mom, I'm missing just about everything, even the stuff I hate.

Dip, he sees me in his rearview mirror and goes, "Hey, Max! Come on up here and keep me company."

So there I am, sitting right behind Dip and we're

seeing what comes down the road. For a while we're going through a place where there are tons of big refineries and factories alongside the highway, and a funny yellow light that makes it look like the sky is burning real slow.

"What a pit," Frank says.

But I think it looks kind of cool, like the end of the world but not quite, and Dip chimes in to say you'd be surprised how beautiful America can be, if you get away from the turnpike. That kind of kills the conversation for a while, until Joanie taps me on the shoulder and goes, "What about you, big guy? What's your story? Is the girl really your sister or what?"

I decide the best thing to do is keep my mouth shut about how we're looking for Worm's father, because the way Joanie is looking at me, so kind and curious and helpful, I'd probably tell her the truth and get us into trouble.

She goes, "The silent type, huh? You're keeping a secret, is that it? Come on, share it with Joanie."

Frank, he's stretched out on one of the couches with all of the pillows to ease the pain. "Leave him alone," he calls out. "He'll talk to us in his own good time, won't you, kid?"

Meanwhile, Dip keeps on driving. Like his hands have melted to the wheel and he can't let go even if he wanted to. He's humming a little song to himself, and it sounds like the tires humming under us and the wind that's blowing his old Prairie Schooner bus across America.

It's just a dumb little song without any words, but it makes me feel peaceful and happy, and I'm thinking there's no place I'd rather be than right here with these people. Like we're all sharing something none of us can talk about or it'll disappear. Like we really are safe and nothing can touch us.

Maybe Worm is right. Maybe there is magic in the world, if you think about it.

When the sun goes down, Worm switches on her miner's light and keeps reading.

I'm kind of dozing off, listening to the hum of the tires and that old bus engine purring along, but I'm awake enough to see Joanie settle down on the couch next to Worm.

"Must be a good story, huh?" she says.

Worm shrugs but doesn't say anything, and she won't look up from her book.

"I bet you've got a story of your own to tell," Joanie says. "You want to talk about it, just us girls?"

Worm ignores her and keeps reading.

"I'm here," Joanie says, her voice going soft. "Whenever you're ready, I'm here."

There's something in her voice that makes me not quite trust her, but I don't need to say anything to Worm. I can tell she feels the same way.

I sleep for a while, but whenever I wake up, Worm's light is still on, and she's turning pages, staying safe inside her book.

13.
There's a Sucker Born Every Minute

There's a place in Indiana where the cornfields look like a big green ocean. Everything is pretty flat except for these low, rolling hills, and when we come over the top you can see just about forever. All there is to see are miles and miles of green cornstalks, millions and millions of them. You can see the wind moving through the corn from miles away, and it looks like waves rolling in from far out at sea.

Dip lets down the windows and you can hear the air moving through the fields. This soft sighing noise like when you put a shell to your ear and hear the ocean. Only it doesn't sound like the ocean to Dip — he says it's the cheering noise from halfway around the world, of all those people who love to eat corn on the cob.

"They're cheering from Maine to Texas, can't

you hear them?" he says, cupping a hand to his big floppy ear. "They're cheering in Tokyo and Timbuktu!"

I don't believe a word of it, but Dip swears Timbuktu is a real place, and there's nothing much there, which is why they joke about it.

Of course it isn't all corn in Indiana, they grow some people, too, and every once in a while a little town springs up out of nowhere, like it crash-landed from a tornado in *The Wizard of Oz*. Usually there's just one street with old wooden buildings that look like cowboys should be inside, except it's mostly these farmer guys buying hardware and tractors and stuff. Guys who look like they don't mind getting dirty and sweaty — in fact, they prefer it. Guys who, when they get a load of the Prairie Schooner chugging down the street, they think it's some kind of joke.

And if they think the painted-up bus is strange, a funny old dude like the Dippy Hippie, with his long hair and his Hawaiian shirt, he really makes an impression in a town full of Indiana farmers.

"Howdy doody," he says to everybody when we stop to get gas or whatever, and people look at him like he just stepped out of an alien spacecraft. Mostly they nod hello and then hurry away.

Dip, he could care less what people think. He says after thirty years as a schoolteacher he's going to play hooky whenever he feels like it.

"I'm free as a bird," he says, "but that doesn't

mean I want to fly with the rest of the flock, if you know what I mean."

I don't know what playing hooky has to do with a bunch of birds. I guess all it really means is Dip is kind of different, and he likes being that way.

Anyhow, one time we come in off the highway to get gas at this place and the bus won't start. That poor old motor keeps grinding and grinding and it coughs a little but it just won't go. "Minor malfunction," Dip says. "Nothing to it," and he gets out his tool kit and opens the hood and starts messing around under there like there's nothing else he'd rather be doing.

Frank and Joanie get out of the bus and watch Dip for a while, but you can see they think it's kind of boring, working on an old motor, and they'd rather be doing something important, like raising money for orphans or whatever.

"Even a little one-horse town like this has opportunity," Frank says. He's squinting into the sun and studying the buildings on the main street like there's something hidden there, if he can only find it.

"Forget it," Joanie says, looking around and yawning. "There's nothing here for us. Just dirt and corn and farmers."

"Then I shall plant a seed," he says. "Come along, children. Make yourselves useful."

The way he marches off, it's hard not to follow.

Worm nudges me and whispers, "You notice

something? Mr. Wonderful isn't limping anymore."

She's right. Frank has gotten better all of a sudden. The ankle that got hurt so bad when he fought the robbers must have healed overnight, because he's walking along like he hasn't got a care in the world.

"A mom-and-pop deal," he says. "This should be perfect."

"Don't be stupid," Joanie says, hanging back.

What he calls a mom-and-pop deal is really a small store with a bunch of dusty cans on the shelf, and a little old bald guy behind the counter watching game shows on this portable TV.

Frank, he marches right in and says, "How's it going, Pops?" Then he takes a newspaper out of the rack and tucks it under his arm and goes, "Where's the tuna fish?"

The old guy points and Frank cuts down the aisle like he's heading for the pot of gold at the end of the rainbow. Me and Worm and Joanie can't keep up with him, he's moving so fast.

We're turning the corner of the aisle when we hear this tremendous crashing noise. *Wham-bam-crash-bang-bing*, as just about every can of food in the place goes smashing to the floor.

"Hellllllp," Frank groans out. "Hellllllp!"

When we get there, he's buried under all these cans and loaves of bread and stuff. You can tell right away he's been hurt bad, from the way his eyes are rolling back and his mouth is hanging open like he can't get enough air.

"Slipped on something," he groans. "Oh God, I think I busted my ankle."

The old guy from behind the counter is all flustered and apologizing and saying how he'll have to call an ambulance, the nearest hospital is fifty miles away.

But Frank groans some more and says a hospital won't be necessary.

"Maybe it ain't really broke," he says. "Probably I just sprained it bad. I'll be fine."

The old guy is fussing over him and saying how sorry he is, and how maybe Frank should at least see a doctor and get the ankle checked out.

"I'll be okay, once I get my breath back," Frank says, but when he tries to walk he almost falls down, it hurts so much. Joanie has to hold up one side of him while I grab the other. "Haven't got time for broken ankles," he says. "We have to be in California in three days, isn't that right, kids?"

He's talking to me and the Worm like we're his kids, but I don't know what to say, so I just nod. The store guy looks pretty worried and you can tell he's a nice enough dude, even if he is an old geezer.

Joanie, she's busy whispering to Frank, but loud enough so you can hear her. "How can we buy groceries if we have to pay for fixing your ankle?" she says.

Frank shushes her. He's acting brave and heroic, like he doesn't want the old geezer to know how poor he is, or how he and Joanie got robbed of every earthly possession. "We'll make it somehow," he whispers real loud. "It's only three days to California. We'll eat when we get there."

The old guy hears that and gets a funny look on his face, like he's thinking hard. I'm worried maybe he's going to call the cops, but instead he fills a couple of bags with groceries. Not just cheap stuff, either, but lots of sliced meats and cheese from the cooler, and cans of tuna, and candy bars for me and Worm.

"This'll get you where you're going," he says, shoving the bags into my arms. "I hope your father has better luck in California. It can't be easy for him, not having enough money to buy food. A man'll do just about anything to put food on the table for his wife and kids, I reckon."

I'm about to tell the old guy that Frank isn't my father and we're not his children, and nobody is hungry, but he feels so good about giving us the groceries I decide to keep my trap shut.

Out on the street Frank waits until we're clear of the store, then he hands me and Worm a chocolate bar. "Good job," he says. "You've got possibilities, both of you."

Worm won't take the candy, but I figure a little chocolate won't hurt me.

You can tell Joanie isn't too impressed with

Frank. "That was just plain stupid," she tells him. "You took a risk and for what? A few slices of bologna?"

But Frank is strutting along like he's the king of the world — that ankle healed really quick this time. When he hears Joanie complaining he just grins and shakes his head. "You're missing the point, sweet buns."

"Yeah? What point is that?"

"There's a sucker born every minute. Right, Max?"

Frank has this look, like he thinks I'm in on the joke. But really I'm thinking he's right.

There *is* a sucker born every minute, and I'm one of them.

14.
The Python in the Toilet Bowl

Good old Dip has got the Prairie Schooner running real smooth by the time we get back. "Dirt in the carburetor," he says. "All those dusty roads. I see you folks have been shopping."

He's eyeballing the paper sacks and you can tell he's thinking this: If Frank got robbed of everything he owned, where'd he get the money to buy groceries?

I could explain the whole deal, but instead I chicken out and keep my mouth shut.

Worm won't say anything either, except to me. "I've read about guys like him," she whispers to me. "They lie so much they don't know what the truth is."

Frank, he must have ears like a cat, because he picks up on it. "The truth is overrated," he tells her, acting like it's a big joke we're all sharing.

"What I do is improve upon reality, and people prefer it. They really do."

After that, Dip says we should hurry up and get back on the road because you never know what might be catching up.

When we're sailing free and clear down that highway again, I start to feel better. Like what we did in the store never really happened. Like it's fading somehow, the farther away we get.

The more we stay on the Prairie Schooner the more I like it. I don't tell Worm, but inside I'm almost hoping we never get to Montana. As long as we're on the bus we're safe, and the rest of the world kind of goes away and doesn't matter as much.

Dip, he's feeling good, too, and he pops in a cassette and plays this golden oldie song about being on the road again. He punches up the volume and starts singing along like he doesn't care how bad he sounds, it's how loud that counts.

"On the road again, de doot de do, nah nah nah nah," he goes, making these electric guitar noises somewhere deep in his nose.

Joanie picks up on it right away, tapping her feet and snapping her fingers. Before you know it, she's standing up in the aisle, dancing to the music and going, "Come on! Come on!" to me and Worm.

She wants us to dance.

No way, I'd rather eat cement. You ever seen

those dancing hippos on the Disney Channel? That's me. But Joanie finally gets Worm out of her seat and makes her move to the beat, and you can tell Worm doesn't mind too much, even if she won't admit it.

"On the road again, de doot de do, nah nah nah nah!" sings Dip.

Okay, I like the song, too, even if it was old before I was born, and it's pretty hard not to sing along, and clap your hands on the beat like Joanie shows us.

Whenever we come to a good part, Dip lets loose a blast of that big old horn, *wooonnnnnnkkkkk!* and the birds fly up from the cornfields right on cue.

Frank is the only one who doesn't care about the on-the-road music. He's stretched out, taking up all of one couch, and he's got his newspaper tented over his face like he wishes we'd all shut up and let him sleep.

The weird thing is, even when he's napping he looks like he's ready to sign autographs. Like he's the star of his own personal movie and the cameras follow him everywhere. And all he has to do is look you straight in the eye and you want to be in his movie, too.

After the song ends, Joanie and Worm flop down on the couch and they're both giggling so hard they can barely breathe.

When Joanie can talk again she goes, "I needed that. Thanks, girlfriend," and pats Worm on the hand. "Who taught you to dance? Let me guess. Your brother?"

Worm shakes her head.

"Maybe it was your dad," Joanie says. "A lot of girls learn to dance from their dads."

Worm shakes her head again. Joanie doesn't seem to notice she's stopped smiling. "Had to be your mom," she says, sort of wheedling for an answer. "Did I guess right?"

Worm gets this frozen look, and her face goes so pale that her freckles look like they hurt.

"Something about your mom, huh?" Joanie says. "What happened, exactly?"

Worm curls up on the couch and covers her face with a book.

"Leave her alone," I say.

Joanie sees how Worm is hiding behind her book and she shrugs and says, "Fine. Okay. I was just making conversation. Nothing wrong with that, is there?"

I don't say anything, but my brain is thinking, *There is something wrong*, only I don't know what, exactly.

Somewhere around Illinois, Frank sits up and starts reading the newspaper. "Look here," he says. "There's a man in Topeka who found a python in his toilet. Amazing, isn't it? It says the python is native to the Amazon and somehow it got all the way to Kansas."

"Yeah," Joanie says. "Amazing."

"I bet I could make money with that snake," Frank says. "Take it on the road, sell tickets. People would pay to see a snake like that."

Joanie goes, "I'd pay more *not* to see it. Especially in the bathroom."

That shuts Frank up for a while, but he keeps rattling that newspaper just to remind us that he can see gold where everybody else just sees a python in the toilet bowl.

Late in the afternoon we cross the Mississippi River, and Dip gets real excited. "There it is!" he shouts. "Greatest waterway on planet Earth! Runs from the Minnesota lakes to the Gulf of Mexico! Passes through ten states! Over two thousand miles long! Mississippi, that means 'Big River'!"

He's talking like a geography lesson until he honks the horn and shouts, "Howdy doody, Big River!" and then he sounds like the Dippy Hippie and nobody else. "Take a look, Max. Drink it in. That's not just a river, it's liquid history. That's your country. It keeps changing paths, making its own way, just like we do."

He's so excited the Worm looks up from her book and smiles when she sees the river, which makes me think she's feeling okay again, now that Joanie has stopped asking her questions.

The Prairie Schooner sails along nice and easy until the sun goes down, and Dip says if we could go fast enough, the sun would never set because we'd chase it all the way around the world. Just thinking about that turns my brain to mush, because I know he's right and I still can't figure it out.

"Tonight we'll splurge on a real campsite," Dip announces. "If I don't get a hot shower soon, they'll put me out with the garbage."

That's how we come to stay at this KOA campground somewhere in Iowa, where they have all these Indian names but not too many Indians, not that I can see. Dip says they mostly live on reservations, but we don't have one, so we'll have to settle for the normal campground. I can tell he's pulling my leg, but I don't let on — why spoil his fun?

When the bus is parked in the right spot, Frank tucks his newspaper under his arm and says to Joanie, "I need a word with you, sweet buns."

He's acting mysterious, and he takes Joanie outside so they can talk private. I can see them under the streetlight and he's slapping his hand on the newspaper and she's listening and nodding, and I figure he's got some new scheme to get something for nothing.

Which he does, only I don't know what he has in mind, or how it's going to change everything for me and Worm and wreck our happy life in the Prairie Schooner.

If I *had* known, I'd have flushed that python right down the toilet, you can bet the ranch on that.

15.
Dip Makes a Promise

That night we're sitting around under the stars with our stomachs full. Worm has put away her book for once, and she's sitting there with her chin on her knees, staring at the little campfire Dip built. Every now and then she glances over at me like she wants to say something important, but she never does. I figure whatever it is can wait.

Frank and Joanie have wandered off somewhere, and it's just the three of us, and I'm thinking how much I want this to go on forever. Sailing that old Prairie Schooner across America, and camping by the side of the road every night, and eating hamburgers cooked over an open fire, and feeling like we're in a place of our own. I'm thinking how my buddy Kevin would have loved this adventure, and I wish he was here, and Grim and Gram, too, but even that doesn't hurt too much, I'm feeling so good.

As long as we're on the bus, the only thing that matters is where we go tomorrow. Yesterday doesn't count, or the day before that. The only thing that matters is me and Worm are safe.

I'm thinking how lucky we are right at this moment, and how no matter what happens next, I wouldn't trade this night for anything.

Dip, he's staring up at the sky for a long time and then he goes, "Guess what I see up there?"

Worm won't guess, but you can tell she's listening.

"I see a girl about your age," he says to her. "See that glow from the Milky Way? That's her hair. Those other stars are her sword and shield. She's fighting a battle. A really important battle. Life and death, I'll bet."

Worm looks up at the sky to where he's pointing. "What happens to her?" she asks.

"I'm not sure, exactly," Dips says. "But in the end she wins because her heart is true. That much I know."

Me, all I see is a bunch of stars, but I don't mind. If Worm can see her dreams come true in the sky, that's good enough. And it makes me think how cool an old dude like Dip really is, to figure it out, and show her where to look.

When Worm starts nodding off, Dip says it's time to turn in. "We have a long day tomorrow," he says. "I expect we'll see Wyoming before the sun goes down. We'll check out the Bighorn Mountains, and Yellowstone, maybe go fishing on the Wind River, if we can find some bait. Sound okay with you?"

It all sounds cool to me.

Worm is sound asleep with her backpack on, and when I pick her up to carry her inside the Prairie Schooner, she's as light as a feather, like gravity doesn't count when you're not awake.

That's when Dip goes, "Oh my."

The way he says it makes the short hairs tingle on the back of my neck. Something is wrong, I can feel it all over.

"Somebody let the air out of the tires," Dip says. "Now why would they do that?"

He's crouched down in the dark, staring at how the Prairie Schooner is sitting low on her rims. I've got Worm asleep in my arms and I don't know what to do. Flat tires are no big deal to fix, but like Dip says, why would somebody do that?

I get this terrible empty feeling like they just let the air out of me, too.

Dip gets up and says, "Wait here," and he goes into the bus and turns on the lights.

I can see him in there checking things out, and then he picks up Frank's newspaper. You can tell something has got his attention. His big friendly face kind of shuts up and I don't know what he's thinking, but whatever he's reading in the paper has made him different.

Then he looks through the bus window out to where I'm standing in the dark, and suddenly I know what's in that newspaper. Dip comes out real slow, and when his feet are on the ground he looks at how the Worm is sound asleep in my arms and he goes, "You've got ten thousand dollars on your head, Max. That's the reward for information leading to your apprehension, and for the recovery of the girl." Then he stops and gives out a big sigh, and when he speaks again his voice sounds small and old. "I knew you were in trouble. I didn't know it was trouble that big or bad."

I don't know what to do or say. It's like my feet are sinking into the ground and the sky is pressing me down and the air feels thick and scratchy in my lungs.

"I read what her stepfather had to say," he says, tapping the newspaper. "You better tell me what really happened."

"I can't," I say, whispering. "Not with her right here. She can't think about it right now, even when she's asleep."

Dip stares at me a long time and then he nods to himself and says, "Well, I guess I've got to trust my instincts on this. I'm not going to turn you in, son. But somebody else might."

That's when the flashing blue lights come gliding into the campground.

"It's my fault," Dip says when he sees those lights. "I never should have let that con man on my bus."

My feet finally come loose and I turn and see the

police car coming around the curve of the campsites. As it passes under a streetlight, there's Joanie in the backseat and Frank in the front. He's showing the cop which way to go.

"I don't know what you're going to do," Dip is saying. "But you'd better do it fast."

Then he shoves some money in my shirt pocket. He pats Worm on the head and he goes, "Trust yourself, Max. I'll see you again someday. That's a promise."

The next thing I know, I'm running off into the night with a girl in my arms, away from the Prairie Schooner and the cop car and the campground. I don't know where I'm running, or why exactly. All I know is this: Worm is still asleep and she's not ready to wake up yet.

My brain has stopped thinking. The only thing inside my head is *Run, boy, run.*

16.
Sometimes the Truth Is Just Plain Stupid

The thing about running at night, you can't even see your feet, let alone the ground. You can't see the holes or the rocks or the old roots grabbing at you. The only thing to do is run faster. Fast enough so that nothing sticks. Fast enough so the shadow things can't find you. Fast enough so the dark is cool in your face, and you feel like running forever.

It's a train that finally stops me.

I'm coming down this hilly area of woods and brush, dodging around low tree branches like I've got radar or something. Like I can feel things without actually seeing them. And then I'm out of the woods and into the open, picking up speed, flying downhill like I'm an airplane getting ready to take off and Worm is my only passenger and she's still asleep.

Ahead of me something big is moving and that's when I put on the brakes and hear the screechy groan of a train grinding along the tracks. Not going fast, but kind of bumping along, *kerchunk kerchunk,* like no hurry, no problem.

There's just enough light from the stars so I can see the long, dark cars moving against the sky. They're so heavy and slow and solid it looks like they'll roll on forever, as far as the track will go.

Worm wakes up and puts her hands around my neck. "I dreamed we were flying and I wasn't afraid," she says.

I figure she'll ask me about what happened and why we ran away from Dip and the Prairie Schooner, but it's like she already knows and doesn't want to talk about it right now.

"Hold on tight," I say and she hangs on with all her might.

I start jogging along beside the track, like we're in a race or something. Me against the train. Which turns out to be going faster than I thought, because I can barely keep up.

In the movies you see dudes jump on moving trains like it was nothing. Believe me, it's not that easy, especially if you've got a girl in your arms and you've only got one hand free.

First, you have to run exactly as fast as the train is going, even though you're slipping in the gravel by the tracks and scared you'll slide under the wheels. Then you've got to grab hold of something and yank yourself aboard and not fall.

By the time we finally climb onto this low-car part of the train, I'm so scared I almost wet my pants. But Worm acts like she wasn't worried, like she knew I could do it.

"You're amazing," she says, and sounds like she really means it.

Yeah, right. The Amazing Dork.

When my heart settles down I look around. There's this big piece of farm machinery chained down to the car, but plenty of room for me and Worm to stretch out. We're barely settled when the train starts to pick up speed, and then we're rolling around this long curve, out into the countryside. I can't see much except to tell it's pretty flat and wide open.

Funny thing about the stars, when you're looking straight up they seem to hold still in the sky, even if you're on a moving railroad car. Like the stars won't change, no matter what happens. A long time ago some old dinosaur, he probably looked up and saw the same stars, mostly, and I bet he had big feet and a small brain just like me.

I know I should feel terrible about getting run off the Prairie Schooner, and having to leave the Dippy Hippie behind, but instead I'm feeling good. They didn't get us and they won't be sending Worm back to the Undertaker, not so long as we're on this train. And it's like the running part is fun, as long as you don't get caught.

Pretty dumb, huh? Well, sometimes the truth is just plain stupid, and you can't help it.

Before long, the train settles into this rhythm, rattling along the tracks, *kerchunk, kerchunk, rackety-roo, kerchunk, kerchunk, rackety-roo.*

For a long time Worm doesn't say anything, but I can tell she's thinking hard, and finally she goes, "I wasn't really asleep when the cop car came."

As usual I go, "Huh?"

"I just pretended," she says. "Because I knew Max the Mighty would come to the rescue."

Suddenly my ears feel hot and my throat is thick and part of me is mad, but I don't know why. "Cut it out," I say. "There's no such thing."

But Worm won't stop. "I heard stories about you," she says, insisting. "Kids talking. Grown-ups, too."

It makes me feel weird to think that people talk about me when I'm not around, and I bet most of it is lies.

"They said your father killed your mom, is that part true?"

I go, "Yeah," and then I'm not going to say anything else because I hate talking about it. But I'm looking at Worm and seeing how the stars make her face glow, and it's like a knot unties inside me and all of a sudden I want to tell her everything.

"It happened when I was a little kid," I say. "My dad got in a fight with my mom and he grabbed her around the neck and he wouldn't let go even though I tried to stop him. Then afterward he put me to bed and told me it was all a bad dream, but

I busted out a window and shouted for the police, and that's how he got sent to prison."

Worm doesn't say anything. She's waiting for me to finish.

"For a long time I never wanted to think about it, until Kevin and me got to be Freak the Mighty. Then he showed me how remembering can be a great invention of the mind. He said you can't forget the bad stuff because it's part of who you are."

"He was a really cool guy, huh?"

"The coolest," I say. "He even saved my life once."

"Yeah? What happened?" Worm wants to know.

"Killer Kane — that's what they call my father — they let him out of prison. Which really flipped me out. And then one night he broke into my bedroom and kidnapped me."

"How come you didn't fight him?"

I shrug. "It was like I was paralyzed or something. I just couldn't."

Worm nods and I'm pretty sure she's thinking about the Undertaker, and how he makes her feel the same way, like she can't do anything to stop him.

"Anyhow, Kevin found out where Killer Kane took me, and he figured a way to get me out of there. He filled this squirt gun with soap and vinegar and curry powder and stuff and sprayed it at my old man and we got away."

"Pretty smart," Worm says.

"Yeah. I lost it when Kevin died. It was like the whole world died, you know? Then I started thinking about all the cool things we did and I wrote some of the stuff down. And then I wasn't angry anymore, just sad. I still think about him all the time."

Worm sees how bad I'm feeling and she takes hold of my hand and gives it a squeeze and then lets go. After a while she says, "You think when you die you really go to heaven?"

"I hope so."

"Yeah," she says. "Me, too."

17.
The Horrible Howl

The *rackety-roo* of the train makes my eyelids heavy, and even though I'm supposed to stay awake and keep watch over the Worm, I fall asleep almost as soon as she does.

When I wake up again, the stars are gone and there's this orange blob on the horizon where the sun is coming up. It looks kind of hot and melted and really old somehow, like I'm looking back in time.

Worm is sleeping on my rolled-up jacket. She's holding her book tight against her chest like she always does. Probably most girls her age would throw a fit if they went to bed without a pillow, but Worm never complains about anything. When you think about what happened to her in the last few days, that's pretty amazing, and it makes me feel even better about being a notorious criminal with a ten-thousand-dollar reward on my head.

They say you can go blind if you stare at the sun too long, but I can't help it. It's like there's this message written in the sunrise and I can't quite make it out. Finally I quit looking and close my eyes, but I can still see the bright orange spot kind of burning a hole in my brain. And my brain, which is pretty irritated with me, goes, *This isn't a cool adventure, you moron! You messed up big time. The whole world thinks you're a monster for kidnapping an eleven-year-old girl. They'll hunt you down like a rabid dog. The smart thing would be to split. Let Worm find her real father on her own. Just leave her and run for your life. Keep on running until they forget all about the son of Killer Kane. Until you forget about yourself.*

I tell my brain to shut up, but it won't listen.

Leave the kid, it says. *She'll be better off without you. Somebody else can take care of her. Somebody smarter and stronger than you are. You're not a hero. Max the Mighty doesn't exist.*

"I know that!" I shout out loud, and that wakes up Worm.

She yawns and looks around and gives me a big smile. Right off she says, "You know what? I bet this train goes forever. I bet it goes to the end of the world."

All I can think to say is, "I dunno. I guess so."

Which is a flat-out lie. Even a total bonehead like me knows the world is round and you can't get to the end. You just keep going around and around and you never get there.

When the sun gets a little ways higher, the train starts to slow down and the clackety-clackety noise changes. We start passing big buildings and you can tell we're getting close to a city. I'm thinking maybe there'll be a train station and I'll be able to buy us something to eat. A hot dog or a hamburger or a candy bar — anything. Because all of a sudden I'm really, really hungry.

But when the train finally stops, there isn't any train station or any food. We're in the middle of this huge junkyard. All these cars crushed up into rusty cubes of steel, and stacked five or six high in row after row.

A wicked-looking barbed-wire fence surrounds the junkyard and I'm thinking who would want to steal a squished-up car? That's when Worm says, "Good doggie. Good doggie."

I go, "Huh?" and then I see the dog.

It's a really mangy-looking animal without a collar or a tag and it looks like it's been rolling in the dirt, or worse. From the way the ribs stick out it doesn't get fed regular and when Worm puts out her hand the dog starts edging closer, keeping low like dogs do when they're afraid.

"Oh," Worm says. "Can we keep it?"

I go, "Be careful."

"I always wanted a dog," Worm explains. "But You Know Who said no."

The dog is growling deep in its throat and its eyes don't look friendly. I grab hold of Worm's jacket and pull her back — just as the dog snaps at her hand.

"Hey!" she says. "You scared him!"

But the growling dog doesn't look scared anymore. It makes a high yipping noise, and then things start to happen fast. Because the yipping was like a signal, and now three, four, five wild dogs come out of nowhere and leap into the railway car, heading right for us.

"Get back!" I yell, grabbing Worm around the waist.

I climb onto the piece of farm equipment that's chained to the railway car and the wild dogs are leaping up and snapping their fangs, lunging at my feet.

One of the dogs grabs hold of Worm's sleeve and tears at her jacket. "Ahhh!" she screams. "Get it off! Get it off!"

The sleeve rips and the dog falls but it doesn't matter because the rest of the dogs are scrambling up on one another's backs, fighting to get higher, wanting to rip us to shreds. It's like they can smell the blood inside us, and it doesn't matter that we're human, all that matters is we might be good to eat.

Worm is crying and holding tight to me, like she thinks I can save her. But there's nowhere to go. We're surrounded, and now the dogs are crawling up the other side of the farm equipment. They'll be able to jump on us from the top.

I want to yell for help but my throat is squeezed so tight all that comes out is a pathetic little squeak. Then a dog has me by the ankle and I'm trying to kick it loose but it won't let go and Worm is screaming and kicking and hanging on to me all at the same time.

I figure this is it, we're going to die, when all of a sudden this loud, horrible howl fills the air.

"Ahhhhh-oooooooooohhhhh!"

And this scrawny little dude with a big stick leaps into the middle of the dogs, swinging the stick and howling at the top of his lungs.

"Ahhhh-oooooooohhhh! Ahhhh-oooooooohhhh!" He's screaming and laughing and yelling like a total lunatic, smacking at the dogs with his stick, kicking at them with his feet.

The dogs don't know what he is and they start yelping and ducking away from his stick, and one by one they jump off the railway car and run off into the junkyard, crawling on their bellies to get under the barbed-wire fence.

The last dog makes a lunge at his stick, but the wild man raises it high and the dog turns tail and runs off.

And that's how we got saved by Hobo Joe.

18.
Keep Us Safe from You Know Who

That's what the skinny little dude calls himself, Hobo Joe. He's got long scraggly hair and scruffy old clothes that are way too big for him and when he smiles his teeth are kind of crooked. Also he's got this wispy little mustache that wiggles when he talks, and he's talking so fast I can barely sort out the words.

"Yes, sir, they call me Hobo Joe and I'm sorry about them dogs! I bet they give you a fright, and I shoulda warned you 'cause that junkyard is famous for the pack of wild dogs. That's right, I seen you two get on back there in Iowa and I says to myself, now Joe, they'll want to rest a bit, so you best wait until morning before you drop by for a visit. See, I been riding three cars up, a nice empty boxcar with a pile of hay to sleep on, it's better than the Ritz Hotel. Got me a room with a view and room service, too. Hey, I'll bet you two ain't had breakfast, am I right about that? Huh? Am I?"

"Excuse me?" I ask, because listening to somebody talk that fast makes my ears ring.

"Food," he says. "Breakfast. I got it if you want some."

Breakfast is this great big can of beans that Joe had been heating up over a Sterno can when the dogs attacked us. Now he heats it up again and pretty soon the smell of simmering beans is thick in the air.

"I know what you're thinkin'," he says. "You're thinkin' a can of beans don't make a breakfast. But that's where you're wrong, because beans is the best kind of food. 'Specially when you're hungry."

Normally I could care less about beans, but we haven't had a thing to eat since supper last night and the sight of those beans bubbling away makes my mouth water. I ask Worm if she's hungry and she nods and Joe shows her how to blow on the spoon so she won't burn her mouth.

"These beans got special vitamins," he says. "Make you grow big and strong."

He's got this old canvas bag he keeps his stuff in, and inside is a loaf of bread. Stale bread with a hard crust. But Joe says it'll soften up good in the bean juice and we tear up the bread and soak it and stuff it in our mouths until we can't eat another bite.

If you're hungry enough, stale bread and beans taste better than birthday cake.

While we're eating, Joe never stops talking and moving around. Like he's got batteries inside that make him keep jumping and fidgeting and twitching his fuzzy little mustache.

"Guests for breakfast," he says. "Who'd a thunk it!" and he rattles on about how lonesome it gets, living on the trains, and how he's glad of the company and how good it is to have someone to talk to because mostly he talks to himself, and how talking to yourself doesn't necessarily mean you're crazy because there has to be an exception to every rule and he, Hobo Joe, is the talking-to-himself exception.

After we spoon up the last of the beans, the boxcar gives a shudder and starts moving again.

"They been shunting off some of the freight cars," Joe explains. "That means they unhook 'em and leave 'em behind. Train'll be lighter now, and faster. By the time we clear Nebraska we'll be flyin', yessir!"

He knows so much about trains because he's been living off the land, he says, and riding the rails from one side of the country to the other and then back again. So he knows what train goes where, and why it stops at one place instead of another, and how not to get caught by the railroad police.

"Don't be thinkin' I'm homeless," he explains to

Worm. "Wherever I'm sleepin', that's my home, and I like it fine." He points at the wide open door of the boxcar, and the prairie grass rushing past like a blurry green river. "Can you beat that? Why it's better than TV!"

It sounds strange, but staring out at the countryside really is better than watching TV, because you never know what you're going to see next. Farms and barns and windmills. Tall silvery silos that look like spaceships ready to take off. Railroad bridges built from giant Erector sets. A herd of buffalo that look like cows with fur coats on. There's even some purple mountains way off in the distance, just like in the song about America.

Everything keeps moving. It never settles into one thing, it keeps moving and turning into something new. You don't need to change the channel, because it keeps changing itself and never stays the same.

After a while I feel like I'm getting hypnotized. Like I'm wide-awake but dreaming. Like the train is standing still and the world is turning under us.

Worm, she gets tired of watching the world go by and takes out a new book. This one is called *The Sword in the Stone*. I know about it because Kevin read it and told me the story back before I could read on my own.

It's about this kid who everyone thinks is a real loser until one day he accidentally pulls this sword out of a stone. And that proves he's going to grow up to be King Arthur, this excellent dude who had a posse of knights in shining armor, slaying dragons and rescuing damsels, which are what they called women in the old days.

"You know what's so cool about King Arthur and his Knights of the Round Table?" Worm says to me. "It's all about fighting for honor and protecting the innocent and never giving up even if the whole world is against you."

I go, "Yeah, that's pretty cool."

"The coolest thing is, they called it chivalry," Worm says, sounding excited. "And that's where we're going. Chivalry, Montana."

She acts like it's this big coincidence, but I'm pretty sure she knew about knights and chivalry, and that's why she picked the book in the first place, so it would remind her of where we're headed.

"You sure your dad is there?" I ask her.

For some reason that makes her mad. "You don't believe me, is that it? You want me to swear on my grave? Okay, I swear on my grave: My father is in Chivalry, Montana!"

I go, "Okay, okay. Take it easy."

Joe hears her and butts in. "Chivalry? That where you two are headed?"

Worm glares at me and then nods. "Yes," she says. "Most definitely."

"Then you come to the right place," Joe says. "This train don't go there, exactly, but I know one that does."

"And you'll show us?"

"'Course I will," he says. "But it ain't exactly right around the corner. We got a good long while before we get there, so if you guys don't mind, I'm gonna catch up on my beauty sleep."

Joe fluffs up his canvas bag like it's a pillow and stretches out his skinny legs and closes his eyes. Pretty soon you can hear him snoring and it blends into the sound of the train.

Worm taps me on the shoulder. "Sorry I got mad," she says.

I go, "That's okay."

"It's just I miss my mom," Worm says.

"Sure," I say. "That's only natural."

The Worm looks fierce. "I miss her but I hate her guts."

I go, "Huh?"

"It's her fault," Worm says. "She didn't have to marry that creepoid. Or let him hurt me. Or lie to the cops."

"She's scared of him," I say. "People do stupid things when they're scared."

"But she's my *mom*. Moms are supposed to take care of you."

I don't know what to say. Moms aren't supposed to die, either, but sometimes they do.

"Everything will be okay if I can just talk to

my dad," Worm says. "My real dad. He'll understand."

"Don't worry," I say. "We'll find him."

Then everything is quiet except for the clickety sound of the train and the wind humming by. It's so quiet I can hear my own heart beating and it seems to go *rackety-roo, rackety-roo* just like the train.

After a while Worm tugs at my arm and says, "You hear that? It sounds like giants talking under the earth."

At first I think it's just another weird thing she got out of a book, but then I start to hear it, too. A low rumble that seems to come off the mountains and roll over the plains. You can't quite make out the words. You can't tell if they're just talking or fighting or maybe the giants are singing and it sounds like earthquakes and avalanches from far, far away.

"It's like they're calling us," Worm says in a whispery soft voice. "Trying to tell us something."

I'm listening so hard my ears are hot, and finally I figure it out. The rumble noise from the train is echoing off the mountains. That's what makes it sound so hollow and deep. It's not giants talking under the earth, it's only the lonesome sound the train makes as it goes through the world.

But I don't say anything and Worm keeps listening, and she's smiling to herself, like she knows what the giants are saying, and that makes everything okay.

I can't hear the giants anymore, but there's a song coming from inside the train. *Rackety-roo, rackety-roo. Keep us safe from You Know Who.*

19.
Wide-Open Country

Joe wakes up fresh as a daisy, he says. He leans out the door of the boxcar and takes a sniff and goes, "Wyoming! I can smell Wyoming just around the bend! Better than perfume! Smells like dry dirt and tumbleweeds!"

He says he's been through this way before but he never gets tired of it. "I love this wide open country," he says. "I bet you can see a hundred miles at least. See that mountain over there, against the dark patch of sky? Seems so close you could hit it with a rock, don't it? Just you try! You could walk all day for a week and still you wouldn't be close. What it is about the West, the real West, the scale is different. The sky is higher up and wider open and that makes everything bigger. Makes a man look to himself because there's nobody else can see him! Yessir!"

So we roll on into Wyoming and Joe says the train is probably making sixty miles an hour. Just humming along, running straight into the horizon, and nothing around but a few scrubby pine trees and these far-off mountains that look like somebody painted them against the sky.

Every now and then the train stops, and Joe always knows where we are and why we stopped, and if we should change boxcars. "They got to fuel up those diesel engines," he'll say. Or, "They're pickin' up a ten-car hitch out of Casper."

Pretty much every time we stop, Joe disappears for a little while and then comes back with some kind of food. He never says exactly where he finds it, but when you're hungry and riding the rails you don't ask too many questions.

He'll heave up this big sack of oranges and go, "Nobody'll miss these little beauties. Got to get our vitamins!"

Maybe he'll bring back a box of stale crackers and a big restaurant tin of honey and give it over to Worm and say, "Nothin' wrong with these crackers a little honey won't fix!"

Thanks to our skinny friend, we never get so hungry we can't stand it. Not that the Worm eats much, but Joe bets I could win one of those flapjack-eating contests where a bunch of lumberjacks eat until they bust. "It ain't just a hollow leg with you," he says, "it's a hollow everything. Which means you're still growing! Pardon me, son, but if you get any bigger you're gonna need your own time zone!"

For some reason I don't mind it when Joe kids me about being big. Maybe because he's so small and scrawny. Maybe because he doesn't have much of anything, but he always shares it without making you feel like he's doing you a favor. And he never asks what me and Worm are doing on our own, or tries to give us a bunch of advice about what we should do and why.

Most important, any time Worm looks a little sad or unhappy, Joe is right there working to cheer her up. "Look over there," he says, getting her attention. "No, farther out. You see that thing moving up and down? Looks like a big tipped-over swing set? That's an oil pump. That's right, they're raising oil out of a deep well. They'll put a pump like that wherever they find oil. Once I seen one right in a churchyard! Talk about an answer to your prayers!"

Worm stares out at the horizon. "They look like giant birds pecking at the dirt," she says.

When Joe hears that, he doesn't make fun of her, he just nods to himself and goes, "I never thought of it that way. Giant birds, huh?"

We're heading out through the wide-open spaces for hours and hours. Pretty soon we'll cross over into Montana, Joe says, where the last of the cowboys live, and the mountains reach all the way to the moon, and that's where we change trains to Chivalry.

Joe says we're on the right track, yessir, and it feels good.

The way night happens out West, the sun kind of disappears all at once and suddenly the stars are shining and the air feels thin and cool. Worm has got herself real comfortable on this pile of hay Joe fluffed up, reading with her miner's light, and before long her chin starts to droop and then she's fast asleep. I shut off the light to save the battery and Joe brings out this old wool blanket and covers her.

Me and Joe are both shivering a little, but it feels good watching Worm sleep so calm and peaceful under that warm blanket.

"I guess you know she's pretty special," Joe says.

I don't say anything because I hate gooey talk like that, but it makes me think about how sometimes you meet someone who really messes up your life but you'd rather have a messed-up life than not know them.

Anyhow, everything will be okay if we can just find her father. And because we got lucky and bumped into Joe, now we're headed in the right direction.

I never do fall asleep. There's something wide-awake inside my head that makes me think of Grim and Gram and how much I miss them, and how rotten it was for me to run off without telling them why, or even saying good-bye. I keep thinking how much they've done for me and how I never did anything much for them, except a couple of lame presents at Christmas or whatever.

When the sun finally comes up, I'm still thinking about home, and how there's no place I'd rather be but hanging out in the down under and reading my comic books for the umpteenth time.

So I'm already feeling pretty low down and sorry for myself when Joe tells me the bad news.

"We're almost there," he says, out of the blue.

I go, "Huh?"

"You kids want to get to Chivalry, right? Well, I got you on the right train. All you gotta do is ride it to the end and you'll be there."

"But what about you?" I ask. "You're coming, too, right?"

Joe shakes his head. "I got business elsewhere," he says. "I got to keep moving, I can't stay still."

Which shows you what a doughnut brain I can be, because I'd been thinking somehow we'd stay on the train forever and just keep riding through the wide-open spaces, and Joe would always be there to tell us where we were, and what was going to happen next.

The train starts slowing down, and gets so slow you could walk beside it.

"There's apples and that tin of American cheese," Joe says, getting ready to go. "I left a big can of beans, too."

"What about your blanket?" I say, looking at where Worm is still curled up and sound asleep.

"Better keep it," he says. Before he hops down from the boxcar he says, "Here's the deal. In about a hundred miles this train dead-ends in Chivalry. Hope you find what you're looking for."

Then he slips over the side and he's gone. The last thing I hear is his voice sounding far away already.

"Yessir!" he calls out. "Don't forget them beans! They got vitamins!"

20.
Chivalry

We're alone again when Worm finally wakes up.

"I dreamed I was home in my own bed," she says. Then she stops herself, like there are parts of the dream she doesn't want to talk about.

I explain about Joe leaving, and how the last stop is supposed to be Chivalry. When I say how everything will be okay once she finds her real father, Worm stares down at her hands and won't say anything. Which really blows my mind, because she's supposed to be happy and excited, right?

Worm has never been a big talker, but the closer we get to where we're going, the less she says. Like she's got this big secret and not talking is the only way to keep it all to herself.

Meanwhile the train takes a long time rolling up toward the end of the line. Moving along in fits and starts. Every time we stop I lean out real careful and take a look around and sometimes I spot these railroad guys waving their arms and shouting out orders. If they suspect anybody is sneaking a ride on their train, it's like they don't care, or they don't want to know.

The mountains are right up close around here. You can see where they start and how they jut up so fast and steep it makes you dizzy looking all the way to the top. The mountains seem like they're made of yellow dirt and yellow rock and a few scrawny-looking bushes here and there, like nothing can grow on a place that steep without falling off.

One time the train stops inside a tunnel and it's so dark it might as well be midnight. Worm switches on her light, but she isn't reading, she's using it to look at me. "I had this weird idea that we all disappear when the lights go out," she says. "Not just you, but me, too."

I go, "That's weird all right."

"Like they say, maybe there's no such thing as a noise if there's no one to hear it."

"Who says that?" I ask.

"Just 'they,' " she says. "I don't know who."

"Well, 'they' sound pretty stupid to me," I say. Which ends the conversation right there. Worm switches off the light and I figure she's hoping I really *have* disappeared.

I'm thinking: What am I going to do with a girl

who doesn't know what's real and what's just in her head? I'm thinking: Here we are in the dark, stuck inside a mountain in a place I've never been and we're about a million miles from home and we don't have the Dippy Hippie to help us, or Hobo Joe, or anybody at all, and I haven't got a clue about what to do.

That's when my brain says, *I told you so, you moron,* and my brain is right, because it's been telling me all along that running away was a big mistake.

After a while, Worm's voice comes out of the dark. "Are you still there?"

I go, "Yeah."

"Good," she says, and then she shuts up again.

Suddenly the train goes *bump-bump* and starts moving again, and we slowly come out from under the mountain and back into daytime.

At first the light makes me squint so hard I can't really see anything. But pretty soon I can make out these shiny roofs and a bunch of chimneys and stuff.

We're looking down on this town full of junky old wooden buildings stuck right up against the bottom of the mountains. There's only one road and it's just plain dirt, no paving. The roofs are shiny because they're made of tin, but when you look closer you can see streaks of rust and dark spots that must be holes. There's a couple of old trucks, but the hoods are up and they look broke down forever.

I keep expecting to see people going in and out of the buildings, or maybe kicking the tires on those old trucks, but the only thing moving is a broken door slapping in the breeze. It looks like everybody just walked away from Chivalry and never came back.

I always wondered what a ghost town was. Now I know.

21. What the Owl Knows

Now that Chivalry turns out to be this falling-down old place where nobody normal would ever live, I'm starting to think maybe Worm's father is going to turn out to be even weirder than she is. He's probably some old hermit with a long white beard, or one of those guys who walk around in camouflage gear talking to themselves about what happened in the war.

Okay, so maybe finding Worm's real dad won't solve everything. But at least I won't be the only one looking out for her. And even if my brain doesn't think so, I'm hoping he can help clear it up with the police, and make it so everybody doesn't think I'm a kidnapper, or worse.

"You sure this is the right place?" I ask as the train rolls through the little town.

Worm nods. She hasn't said a word since we

came out of the tunnel, and she's not reading her book, either. Her eyes have this look that's either scared or excited, maybe both.

The old train station is built right up against the side of the mountain. It's all boarded up with plywood covering the doors and windows. Which doesn't do much good because part of the roof has caved in.

Near the train station I notice a faded sign that says,

CHIVALRY MINING CORPORATION
"We're Digging for the Future!"

I doubt this is the future they had in mind, with everybody gone and the whole town falling down. From the look of everything, they must have run out of stuff to mine, and that's why nobody is around.

All of a sudden the train motors stop and you can feel the way everything goes dead quiet.

"We better get out of here," I say. Because sooner or later those railroad guys are going to check the boxcars and never mind what my stupid brain says, I'm not ready to get caught yet.

Worm helps me load up with apples and cheese and the other food Joe left behind.

"You know where your father lives?" I ask.

Worm shakes her head no.

"But you're sure he's here?" I ask.

"I'm sure," she says, but her voice sounds so small it's like she swallowed something the wrong way.

We slip away from the boxcar without being seen and skid down this gravel embankment until we're out of sight of the train. Worm stays close to me while I check out the old buildings, looking for a good place to hide until we can find her real father, or until he finds us.

I'm kind of spooked, because it feels like something is watching us from inside the ratty old buildings, like the empty windows are really eyes. The sound of a broken door slamming in the wind is driving me nuts.

"Come on," I say, and we head straight for the banging door. It's on the back side of this boarded-up building that has gray clapboards peeling off and a saggy old front porch that faces the dirt street.

The first step through that busted door almost breaks my leg.

Wham! My foot goes through the floorboards and I fall sideways. The air gets whumped out of me so bad I can't say anything, I just have to lie there and wheeze for a while.

Worm asks me four or five times if I'm okay, which I am once my breath comes back.

The place is pretty dim except where beams of sunlight come through the boarded-up windows and the holes in the roof. The inside is basically one room with a few broken chairs and a tipped-over table with three legs. There's a big wooden counter along one wall that looks kind of familiar. Then it comes to me.

"I bet this used to be an Old West saloon," I tell Worm. "Only it was probably miners instead of cowboys."

The only thing is, it looks a whole lot crummier than the neat old saloons you see in the movies, where Maverick and his buddies are sitting around playing cards and acting cool. You couldn't act cool in this place no matter what you did.

"How will your dad know you're here?" I ask.

"He'll know," she says. Like that's final, end of discussion.

I'm feeling my way along in case there's any more soft spots in the floor. The more I look, the more junk I see. Empty bottles, cracked mugs, a box of candles, a broken mirror in a fancy frame, an old tin of wooden matches.

Worm has her head cocked to one side, listening hard. "Can you hear them?" she whispers.

"Hear who?" I ask.

"All the people who went away. It sounds like they're whispering."

"That's only the wind," I say.

"I hear *something*," she insists.

I go, "It's just your imagination."

That makes her frown at me, but she does shut up about the whispering ghosts.

Probably this whole town has been checked out, and everything valuable got swiped. But you never know what might get missed, so I'm poking around behind the old wooden bar when suddenly I feel somebody watching me.

I turn around real careful and slow.

Eyes!

Right in front of me, close enough to touch, these big yellow eyes are looking at me. Real eyes. Eyes that are alive inside. The eyes blink and I can't breathe or talk or scream out how scared I am.

Below the staring eyes is this strange, sharp-curved nose. Then I realize it isn't a nose, exactly. It's a beak.

Owl. I'm staring at an owl, a great big brown-and-white owl, and he's looking at me like he could care less. It comes to me so sudden that I fall back on my heels and sort of tip over backward, *thump!*

The noise startles the owl from his perch under the bar and he opens his beak and goes, *"Hoooooooo!"* He unfolds these huge wings and launches himself up into the air and takes off.

"Hooooooo!" he goes. *"Hoooooooo! Hoooooooooo!"*

The big owl flaps around the inside of the ratty old saloon and his wings make a whispery sound like *"Wissshhhhh! Wisssssshhhhh!"*

The Worm never screams, not once. She just stands there and watches, her eyes almost as big around as the owl's.

After I get over being scared to death, the big old owl starts to look sort of beautiful. It's amazing how it swoops so calm and cool around the room, wings never quite touching the walls. It doesn't look like a normal bird, it looks more human because both eyes are in front. It makes you understand why they say owls are wise. Man, this bird looks like it knows everything. How old the earth is, why the sky is blue, where you hid your favorite comic book, everything.

The owl goes, *"Hoooooooooooooooooooooooo!"* and swoops up into the wrecked part of the roof and then he's gone.

"Wow," I say, and let out the breath I've been holding.

I look over to see Worm staring up at where the owl found a way out to the sky. She's got this secret look on her face like somehow she knows what the owl knows.

22.
Magic Believes in Me

Nothing tastes better than apples and good old American cheese when your mouth is dry and your stomach is growling. After the owl takes off, me and Worm decide it's time for lunch. I'm expecting she'll want to go look for her dad first thing, but she doesn't seem to be in any hurry to find him now that we're here.

Mostly she just watches me eat. Worm doesn't seem to have much appetite.

"Apple a day keeps the bad guys away," I say, trying to joke her into eating.

She just scowls at me and gnaws her apple a little.

"Beans?" I ask. "We could heat 'em up over a candle."

She shakes her head.

After a while, when my stomach isn't so empty

anymore, I lean back and go, "How come your dad lives in an old ghost town?"

Worm stares at her hands. "Because he does," she says. "I don't want to talk about him right now, okay?"

"Okay," I say.

I'm not exactly surprised when Worm pulls a book out of her backpack. When she doesn't want to talk about something, she always goes right for her books.

"What are you reading now?" I ask.

She holds the book up. "*The Hobbit*," she says. "I've read it before."

"Me, too," I say.

Worm gets this look like she can't believe the big goon can actually read a book, and for some reason that really burns me. "What," I say. "You think you're the only one who ever read a book?"

She shrugs. "I didn't say that."

"No, but that's what you're thinking, right? Because I'm this big goofy-looking guy who doesn't talk that much, I must be dumb."

She goes, "I never said that."

"No, but that's what you're thinking," I say. Then I shut up quick, because Worm looks like she's going to cry. Which proves that I really am a big doughnut brain, even if I do know how to read.

She sits there with her chin on her knees and her eyes closed, not moving at all. I'm starting to wonder if she's fallen asleep when she goes, "You know what? The first time I read *The Hobbit* I wanted to *be* Bilbo Baggins, you know? And live in a hobbit hole underground and have friends like Gandalf the wizard, and go on adventures to the Lonely Mountain, and fight Smaug the evil dragon."

"Really?" I say. "That's what I thought, too."

After that something breaks loose and she can't stop talking about all these books she's read, and how much it means to her, and how she's probably a book addict but she doesn't care, and how she doesn't even mind everybody calling her Worm because it's an honor to be a bookworm even if nobody understands.

"You know what's really weird?" she says. "All those kids who make fun of me and act like such jerks, they really feel sorry for me, right? But *I'm* the one who feels sorry for *them*. They're the ones who don't know about how Charlotte saved Wilbur. Or why Old Yeller had to die. Or how the boy saved the dog named Shiloh."

Worm is so excited she's punching her fist in the air and her eyes are blazing and her hair is so red and wild it looks like her head is on fire. I'm ready to applaud but I figure she'd probably take it wrong and punch me out. It's like there's a whole other person living inside her that only comes out when she talks about books, and that person is so brave that nothing could scare her.

It must have been really miserable being a caveman, before fire got invented. I know because when night comes and it starts to get cold, the first thing we try to do is make a fire and get warm. There's this little potbellied stove in the saloon and plenty of busted-up chairs and old newspapers and stuff, so I figure it won't be hard.

Wrong.

The wooden matches are so old they keep falling apart. I'm scratching the side of the box and the heads keep snapping off or going soft or whatever and before you know it we're down to one match.

One measly crummy match.

That's when I notice Worm is sitting there grinning in the dark. "We'll have to use magic," she says.

"There's no such thing as magic, except in books."

Worm shakes her head. "Not true," she says. "Book magic escapes into the real world."

She sounds so convinced I decide not to argue. If you think about the raw deal Worm has been getting, you can't blame her for wanting to believe in magic and wizards and hobbits. If she can fill her head with stuff like that, she won't have to think about the bad things that have already happened, and what might happen next if we don't find her real father.

"I'll show you," she says, and holds out her hand.

I shrug and give her the last match.

"Watch and believe," she says.

Then she takes all of her books out of her backpack and makes a pile on the floor. She opens each book and waves the match over it and goes, "Humnahooah, humnahooah, give us fire, give us light, keep us warm on this cold night!"

After she's waved the last matchstick over each and every book, she hands it back to me.

"That's it?" I ask. "That's the magic?"

She nods. "No problem. Guaranteed to light."

I look at the measly match and I'm thinking, Go ahead, what have you got to lose? But then my brain says, *Don't be a dodo, you big moron. If the match doesn't light, that will mean books aren't magic, and where does that leave the Worm?*

Now I wish I'd never tried to light a stupid fire. But it's getting colder by the minute and all we've got is that one old blanket Joe left us, so what choice do I have?

When I scratch the last match on the side of the box, *poof!* a blue flame pops up and I'm so surprised I almost forget to put it in the stove and light the fire.

"It's like clapping for Tinkerbell," Worm explains when we're warming our hands in front of the stove. "You don't dare not believe it."

The real truth is, I still don't believe in magic. But I'm starting to wonder if maybe magic believes in me.

23.
The Secret of Chivalry

Just when I'm falling asleep, the owl comes back. He flies in through the hole in the roof as quiet as a whisper. His wings seem to fill up the night. Normally I'd be scared, a big thing like that swooping around in the dark, but there's a lot of other stuff crowding my brain lately.

So I lay there staring at the glow from the woodstove, trying as hard as I can not to think about the trouble we're in. Like running away from the scene of a crime and lying about who we are and believing a phony like Frank and escaping from the police. Stupid stuff like that.

My brain is thinking, *You better start acting smart, you big jerk,* and it won't let me sleep. It makes me count the stupid things I've done instead of counting sheep or whatever. I'm counting every stupid thing I ever said or did in school that made everybody laugh at me, and all the words I didn't understand back then, and all the books I never read, and all the cool things I wish I'd said but didn't, and all the time I wasted being mad at the world when I was really mad at me, and that day my pants fell down in gym class, and the time Kevin dared me to eat a tadpole for scientific purposes, and I did and got sick.

All of it starts whirring around inside my brain, the really bad stupid stuff and the just plain stupid stuff and the who cares stupid stuff, until it feels like there's an eggbeater inside my head turning my brain into scrambled eggs. Which makes me feel even *more* stupid.

Then my brain has an idea. *Leave the girl here and turn yourself in,* it tells me. *You know that's the smart thing to do.*

You mean leave Worm on her own? I ask my brain.

She's the one who wanted to run away. She's the one who wanted to find her real father. So let her. If you stay with her, you're the one who will get the blame.

Just go? I ask my brain. Sneak away while she's sound asleep?

Do the smart thing.

Sorry, I tell my brain. I can't leave Worm, not now. Not here. Not when we've come this far. Her dad is going to fix everything.

You're hopeless, my brain says. But finally it lets me fall asleep, and in my dream we're back on the Prairie Schooner with good old Dip, and Joe is there, too, and we're all going home and everything is going to be okay, just like on TV.

In the morning Worm says it's time to find her real dad.

"He's waiting for me," she says. "Out there."

She's staring at her hands again, like she doesn't want me to see what she's hiding in her eyes.

I go, "You know where he is?"

Worm nods.

"I don't get it," I say. "If you know where he is, why didn't we go there right away?"

Worm shrugs. "I wasn't ready."

She's not going to tell me what's really going on, or why she's being so mysterious.

Outside the old saloon, Worm takes a deep breath, squints into the sunlight, and starts marching up the street, like she knows exactly where she wants to go.

I'm tagging along, tripping over my big feet, and saying stuff like, "So what's the deal? Where are we going?"

Worm doesn't say anything, she just balls her hands into fists and keeps on marching.

We pass all of these falling-down old buildings, places that once upon a time were a general store or a barbershop or whatever, and we're heading up the slope toward the mountain that looms over the whole town.

"The railway station," I say. "He's at the railway station? Why didn't you say so?"

The old railway station is the biggest building around, with tons of fancy trim and a steep roof with a big chunk missing. It looks kind of like a gingerbread house except all the icing has melted off. You can tell the people who used to live here must have sunk everything into this one building, to make an impression when visitors came to Chivalry, and maybe to kind of inspire the rest of the town. It didn't catch on, that's for sure, and now the train only comes here because it's a good place to turn around, which is pretty pathetic, if you think about it.

Anyhow, when we get to the railway station I'm expecting some weird old guy to pop out of the woodwork and go, "Hey, kids! I'm Rachel's dad!" or whatever, and we'll have to go from there. But when we get there, nothing happens. There's nobody waiting for us.

Worm stares hard at the building. "Inside," she says.

"It's boarded up," I point out. "We can't get inside."

But Worm won't take no for an answer. It's pretty clear she's going to find a way into the railway station or die trying, so we go around back. Only there isn't any back to the building because it's built right up against the side of the mountain. And everything is boarded up and nailed shut with these big spikes you couldn't pull out with a crowbar even if you had one, which I don't.

Finally Worm finds a hole in the wall. "Here goes nothing," she says.

"Wait up!" I say. "Hang on!"

But she's already inside.

It turns out the hole is just barely big enough for a doofus like me to wriggle through if I hold my breath. I end up facedown on the floor with dust in my eyes and that makes it hard to see. But even without seeing you can feel how big it is inside the railway station, much bigger than it looks on the outside.

When my eyes start to clear up I can make out the rows of old benches where people must have waited for the train, and the ticket windows. Everything else seems to blend into the shadows. It can be anything you want it to be, or nothing at all.

But the inside of the station isn't all dark places. There's this one beam of sunshine coming down through the hole in the roof and the Worm is standing right inside the light.

"Dad!" she calls out. "It's me, Rachel! Are you there?"

And then she says it again and again, *there-there-there-there*. Except her mouth isn't moving. It's an echo coming back from someplace deep inside the earth.

Which is impossible but true.

My eyes have gotten used to the dim and dusty light and I can see it now.

A tunnel.

The echo is coming from a mining tunnel that goes straight back into the mountain. A tunnel so big and dark it looks like it wants to swallow up all the light in the world, and us, too.

Something about that old mining tunnel scares me like nothing ever scared me before. Somehow I know there's evil and misery inside, just waiting until somebody comes along and lets it out.

"Dad!" Worm shouts, and it comes back *Dad-Dad-Dad-Dad*.

I may be big and dumb, and a lot of times I won't listen to my brain, but it doesn't take me long to figure out that if her real father is down in this old mine, he probably isn't coming out.

When I get to Worm, she's shining her miner's light on a bronze plaque near the entrance to the mine, where the railroad tracks curve into the darkness and disappear.

On the plaque it says:

BURIED IN THIS SHAFT
ARE THE REMAINS
OF SIXTY-SEVEN MEN
WHOSE LIVES WERE LOST
IN THE GREAT CHIVALRY
MINE DISASTER.
MAY GOD HAVE MERCY
ON THEIR SOULS,
AND ON THOSE
THEY LEFT BEHIND.

Worm goes, "Daddy, I miss you so much. Please tell me what to do. Please?"

The echo comes back *ease-ease-ease*.

My brain tells me I should have known it all along. The reason Worm's real father has never been there to help her is because he's dead. We've come all this way just so she can visit his grave, and we can't even do that because he doesn't have a grave of his own, not like in a real cemetery.

Worm finally notices me and takes a tight grip on my hand. "I was so little when it happened I can barely remember him," she says. "All I remember is he had this miner's helmet with a light, and I wanted one, too."

There's nothing I can think to say except, "He must have been a pretty cool dad, giving his kid her own miner's helmet."

Worm squeezes my hand so hard it hurts, and it makes me think she's a lot stronger than she looks.

"Do you think he knows about my mom?" she asks. "And You Know Who?"

I never get to answer that one because a new sound comes into the old railway station and starts echoing back out of the tunnel.

It's a siren. A cop car siren.

24.
Officer Friendly

I find a crack to look out through the boarded-up windows. The siren has stopped whooping, but there it is, a white cop car kicking up dust as it comes down the main street, heading for the railway station. The cop car has a big star on the side, and SHERIFF spelled out in gold.

Worm is looking out through the same crack and she's not making a sound. She doesn't act scared, exactly. It's like she's got a switch inside and she just turns herself off somehow.

The sheriff car pulls up to the front of the station. The sun glints off the windshield so you can't see inside, but the driver's door opens right away and this short, stocky dude gets out, wearing a white cowboy hat and a gold star on his shirt pocket.

He cups his hands to his mouth and calls out, "Anybody home?"

When nothing happens, he looks around, squinting at the broken-down town. He snugs down his hat, hitches up his belt, and spits in the dirt, which I must admit he does in a pretty cool way.

Then he kind of shrugs to himself and walks back to his cop car and opens the door like he's going to get inside and drive away.

But he doesn't drive off, not yet. He comes back out of the cruiser with this shiny metal thing in his hand. At first I think it's a gun, but then he holds it up to his mouth and clicks it on.

Megaphone.

"Howdy, folks. This is Sheriff Goodman. I'm the law here in this county. If there's anybody around, please come out and say hello. Nobody gets arrested, nothing like that. Just want to make sure you're okay."

The last word echoes up from the tunnel behind us, *kay-kay-kay*, and there's nothing I'd like better than to give myself up to Officer Friendly here. Let him figure out what to do about Worm. A dude who can spit so cool can probably figure out most anything, right?

Wrong. Because my brain knows he's just acting friendly so he can get us to surrender, and then he'll lock me in jail and throw away the key and send Worm back to her rotten stepfather because in real life stuff never has a happy ending like it does on TV. I learned that a long time ago and my brain won't let me forget it.

You can tell Sheriff Goodman is listening hard,

so me and Worm don't make a peep, we hardly breathe. When he doesn't hear anything he switches on the megaphone again and goes, *"Maybe I got it wrong and there's nobody here, but if there is, please remember one thing. The old mining tunnels are very dangerous. Repeat, stay out of the tunnels."* He starts to lower the megaphone and then remembers to say, *"Have a nice day,"* before he turns it off for good.

The sheriff looks like he's about ready to give up when suddenly the passenger door swings open. At first I can't see who's there, all I can do is hear one boot hit the dirt, then the other. And then he's unfolding himself from inside the cop car and standing tall and thin and dark as a shadow.

The Undertaker, come to get us.

25. *Things That'll Turn Your Bones into Jelly*

Beside me Worm makes a small whimpering sound.

"I'm not here," she whispers to herself. "I'm somewhere else. I'm somewhere else." Except she doesn't sound like she believes it.

I've got my face against the crack in the window boards, trying to keep an eye on things. Sheriff Goodman is still there, but I can't see Worm's stepfather, like he's moved out of range.

Suddenly the board gets yanked off the window and a blast of daylight hits me right in the face.

The Undertaker is on the other side of the window, looking in at both of us. He lifts up his hand and points at me and shouts, "There he is! The monster who kidnapped my daughter!"

His raggedy lightning voice goes through me like a hot bullet and for a moment my heart just stops. I can't move.

Sheriff Goodman goes, "You'd better come out of there. I'll bet you're pretty hungry, huh? We'll get us some food and then we'll talk."

Worm bolts. Running away as fast as she can.

Before my brain knows what's going on, my feet are following her, running into the darkness, into that old mining tunnel, into the place of the dead.

The sheriff is yelling, begging us not to go into the mine, but he's so far away he sounds like he's shouting from another planet. I'm barreling along like an out-of-control locomotive, heading for the tunnel. Racing across the floor of the old train station with the terrible darkness getting closer and closer, that's when my brain tries to put on the brakes.

Don't do it! my brain screams. *If you go down into that mine, you'll never come out alive!*

Shut up, I say to my brain, and keep on going.

But my brain won't shut up. *There are terrible things down there,* it says, *things you can't think about or you'll die. Things that'll turn your bones into jelly. Things that'll eat you up and spit you out. Things that'll make you wish you'd never been born.*

But it's too late to stop, no matter what my brain says. I'm already inside the entrance to the mine, trying to catch Worm before the shadows swallow her up. The air feels different, and the darkness feels different, and I'm running so fast there's no turning back.

I can't stop. It's like gravity is sucking me down into the mining tunnel, under the mountain, into the earth.

"Wait! *Wait-wait-wait. . . .*"

Sheriff Goodman's voice turns into an echo. The words chase us underground. I'm still running as hard as I can, down into the darkness, and the last thing I hear is him shouting, "Be careful-*ful-ful-ful. . . .*"

Too late for that. I'm way past being careful.

And that's the last thing in my head before something comes out of the dark and *whams!* me so hard my bones turn to jelly, just like my brain promised.

Some people see stars when they get knocked out. Me, I see mosquitoes. Shiny mosquitoes buzzing around my head.

They're still buzzing when Worm wakes me up. She doesn't say anything, but she's tugging on my ear so hard it almost comes off, and that wakes me. I can't see anything but the dark and the sparks of light from banging my head.

I try to sit up, but that turns out to be a bad idea because it makes me dizzy and I have to lie down again or puke. When I try to say something, Worm puts her hand on my mouth and shuts me up.

Footsteps. I can hear footsteps, and whispery voices.

"Must have gone this way," somebody whispers.

It's so completely dark I can't see a thing, but the voices have shapes. One belongs to the sheriff, the other to the Undertaker. And whenever *he* talks, Worm gets very, very quiet and still.

"No telling what evil things that boy has done," the Undertaker is saying in a voice so smooth it makes my brain itch. "He may have turned her mind against me."

The sheriff says, "Never mind that now. Get 'em out of this death trap alive, then we'll worry about sorting it all out."

The Undertaker doesn't like that. "The girl belongs to me," he insists. "Don't matter what happens to the boy."

It's hard to tell in the dark, but they sound real close, and getting closer. I'm thinking about what to do next when suddenly the whole tunnel *creeeaaaaaaks!* and the Undertaker shrieks out, "What's that?"

"Old timbers," the sheriff says. "They had a really bad cave-in here already, the same one that killed your stepdaughter's father. The rest of the place is ready to collapse any day now. Bump into the wrong timber and the mountain comes down on our heads."

"What do we do?" the Undertaker asks in a shaky voice.

"We get out of here before we make matters worse. Organize a search party. You were right about the girl heading here, but you gotta let me handle the police work, okay?"

The footsteps start to fade away. Then I hear the sheriff calling out, "Maxwell Kane, if you can hear me, listen up! Give yourself up and nobody gets hurt, not you or the girl. You've got my word on that!"

Me and the Worm keep still until the footsteps are gone. Until there's just us and the darkness and the wind in the tunnel.

When I try to stand up, my head gets bumped again, but not so hard this time. With my hands I can feel the busted timber sagging down from the roof of the tunnel. That's what clobbered me.

A light comes on, pointing right in my eyes.

Worm has turned on her miner's hat, and she's aiming it so I can see. Which should be good, right? Except the trouble is, now that I can see the rotten old timbers that hold up the tunnel, it makes me feel sick inside.

Here I am trying to keep Worm safe and we end up in a place that could bury us alive if we sneeze too hard.

"I'm not going back," Worm says, real fierce. "I don't care what happens, I'm never, ever going back to him."

I go, "We could get killed down here."

"You go on back," Worm says.

"The both of us," I say. "We'll go back together."

The light weaves as Worm shakes her head. "No way. I'd rather die."

Something in her voice makes me think she doesn't care if she does die, or maybe she even wants to, just to get away from being afraid. And that makes me decide to stick with her no matter what, even if my brain thinks I'm being stupid.

"We can't just stay here," I say. "They're coming back with a search party. They'll find us for sure."

"I told you. Go if you want to," Worm says, acting stubborn and fierce.

"That's not what I mean," I say. "Come on."

And then I take her hand and lead us deeper into the tunnel, into the dark places under the earth.

26. Catch a Dragon by the Toe

The wind. That's what gives me the idea there might be another way out. The cool air sighing into my face. I figure it has to come from outside, and if we follow the wind we'll find it.

Worms sniffs at the air. "Smells like dragon breath," she says.

I go, "Huh?"

"Sulfur and rotten eggs."

I go, "Nah," but she's got me thinking about dragons and things that live in the dark, or die there.

It turns out there's more than one tunnel that goes down into the mine. There's like a maze deal going on, with tunnels branching off all over the place.

It reminds me of this ant farm I had once, until the ants got out and started snacking on Gram's homemade raspberry jam. Anyhow, before they escaped, the ants were digging a bunch of little tunnels and paths, and they kept streaming in and out, carrying grains of sand that were as big as boulders, if you happened to be an ant.

So I guess miners are like the human version of ants. They just keep digging until they find something good, and then they dig some more. They probably knew exactly where they were going, but I sure don't. It's not like they left behind signs that say THIS WAY TO ESCAPE or anything.

All we can do is follow the wind. And that's not easy because sometimes it's so faint you can barely feel the air moving, or you think it's your imagination and not the wind at all.

The Worm, she's got a talent for it. We'll be creeping along real slow and careful, making sure not to bump into timbers that hold up the roof, and then we'll come to a place where the tunnel branches off in two or three more directions. And Worm will stand there, her miner's hat shining like a lighthouse in the dark. She'll close her eyes and feel the air on her face, and then finally she'll point at the right tunnel.

At least I hope it's the right tunnel. Because the light-beam batteries aren't going to last forever, and even if Worm isn't scared of the dark, I am.

I figure once her light goes out, the whole mountain will probably come down on top of us. I can feel it all around me, how much the mine wants to bury us. Partly that's because I can't stand up straight, I have to move along hunched over. Whoever dug these tunnels made them for normal-sized people, not for me.

We're shuffling along, being careful not to bump into any of the old beams that hold up the mountain, when we come to another fork in the tunnel.

Worm shines her light into the tunnels but we can't see to the end. And I can't feel any air moving at all.

"Wait," Worm says, and she closes her eyes and tries to feel the wind on her face. When that doesn't work she starts counting off the way little kids do, except she does her own version. She goes, "Eenie-meenie-miney-moe, catch a dragon by the toe. If he saves us, let him go. Eenie-meenie-miney-moe."

"Are you serious?" I ask.

"It's better than just guessing," she says. "You got a better idea?"

I don't have a better idea, so we go down the "moe" tunnel. Which at first seems like all the other tunnels, with these rotten old timbers and boards holding up the roof, and piles of dirt and rock that have seeped down through the planks. But before we get very far, the floor starts getting damp. There are wet-looking streaks along the sides, and if you listen carefully you can hear the *bloink-bloink* of dripping water.

I go, "I dunno about this," because the dark is bad enough when it's dry, but Worm keeps scooting along and it's hard for me to keep up because the top of the tunnel keeps trying to wham me on the head. I'm going, "Hey, wait up!" but she won't slow down.

"We're almost there," she calls back. "I can feel it."

I go, "Slow down, please? I'm tired."

Worm finally slows down and waits for me to catch up. Which turns out to be a good thing. Because right around the next curve in the tunnel there's this big hole in the floor. At first I think it's just a shadow, but the Worm's light doesn't touch it and I go, "Whoa!" and pull her back from the edge just before we both fall in.

It's an old mine shaft going straight down into the deepest, darkest place in the world.

Worm aims her miner's hat into the hole, but the beam of light fades out before it hits bottom, that's how deep it is. When I drop a rock and listen for the clunk, there is no clunk. Like maybe the rock will keep falling forever, until it gets to the very center of the earth. There's an old ladder built into the side of the shaft, but some of the rungs are busted and you can see where the dampness has rotted up the wood.

"I bet that's where it happened," Worm says. "The cave-in. Way down there."

I don't know what to say. Maybe she's right,

maybe this is as close as she'll ever get to where her father died. I'm trying to think what it means to me when I visit my mom's grave in the cemetery. I always bring flowers, but today we don't have any flowers with us. We don't have much of anything.

"We could pray," I say, and Worm seems to like the idea. So we get down on our knees and fold up our hands, and when Worm nods her head to pray, her beam of light shines down into the shaft, and it looks scary and beautiful all at the same time.

Worm is praying silent, so I don't know exactly what she's thinking or saying inside her head. But whatever it is seems to change her. She kind of relaxes all at once, like she's been waiting all her life to do this, and now that she's finally here she can let go and not be scared anymore.

I don't know what to pray, so I just thank God that her dad gave Worm the miner's light to find her way, because we sure would be lost without it.

When we're done, Worm gives my hand a squeeze and says, "Thanks."

Like a dummy I go, "Thanks for what?"

"For being Max the Mighty."

I go, "Look, I told you, there's no such thing as Max the Mighty. I'm just plain Maxwell Kane, okay?"

"Sure, okay. But when things got really bad I told myself Max the Mighty would come, and you did."

"I couldn't think of anything else to do," I say.

"I know," she says. "That's why you're Max the Mighty."

I'm about to tell her she's cracked in the brain if she really thinks that, but she goes, "Ssssh. We'll argue about it later. Right now we have to follow the wind. I can feel it, can you?"

I really *can* feel the wind. It smells cool and dry and it makes me think we're getting closer to the outside. Because I can't really explain it, but the air smells like it comes from the sky.

We edge around the mine shaft — there's barely enough room for my big fat feet — and head on up the tunnel.

"We'll come back here someday," she says. "You promise?"

I go, "Sure thing," but really I'm thinking *no way*. We get out of this place, I'm never coming back, not for all the TVs in China.

The tunnel starts to slope up and the wind feels even cooler and fresher, and I'm thinking, Way to go, you big goon, you were right for once in your life, maybe you aren't so dumb after all.

Then the tunnel starts getting wider, wide enough so the sides kind of melt away into the shadows, and I swear it's starting to get lighter. The roof part gets higher, too, and stops trying to wham me on the head, and it's all I can do to keep from running.

Easy does it, I'm thinking. *You're almost there.*

"Uh-oh," Worm says.

Uh-oh is right. Because suddenly the wind starts pushing hard against us, like something big is coming into the tunnel.

Worm goes, "The dragon! He's coming back!"

The ground starts shaking under my feet and the wind is coming faster and I can hear this low kind of growl, like a giant monster really has entered the tunnel, and we're in the way of where it wants to go.

Grrrruhhhruhhhhruhhhhhhh!

Coming to get us, making the shadows go crazy and filling the whole tunnel with wind and noise.

Then it starts to ROAR.

My brain keeps telling me, *There's no such thing as dragons*, but this sure sounds like one.

I pick Worm up and hold her tight so the wind doesn't blow her away. I'm so scared, my feet won't run.

That's when the glowing eyes find us. Eyes so bright they paint us with light. Eyes so bright it's like looking into the sun. Which must be what dragon eyes look like when they want to eat you up, or burn you to a crisp.

That's when I know we're going to die and there's nothing I can do about it.

27.
The Flower-Power Fogeys

Just before it kills us, the dragon honks.

I'm standing there like a total doughnut head, holding tight to Worm because we're dragon bait, we're history, when the monster with shining eyes honks at us.

Then it beeps.

I'm pretty sure dragons don't honk and I'm completely positive they don't beep. Cars beep, trucks beep.

Buses beep.

My brain has barely figured it out when Dip leaps out of the Prairie Schooner and gives us both a hug.

"Howdy doody, kids! Man, are we glad to see you!"

By now my eyes have gotten used to the headlights and I can see the old painted-up school bus filling up the tunnel. And behind Dip is this other old dude I can't quite make out. He's coming at us real careful, like he's afraid we'll disappear, or run away.

"Max," he says, and then I know.

It's Grim, my grandfather, which is like impossible. I'm so confused about how he could be here with the Dippy Hippie, or why the Prairie Schooner came roaring into the mine like a mean old dragon, that I can't think of anything to say.

Grim, he's not too cool with words either, so he just gives me this stiff kind of hug, and then he clears his throat and says, "Well. So. Fancy meeting you here, huh?"

It feels like I swallowed an apple or something, my throat is that choked up. Which is totally stupid because I should be happy, right? But instead it's like somebody punched me in the chest and I can hardly get my breath.

Dip, he takes charge and herds everybody into the bus. "We may have to make a sudden getaway," he says. Making it sound like a joke except it turns out he's not joking.

What happened is, after Frank and Joanie tried to turn us in for the reward and we had to run away or get arrested, Dip decided it was all his fault and he had to do something about it.

"Finally I did the right thing," Dip explains. "I called the police in your hometown and they gave me your grandfather's phone number. He hopped a plane and met me at a campground in Nebraska and we've been driving ever since." He looks over at stern-faced Grim and shakes his head. "Your grandpa is a funny old codger, but we get along okay."

Grim goes, "I'm no older than you are, you flower-power fogey." And Dip starts laughing so hard his glasses fall off and his big belly shakes. "That's it!" he says, "We're the flower-power fogeys!"

Grim makes a face and snorts, but you can tell he kind of likes the idea even if he won't admit it.

"We heard you'd been sighted in Chivalry, and when we got here the sheriff told us you'd run down into the old mining tunnels," Dip explains. "We thought you were goners, both of you. But we started searching for another way into the mine and got lucky. Then what do you know, our prayers were answered and you're both okay."

Worm has flopped down on the old sofa, testing the springs, and when Dip mentions the part about prayers being answered, she grins like crazy and her eyes are so bright and green you can hardly stand to look at her.

Grim clears his throat and goes, "Anybody got any ideas?"

"I hadn't really thought beyond finding these two," Dip whispers to him.

Grim nods to himself. "At this point it's their

word against, uhm, that man," he says very quietly.

Dip fiddles with one of his pigtails like he does when he's thinking hard. After a while he goes, "We need to find Max a good lawyer. I've got a little money saved up and you're welcome to it."

"We'll manage," Grim says. "But thanks."

The amazing thing is, somehow they both know I didn't do anything wrong, even without me telling them. Which makes me think if you stick to the truth you'll be okay, even if the rest of the world thinks you're a liar.

Dip brightens up and says, "I've got another idea." We're all expecting something really amazing, but he says, "One word. Pancakes."

Grim grumbles and goes, "That's your big idea?"

"These kids look half-starved," Dip points out. "We'll all think better on full stomachs. So I vote we head for the nearest pancake house, eat till we bust, and then we'll figure out what to do next."

"Pancakes sound good," Worm says.

Dip says it's settled and he fires up the Prairie Schooner and backs it out of the tunnel, going extra careful so he doesn't scratch the paint, which probably nobody but him would notice.

When we're almost out of the tunnel the back windows start to turn orange, which looks weird until I realize the sun is going down. So me and Worm were lost in the mine for a whole day. If you asked me how long it was, I'd have said somewhere between ten minutes and forever.

I'm thinking the sunset is pretty cool, the way the sky looks on fire, and the clouds could be giant castles made of smoke, when all of a sudden Dip says a bad word and jams on the brakes.

Grim goes, "Everybody stay calm," but there's no way I can stay calm when I see the white cop car blocking our way.

Dip is tapping his fingers on the wheel and looking in the rearview mirror and saying, "Darn. I really had my heart set on pancakes."

My stomach feels like I've been eating tadpoles again, which I haven't done since I was too dumb to know any better, but my stomach doesn't know that, and my brain is having a great time laughing at me. *You big moron*, it says. *What did you expect? A happy ending? Did you really think you could drive off into the sunset and nothing would happen? Huh? Are you really that stupid? Answer me, you big moron.*

I want to tell my brain to shut up, but it's too late, Sheriff Goodman is already knocking on the door of the bus.

"Open up!" he says. "I want you all to come out real peaceful. One at a time. No sudden moves and no fooling around."

Dip opens the bus door. "No problem," he says to the sheriff.

Dip gets out first. Then Grim. Then me. The

sheriff is giving me this look, like if he stares hard enough the truth will just melt right out of me.

Grim goes, "There's been a mistake, officer. Max never meant any harm. He was trying to protect the girl. Her stepfather is the real culprit."

"Could be," the sheriff says. "That's for a court to decide."

He unsnaps a pair of handcuffs from his belt. "Maxwell Kane, you're under arrest."

The weird thing is, even though I should feel really terrible and low and miserable, I don't. Not even close. I'm too happy that Grim and Dip are there to take care of Worm, and anyhow, sleeping in a jail cell can't be much worse than sleeping in a freight car or an old saloon with holes in the roof, and I did both of those and came out okay. I'm thinking maybe prison won't be so bad after all, and they'll probably let me read books and maybe I'll take up a hobby and be the Bird Man of Alka-Seltzer or whatever.

"Hold out your hands," the sheriff tells me.

He's just about to put the cuffs on me when the cop car door creaks open. "I told you to stay in the car," the sheriff says, real sharp.

But the Undertaker gets out anyhow. With his black clothes and his black hat. His face is pointed like a hatchet and his eyes are full of hate.

He comes barging up, jamming his finger at me like a gun. "Where is she?" he shouts, spit flying from his mouth. "What have you done with

Rachel? You've been brainwashing her, haven't you? Turning her against me!"

That's when Worm sneaks out of the bus, holding her bag of books. She tries to hide behind me, but the Undertaker makes a grab at her and she ducks away. She won't look at him, no matter what.

"Rachel?" he says.

"I'm not Rachel!" she shouts. "Rachel is dead!"

Then Worm moves so quick that nobody can stop her.

I go, "No! Don't!"

But it's too late. The darkness has already swallowed her up.

28.
Suddenly Worm Says Good-bye

Only a total moron would run into a deep dark mine without a flashlight. But I don't have time to think about it, because I know where Worm is going.

The mine shaft. The place where we prayed and she felt she was safe from all the bad things in the world, and nothing could touch her.

I've got this terrible empty feeling inside, like that falling dream you have just before you go to sleep, only I'm wide-awake and it won't stop.

"Rachel!" I'm calling out. "Wait up! Wait for me!"

But her running feet keep skittering ahead of me in the darkness. The thing is, because I have to scrunch down to keep from bumping my head, Worm can run a lot faster than me. And even scrunched over, I keep banging into things, the sides of the tunnel and the timbers and stuff.

I'm not the only one chasing Worm. The others are back there behind me. Grim and Dip and Sheriff Goodman and the Undertaker, too. Which makes me run all the faster, because if *he* gets to her first, there's no telling what will happen.

Running faster turns out to be a mistake. *Smack!* Before I know what's happening, I'm flat on my back with my nose swelling up like a banana where I smacked it against the wall. Fork in the tunnel and I hit it face first.

So now I've got two tunnels to choose from and no time to mess around. I try to shake the ringing out of my ears and listen for those running feet. *Pitter-pat, pitter-pat*. Hide-and-seek, except for her it's just the hide part. She doesn't want anybody to find her, not ever.

Go right, my brain tells me.

The tunnel slopes down pretty steep, which makes sense because when we came from the opposite direction it slanted up. Up toward the light. Down into the darkness.

"Rachel! Please wait!"

That's when I notice a faint beam of light flickering far ahead. Worm has her miner's light on. Which makes me feel a little better because at least she won't fall into the mine shaft, not if she can see it first.

Or that's what I'm hoping. That's what keeps me going, even though I can't seem to get enough air to breathe and my feet feel like they're made of lead. Mostly what's wrong with me is I'm afraid. Afraid Worm is going to get hurt or killed and it'll be my fault.

Your fault? my brain says. *Don't be a bonehead. How could it be your fault?*

Because I made her think I'd keep her safe, and then I didn't, that's why. Because even though I said there was no such thing as Max the Mighty, I really thought there was, and it turned out to be a lie.

But you didn't mean to hurt her, my brain says.

So what? It's still my fault, I'm thinking. If you want to be a superhero, you have to get it right, that's the deal.

I'm thinking so hard my feet get tangled up and I go down, skidding along the slanted floor, getting closer and closer to the flickering light.

When I finally come to a stop, I put my hands out to push myself up from the floor, but there is no floor.

I'm right on the edge of the mine shaft.

Inch by inch I wriggle backward until I'm clear of the edge and my heart can start beating again.

"You shouldn't have come," Worm says. "I have to do this by myself."

At first I can't see her. All I can see is the miner's light bobbing around. After a while I can make out a shadow that has the shape of her, and that's when my heart wants to stop again, because she's standing right on the edge of the mine shaft.

"Be careful," I say. "You'll fall in."

"So what?" She says softly. "My dad is dead. My mom might as well be dead, married to a creep like that. Things would be a whole lot easier if I was dead, too."

She's on the other side of the shaft, where I can't get to her right away.

Say something, my brain tells me.

I want to tell her that life is like the books she reads, and no matter how bad things look, it will all work out in the end. That's another big lie, but I'll say anything to stop her from going over the edge. The problem is, I'm so scared that my mouth won't work.

"I know you tried," she says. "And I kept pretending it would be okay. But it isn't okay. He'll get me. Nobody can stop him."

I'm on my hands and knees, creeping along in slow motion, no sudden moves. But the closer I get to her, the closer she gets to the edge.

I go, "Max the Mighty can stop him. Max the Mighty can save you."

She moves even closer to the edge. "There's no such thing," she says. "I made it up, remember?"

That stops me in my tracks. Because I know in my bones that if I don't have an answer, Worm will slip over the edge. And it has to be the right answer and it has to be true.

I'm kind of surprised when my mouth starts talking, like it already knows what to say without me having to think about it.

"You're right," I say. "You made it up. I'm just plain Max, and I'll never read as many books as you, or be as smart as you, but I do know one thing. You know how bad you feel about your father, and how much you miss him? I feel that bad about my mom and my best friend Kevin. And if I lose you, I'll feel even worse, all the time. Every day for the rest of my life. And that's the truth."

I'm staring across the mine shaft at her miner's light. Staring with all my might, hoping I said the right thing.

Suddenly Worm says, "Good-bye," and then the miner's light is falling. It spins end over end, falling down and down and down, getting smaller and smaller, until the darkness swallows it up, and I'm all alone in the dark.

Inside it feels like part of me is falling with the light, and will keep falling forever.

Stupid, stupid, STUPID.

And then a warm hand finds my big stupid face in the dark and Worm says, "I gave my father back his light. So he can find his way in the dark, like I did."

I've got Worm by the hand and we're going slow and careful, heading up through the shadows to the surface of the world.

She's afraid but that doesn't stop her. "You've got to promise," she says. "Friends for life. No matter what. No matter how many fights we have or how many stupid things we say to each other."

"I hate fights," I say. "But I can't help saying stupid things sometimes."

"But you promise?"

I go, "Promise," and then Worm asks me to crouch down and she gives me a quick little kiss.

"For luck," she explains. "We're going to need it."

We're coming into the rosy light of sunset when the ground starts shaking under our feet.

Rrrrrrrrummmmble.

Like the whole mine is clearing its throat and getting ready to cough. There's a sound like wood splitting, and then something heavy falls *thump!* and makes the ground shake again.

Up ahead of us, not too far away, somebody groans.

"Help . . . me," a familiar voice says. "Help me or I'll die."

29.
The End of Maxwell Kane

All I can see of the Undertaker is his long, black-covered legs sticking out from under a huge beam. Part of the mine has caved in and he's trapped. His boots are twitching so I know he's alive.

"I can't breathe," he gasps. "Get this off me, please."

Feet come running up behind us.

"Don't touch anything," Sheriff Goodman says. "The whole place is ready to come down on our heads."

Dip and Grim are both panting so hard they can barely talk, but Grim sees Worm is safe and sound and he gives me a thumbs-up. Which is pretty cool for Grim.

The Undertaker groans some more. The way the beam has got him pinned, I can't see his face, but I can hear him moaning and groaning, and it sure sounds pitiful. Even though I can't stand the guy, I feel bad for him, the way you'd feel if a really mean dog got hit by a car and needed help. Part of you is glad the dog can't hurt you anymore, but you don't want it to die.

I go, "Maybe we can dig out from under him," but the sheriff thinks that's a bad idea, that it might make matters worse.

"Everybody out of the mine," he says. "I'll call backup, get a rescue team in here to do it right."

"Don't leave me!" the Undertaker wails.

Worm, she's been standing there real quiet, not moving. But after a little while she lets go of my hand and edges a little closer to him. Not too close, like she's worried he's playing a trick.

"You were the one who beat up my mom," she says. "You were the one who hurt me. It was you! Not Max. You lied about that. You lied about everything."

The Undertaker groans and then goes, "Your momma was asking for it! She was going to call the cops! It was all her fault!"

When Sheriff Goodman hears that, he looks at me and nods, like he knew all along that I wasn't really a criminal. Then he tugs down on the brim of his cowboy hat and says, "Let's move along, folks."

We're starting to go when suddenly I can feel it coming up through my feet. This rumbling from deep underground, like the whole mine has decided to cave in, starting at the bottom.

"Please!" the Undertaker groans. "Somebody help!"

The timbers and planks are shaking. Clouds of dust belch up from down below.

Creeeeak! And a huge *kerchunk!* of rocks smashing together. Everything is breaking, falling apart.

"She's going!" the sheriff cries. "Get out of here! Run!"

Dip grabs hold of Worm and takes her away and I can hear Grim shouting at me through the roaring dust. Shouting to leave while I've got the chance.

There's nothing I want more than to get out of that mine while the getting is good, but just as I start to go, a strange thing happens.

This pale white hand reaches up through the dirt and the dust. The Undertaker. He can't talk because his face is covered with dirt, but his hand is begging me for help. *Don't leave me,* it says. *Please, please.*

Grim screams, "Max! Don't!"

My brain screams, *Run! Run!*

But it's too late, because I've already got my arms under the fallen beam, and I'm yanking it up with all my might. With so many rocks pinning it down, it must weigh a ton. It's like trying to move the earth, but I have to do it, there's no one else who can.

So I yank harder. Harder.

The beam moves.

The thing is, once you start lifting something really heavy, you can't stop when you're halfway done. You have to lift it all the way up. My knees feel like old tires about to blow out, but I can't stop until the huge old timber is up on my shoulder.

Grim screams, "Got him!" and drags the Undertaker out and helps him to his feet.

Then the ground is shaking again. Dust blows down from the ceiling and timbers start popping out of the walls, snapping like toothpicks.

Of course I want to let go of that beam and run, but it's like I'm pinned to the ground by the weight of everything. Stuff is coming loose all around me but I can't move. All I can do is keep holding up the timber and the roof above it and the mountain above that. Which nobody can do, not even a big huge doofus like me.

The last thing I remember is how much it sounds like the ocean. Like waves crashing, and seagulls screaming, and gravel caught in the undertow. The dust is real bad, but I can make out a couple of shadowy figures running toward the light, and I'm glad Worm is okay, and Grim and Dip got out in time. This is really dumb, but it doesn't even bother me about the Undertaker getting out alive.

I'm thinking this is the end for Maxwell Kane,

too bad he never got a chance to be Max the Mighty, and that's when the beam finally slips and the whole world crashes down on me and it really is the end, the end,

the end.

30.
After the End

They say Grim and Dip and Sheriff Goodman dug through all that dirt until their hands were bleeding, and finally got me out in one piece, more or less, and that I kept saying something really stupid like, "I hear the ocean, I hear the ocean." I don't remember because I was so out of it.

When I woke up in the hospital, this nurse told me I'd broken my shoulder and my leg, and could she please autograph my cast, which I thought was pretty weird, her being a nurse and all.

Then Grim and Gram came in, and Grim said he guessed I wouldn't be dancing in the ballet, on account of my leg. That's his idea of a joke, ha ha.

Worm, she was real upset with her mom for going along with all the Undertaker's lies, even though she was so scared of him she couldn't help it. But then she felt a lot better about everything when her mom finally got up the courage and testified in court about what really happened, and the Undertaker got convicted.

It turns out he'd done the same kind of creepy stuff to another kid and her mother years before, and so he's going to be in prison a long, long time, which is just fine by me.

The best thing is that Gram made a big fuss and insisted that Worm and her mom come live with us, at least for a while, until they get on their own two feet again. Gram said she and Grim had always wanted to have a big family, and this was the chance of a lifetime.

At first Worm's mom said she couldn't possibly, but Gram wouldn't take no for an answer, and now Worm's mom says that moving in with us was the best thing for all concerned, and even though Grim is an opinionated old coot, she wouldn't trade him for the world.

So the way it all worked out, now I've got a little sister for the time being, and who knows, maybe forever. Which is pretty cool, if I do say so myself.

Sometimes when I get bored and there's nothing to do in the down under and we're out of books to read, I ask Worm if she wants to do it all over again. Just stick out our thumbs and see where the road takes us.

You know, have another cool adventure.

When I say that, Worm looks at me and goes,

"Are you cracked?" Then she'll kid me and say why don't I grow up and get a brain like normal people?

That's when I tell her I'll never be normal, not in a million years, and I like it that way just fine, thank you.

And that's the truth. The unvanquished truth.

Rodman Philbrick is the author of several books for young readers. His first novel, *Freak the Mighty* (Blue Sky Press, 1993), was received with great acclaim and won the California Young Reader Medal, as well as several other state awards. It was also made into the feature film *The Mighty* (Miramax). Philbrick's sequel, *Max the Mighty*, received starred reviews, and his novel *The Fire Pony* was named a 1996 Capital Choice. His most recent books include *The Young Man and the Sea*, *REM World*, and *The Last Book in the Universe*, which was named an ALA Best Book for Young Adults and a Notable Social Studies Trade Book for Young People. He and his wife, also a writer, divide their time between Maine and the Florida Keys. You may contact Rodman Philbrick at www.rodmanphilbrick.com.